PROM QUEEN

Laura Wolfe

Published by Bookouture in 2023

An imprint of Storyfire Ltd.
Carmelite House
50 Victoria Embankment
London EC4Y 0DZ

www.bookouture.com

ISBN: 978-1-83790-285-9
eBook ISBN: 978-1-83790-272-9

For JP, Brian, and Kate (& Milo)

PROLOGUE

The tiara fell first, rhinestones glittering through the darkness as it spiraled toward the tracks below. An oncoming train rumbled, rattling her bones, its horn screaming at her to get out of the way. But Bailey couldn't stop her falling body. Time stretched slowly as if moving through water. She touched her bare neck, feeling the spot where the necklace had been. Her warmest memories flashed through her mind one last time—the glow of the beach at sunset, her tenth birthday party at the roller rink, and years of Friday night sleepovers. She tasted the salty-sweet butter pecan ice cream from Scoops and tensed at the shock of the frigid lake water during the first swim of the summer. She felt her boyfriend's warm lips on hers and listened to the applause of her drama class after performing her monologue.

In the moment before she died, Bailey accepted her fate, that the best day of her life had turned out to be her worst. The betrayal stung almost as much as her impending death. Because a split second earlier, up on the bridge, she'd sensed a presence behind her, the ragged breath of someone standing a little too close. And that was just before she felt the pressure of the palms on her back.

ONE

NOW

My spine straightened at the sight of her necklace reflecting in the morning light. A splash of coffee spilled from my cup and dribbled over my fingers. I hunched lower to get a better view of the woman who sat on the far side of the café near the window. A silver pendant dangled from a mismatched chain on her neck. I pretended I was looking beyond her, toward the old-fashioned barber shop across the street or the marina in the distance. But even as I dried my hand with a napkin, my eyes were on the necklace.

The woman's blue-painted fingernails flicked across her phone. She had a dazed look in her eyes as if she were oblivious to everything around her, including my stares and the hiss of the espresso machine. Just as the door of Drips Café slammed shut behind a young family, another flash of silver caught in the sunlight, causing me to lose my breath. Was that a speck of purple? I squeezed my cardboard cup and craned my head around a man waiting for his hazelnut latte, confirming again that my eyes weren't playing tricks on me. A tiny silver puzzle piece hung from the end of the chain, dangling into the woman's V-neck T-shirt. I bit my lip, composing myself. Striking up conversations with strangers had never come naturally to me, but I took a breath of courage and stood, approaching the woman scrolling on her phone.

"Hi," I said, standing next to her now.

Her head jerked up, shiny black hair settling into a sleek line beneath her shoulders.

"I'm so sorry to bother you, but I couldn't help noticing your necklace. It's so unusual."

The surprise on the woman's face melted into a bemused smile as she tugged at the pendant. "Oh, this. I bought it a couple of days ago at the thrift shop near the train station. Do you know the place?"

"I think so."

"It's basically like a garbage dump run by this weird old lady, but everything is super cheap."

"Yeah. I've walked past it before." I pointed to the necklace, struggling to keep my voice even. "I guess you found a treasure."

"It's..." She paused and bit her lip as if contemplating how much to share. "It's really just a cheap necklace that I'm using as inspiration for my podcast. *All the Dark Corners*." She said the name as if I'd heard of it.

I nodded to be polite.

"I'm Hannah Mead." Her hand shot toward me.

"Nice to meet you." I shook it, then took a sip of my coffee instead of offering my name. My gaze gravitated back to the puzzle piece, my pulse accelerating as I confirmed a minuscule dot of purple marring the silver pendant. "This is going to sound strange, but do you mind if I buy that off you?" I angled my head toward the necklace. "I'll pay double whatever you paid for it. It's for my daughter. She loves jigsaw puzzles. And I always try to bring her back a little present whenever I travel somewhere."

Hannah waved me off. "You don't want this. It's not in great shape, and the chain doesn't even match. I'm sure you can find something better on Amazon."

"The ones on Amazon won't work." I bit my tongue, reminding myself to soften my voice, not to sound panicked. "My daughter likes unique items. You know, things that tell a story."

Hannah tilted her head, lips twisting. "Oh."

"It would really mean a lot to her."

She tapped a blue nail against the table. "Okay. Yeah. Why not? I already have all the photos and videos I need for social media." She reached back and unclasped the back. "You don't have to pay me anything, though."

"Are you sure?"

"Yeah. Of course. It was only three dollars. This coffee cost me more." She handed me the necklace and motioned across the table. "Want to sit for a sec and finish your drink? I've been hanging out by myself for a few days and could use the company."

"Sure." I ached to get out of there, but she had just given me the necklace, no questions asked, and I didn't want to be rude, so I sat across from her, gripping the flimsy chain in my hand. "How much longer are you in Cove Haven for?"

Hannah pushed her phone aside. "Probably for a couple of weeks. Or as long as it takes me to record six episodes, I guess. Do you live here?"

"Just visiting. I live a few hours away, in the Detroit suburbs." I glanced away from her, even though it wasn't a lie. "What's your podcast about?"

Hannah leaned forward as if telling me a secret. "It's a true crime investigative podcast. I'm looking into the tragic death of the prom queen of Cove Haven."

"Oh?"

"Haven't you heard the story of Bailey Maddox, who jumped in front of a train just hours after she was crowned prom queen? It happened under that bridge behind the old train station twenty years ago."

She stared at me as another customer burst through the door, a cool breeze whipping past my face.

"How horrible."

"Yeah. And it gets even worse because some think she was murdered."

I raised the chain in my clenched fist. "And what does the necklace have to do with anything?"

"The prom queen was wearing an interlocking necklace similar to this one—I'm guessing much better quality—the night of the prom. But just hours later, when they recovered her body, or what was left of it, the necklace was nowhere to be found."

"Someone took it?"

"The police said she must have thrown it away. Or maybe it got caught in the wheels and carried further down the tracks, never to be recovered. But I don't know. There were so many people with motives. Maybe one of the other girls who thought they would win the title took it. Or a jilted boyfriend. Or maybe a former friend."

I raised an eyebrow as Hannah continued talking.

"Bailey's best friend, Brooke, had the matching necklace. The pendants on the two necklaces were supposedly custom-made to fit into each other. But here's the thing, the two of them had a falling out a few months before the big dance, and Bailey basically ditched Brooke that night to hang out with a more popular crowd."

"So, you think the best friend stole the necklace back?" I touched the back of my neck, my skin clammy.

Hannah flicked her fingers in the air. "That's what some people have guessed over the years. It's one theory of many, and it's going to be one of the first I examine in the next episode."

"Wow."

"And now I'm under a time crunch because a developer is

building a hotel where the old train station stands. They're tearing down the bridge from which the prom queen supposedly jumped. And just between you and me, I might have skipped this case altogether, given that most people accepted the prom queen's death as a suicide, even the girl's parents."

"So why look into it?"

Hannah's berry-stained lips puckered as she leaned closer, lowering her voice to a whisper. "Because a few weeks ago, I received an anonymous tip. It was from someone who knew Bailey back then. Someone close to her believes she was murdered."

"Who?" I hugged my arms around myself, suddenly dizzy. The hard-backed chair was the only thing keeping me upright.

Hannah sighed. "Don't know."

"A man or woman?"

"Can't say for sure. It was a text. Untraceable. Probably sent from a burner phone."

"That's strange."

"But given the tantalizing tip, the new hotel development about to happen at the site of the tragedy, and the recent twentieth anniversary of the prom queen's death, I thought it was crucial to look into this mystery one last time before the entire scene and any remaining evidence no longer exists."

"I'll have to tune in."

"*All the Dark Corners* podcast," she repeated. "Episode one just dropped yesterday." Hannah's brown eyes took on a darker hue. "It's such an elusive case. So many unanswered questions."

"I'm sure it will get tons of listeners."

"That's what I'm hoping," Hannah said with a wink.

I scooted my chair back a few inches, struggling for air. "I'm sorry. It was nice chatting with you, and thank you for the necklace, but I've got to meet a contractor in a few minutes."

"Oh." She raised an eyebrow. "I thought you didn't live here."

"No. I don't. I'm working on flipping a house. You know, to hopefully make some extra money. I'm doing a few quick renovations before putting it on the market."

"Cool. In that case, maybe I'll see you around."

"Sounds good." I waved with one hand as I slipped the necklace into my purse with the other, hoping I'd never see her again.

"What was your name?" Hannah asked.

My back was turned to her, and I pretended not to hear the question. I threw my cup into the trash bin, nodded toward Gabe behind the counter, and darted out the door.

I ventured out of the shadows of the café and into the early June sun. As soon as I was out of view, I picked up a jog, hurrying past the quaint storefronts and the trendy new restaurants, turning down a residential street, and reaching the front door of my childhood home a few minutes later. With a quivering hand, I turned the key and raced up the stairs to my old bedroom, locating the locked box in my drawer and retrieving a smaller key hidden inside a pair of never-worn slippers in the back of my closet. As I pried open the lid, a nearly identical necklace stared back at me. I grasped the silver puzzle piece from my purse, removing the other one from the box. Then I slid the two pieces together, hearing the click. A perfect fit. I turned them over, examining the dot of purple nail polish on the pendant I'd taken from the podcaster, the exact same shade of purple as the B on the pendant that I'd saved in my box for two decades. B & B for Bailey and Brooke. We'd painted the letters in purple nail polish across the backs.

This was the necklace I'd given to Bailey for her seventeenth birthday. It had been missing since the night she died twenty years ago. Now somehow—inexplicably—I was holding it in my hand.

TWO

NOW

It took a minute to steady myself, to stop shaking. My thoughts spun back to the woman at the coffee shop who'd been wearing Bailey's necklace. It hadn't been custom-made as Hannah had stated, but I had purchased it for Bailey with my babysitting money from a vendor at an art fair the summer before our senior year. It was meant to be a symbol of our everlasting friendship. Acid swirled in my stomach, and I rushed to the bathroom, leaning against the counter, worried I might throw up. The mirror reflected the panic in my eyes as I set the interlocking necklaces on the counter, waiting for the nausea to pass.

I splashed cold water on my face and used one of Mom's old towels to pat my skin dry, Then I turned back to the long-lost relic on the counter, touching it to confirm again that I wasn't hallucinating. The chain was different now. Someone had replaced it with a longer one that felt cheaper than the original, but I would have recognized the puzzle piece anywhere, especially with the faint nail polish still visible.

A strange combination of terror and nostalgia shuddered through me. I couldn't pull my stare from the interlocking pendants. The police had been so sure that Bailey had killed herself, so certain she'd jumped in front of the train to end her suffering. I'd witnessed her depression, her downward spiral, firsthand. With all the damning rumors swirling through town in the days and weeks after the tragedy, suicide had been the safest and most logical theory to cling to. But I'd never been completely convinced that Bailey took her own life. The circumstances had been too strange, our classmates had too many motives, and the verdict of suicide had been too rushed. I'd accepted the outcome despite the niggling in my gut because everyone else had too. It was the path of least resistance, the quickest way to get the spotlight off me and move on with my life at a time when merely getting myself out of bed in the morning was a struggle.

I'd shunned the emails and phone calls over the years from several people just like Hannah Mead, people who wrote articles or hosted podcasts questioning whether Bailey's death was really suicide and whether whoever took her necklace that night was the person responsible for her death. I never spoke to the armchair investigators except to tell them I'd lost my best friend and to please leave me alone. But now Bailey's missing necklace had resurfaced just as I returned to Cove Haven on the twentieth anniversary of her death. Someone had left an anonymous tip for a true crime podcaster claiming Bailey had been murdered. It couldn't be a coincidence.

Unanswered questions fluttered through me, emerging like ghosts from long-forgotten hiding places. I could almost hear Bailey's voice whispering for me to try harder, to do right by her. My doubts had been warranted all along. Someone had kept Bailey's necklace hidden all this time. Someone had lied. The realization speared through me, hardening my resolve.

I'd failed my best friend once, but I wouldn't do it again. I was older now. Wiser. More confident. My fingers tightened around the silver pendant. I'd spent years avoiding the truth, sometimes with drastic consequences. But now with Bailey's necklace in my hand, the overwhelming urge to find out what really happened to her on the night she was crowned prom queen overtook me.

I zipped the jewelry into the pocket of my windbreaker, my fingers still trembling. An unknown force drew me back and forth along the upstairs hallway, as I zig-zagged from window to window, not entirely sure what to do with the discovery. I peeked into Mom's bedroom, willing her to offer some advice, but was only greeted by specks of dust floating above a sagging bed, an empty dresser, and the lingering scent of moth balls. Sometimes I still forgot she was gone.

I ventured down the dimly lit staircase, the wooden steps covered with a worn carpet runner. I'd only been in Cove Haven for three days, which had been consumed by phone calls with my contractor and trips to Goodwill. After graduating high school, I avoided returning to this place as much as possible, dodging the rumors that I'd killed Bailey, if not literally, then by being a bad friend who was unaware of the depths of her depression. I'd escaped to art school, where no one knew my past. Then I'd built a new life for myself, hours away.

But Mom had passed away six months ago and left the house to my younger brother, Derek, and me. Derek, who lived in Seattle and made more money than me, offered to fund some bare-bones renovations if I spent the summer in Cove Haven overseeing the work. We'd sell the place in the fall and split the proceeds. Given the recent tourism boom in Cove Haven and the soaring property values, it was an offer that I couldn't refuse. I'd taken a two-month leave-of-absence from my position at the art museum. I wished Ruthie could have been with me these couple of months, but my eight-year-old daughter was with my ex-husband Shane for the summer, pursuant to our custody agreement.

My chest heaved at the thought of my daughter, but I swallowed back the emotion. As I reached the bottom step, the foyer's walls closed in on me, dark and suffocating. I exited the house and sat on the wooden bench on the front porch, thankful for the sunshine and a light breeze. A woman about my age dressed in running clothes emerged from the house next door. She waved and said good morning, then jogged away. It was the house where Bailey used to live, although it had undergone a facelift. A gray coat of paint now covered the red brick, and a fancy new front door had been installed. Mr. and Mrs. Maddox had moved to Florida at least fifteen years earlier, and Mom told me the new owner rented the house by the week to tourists.

I pressed my hand against the necklaces in my pocket, confounded by how Hannah Mead had so easily happened upon it. Curiosity getting the better of me, I pulled out my phone and located *All the Dark Corners* podcast, slightly alarmed by the latest season's relatively high position in the Spotify charts after only one episode. My earbuds in place, I pressed play, Hannah's high-pitched, sing-songy voice sounding loud in my ears.

All the Dark Corners *Podcast*

Season 8: The Prom Queen of Cove Haven

Episode 1: The Mysterious Death of the Prom Queen

Hi, everyone. It's Hannah Mead, your favorite true crime investigative podcaster, with season eight of All the Dark Corners. *Welcome back. I'm so glad you tuned in because this season, I'm visiting the quaint lakeside town of Cove Haven, Michigan, to bring you one hell of a story. It's the harrowing tale of the prom queen of Cove Haven, a mystery that contains some serious Stephen King vibes. You all remember* Carrie, *right? The classic horror movie with the pig's blood. Ugh. I get the creeps just thinking about it. Anyway, there's no pig's blood in this one, thank God, but there's plenty here to make you squeal.*

My weight sunk into the bench as I listened to a stranger describe a glossed-over version of the worst events of my life. First, Hannah portrayed Cove Haven as an idyllic small town on the shores of Lake Michigan, whose locals placed a premium on church potlucks and Friday night high school football games and who never felt the need to lock their doors. She described Bailey as a fun-loving, all-American girl who strived to please her parents and friends, watched too many episodes of *Law and Order*, and dreamed of becoming a prosecuting attorney. Hannah recounted Bailey's close relationship to me, the girl next door, and described the friendship necklace I'd given to Bailey just before the start of our senior year at Cove Haven High School. She depicted Bailey's social climb from a low-key, no-nonsense student to a popular cheerleader, and Bailey's increased partying and corresponding loss of interest in school. Hannah's voice lowered as she recounted the events of that fateful prom night—Bailey in her eggshell-blue prom dress, donning the friendship necklace I'd given her nine months earlier. Hannah described how I'd watched from the shadows— along with Bailey's jilted prom date, Spike—as Bailey was crowned prom queen in a surprise triumph over the expected winner, the popular head cheerleader Mikayla. I noticed Hannah only used first names, which theoretically provided some anonymity to outsiders but wouldn't fool anyone in this town.

With broad strokes, Hannah painted the scene of the after-party—a bonfire in a clearing in the woods behind the train station with plenty of cheap beer to go around. She described how ten people were at the bonfire, including two of Bailey's cheerleader friends, Zoe and Liz. But others were noticeably absent—Mikayla and her boyfriend, Trevor,

Bailey's prom date, Spike, and Bailey's former best friend, Brooke.

I bit my tongue at the frequent mentions of my name but kept listening. Hannah described Bailey's heavy drinking and somber demeanor as the rain began to pour atop her glittering tiara, breaking up the after-party, and how Bailey rejected offers to walk home with the others, claiming her mom was picking her up at midnight, which turned out to be a lie. Hannah told of the frantic 911 call that came in from a train conductor minutes later, stating that a girl had jumped from a bridge in front of the train, that they couldn't stop in time. Finally, Hannah huffed over the small-town police department's quick determination of suicide. She promised to delve deeper into the prom queen's mysterious death, examining a long list of suspects and their motives and asking viewers to subscribe so they would be alerted as soon as the next episode dropped.

I removed my earbuds, simultaneously disgusted and impressed with Hannah's account of the most painful period of my life. The episode was merely an overview, but Hannah's style of reporting was smooth, and the information she presented was relatively accurate. My first impression of the podcaster had been that she was more concerned about building an audience with a flashy story than she was about getting the facts right. But maybe I'd judged her too quickly.

My feet shifted underneath the bench. She hadn't mentioned the anonymous tip, and I wondered again who had contacted her. I wanted to stay one step ahead of her. Once word got out about her investigation, the locals were sure to either clam up or throw gasoline on wild theories that should have burned out decades ago. While Hannah's motives were different than mine, we shared the same goal. Maybe something on her podcast would spark my memory or cause me to look at familiar facts in a new light. She'd already inadvertently led me to Bailey's missing necklace. Cove Haven was painfully small, and Hannah asked a lot of questions. It was only a matter of time before she figured out my identity, before she realized that the necklace she'd given me wasn't a knock-off.

I needed to talk to Willa, the owner of The Treasure Cove thrift shop. The place was a mishmash of junk and antiques sold out of the front room of her house, and I couldn't believe it was still in business. But someone had dropped Bailey's necklace at the shop, and I had to know who it was.

THREE

THEN

August 2002

Bailey's knee brushed against mine as she stretched back on our shared beach towel. The sand radiated heat, soothing my legs through the terry cloth fabric. A summer breeze whipped off the lake, carrying the scent of coconut sunscreen. Two seagulls waddled toward us, looking for food, but Bailey shooed them away. I hadn't seen much of my friend in the last few weeks because she'd taken on extra shifts at the ice cream shop, and I usually babysat in the mornings when she wasn't working. But so far, this was my idea of the perfect afternoon.

I scooped a handful of sand, enjoying the sear of the sun on my skin and the nearby waves lapping in a quiet rhythm. "It's so nice out. I don't want to go back to school." It was mid-August, only two weeks remaining before the first day of twelfth grade. I could almost feel the freedom of the long summer days slipping through my fingers along with the sand.

"But we'll be seniors. We'll basically rule the school." Bailey flashed her white teeth at me. Her baseball cap was tattered at the edges, and her curves filled out her bikini top better than mine. I could see that she wasn't nearly as anxious about returning to the bleach-scented hallways of Cove Haven High School as I was. "Hey, guess what?" she asked.

"What?"

"I made the cheerleading squad."

"Really?" I knew Bailey had gone to the tryouts last week, but I didn't think she stood a chance of breaking into the tight-knit group of cheerleaders, especially as a senior with little or no experience. Then again, Sherri Stevens had gotten knocked up and had dropped out of school last spring, leaving a spot open for an incoming senior.

Bailey batted my arm. "Don't act so surprised, jerk."

"I'm not surprised." I injected some enthusiasm into my voice. "That's great. I'm happy for you."

"So, I won't be able to walk home with you most days after school because of practice."

"Okay." I smiled even as my chest swelled at the thought of missing out on our afternoon talks. "So is Mikayla your new best friend?" I asked, half joking.

"Don't be stupid." Bailey shook her head, smiling. "Those girls aren't that bad, you know? Seriously. I think we've pegged them wrong."

I knew who Bailey meant by "those girls." While there were several cheerleaders who were kind, intelligent, well-rounded people, including my friend Libby who took all the same art classes as me, there was also a handful of them who were not. Their names were Mikayla, Liz, and Zoe, and they ruled the school. They wore too much makeup and laughed a little too loudly, usually at other people's expense. They went to parties where people like me weren't invited and where I imagined the alpha males flirting with them and asking them on dates.

Bailey and I sat without speaking as a boy ran past us with a bucket to gather lake water. I dug into my canvas beach bag and pulled out a small, square box, handing it to her and hoping to lighten the mood. "Here. Happy birthday! You're finally seventeen."

She turned the package over. "But my birthday is tomorrow."

"You said you're working tonight, and you have family stuff going on tomorrow. Just open it."

Bailey loosened the blue ribbon and opened the lid, revealing two silver necklaces with puzzle piece pendants. "Cool." She held them up, letting them dangle between us. "Matching necklaces."

"One is for you, and one is for me. The puzzle pieces fit together. You know, so we can always remember that we're best friends, even if we go away to different colleges and all that."

"I love it." Bailey's blue eyes mirrored the water as she looked at me. "Where did you get them?"

"At that art fair in Petoskey my parents took me to last month. I should have had our initials engraved, but I ran out of money."

Bailey leaned forward. "I know what we can do." She reached into her bag and pulled out a bottle of purple nail polish. "We'll paint B & B. Remember?"

"Of course, I remember." We'd referred to ourselves as "The B's" all through elementary and middle school, a secret nickname for the pair of small-town superheroes we'd imagined ourselves to be, ones who lacked any actual superpowers, but who rescued stray dogs, distracted screaming toddlers with candy, and alerted women on first dates if they had pieces of spinach stuck between their teeth. We laughed about the idea often, certain that no one would suspect The B's for all the good being accomplished in Cove Haven.

We laid the necklaces on a paperback book I kept in my beach bag and painted two small Bs on the backs of the puzzle pieces, leaving them on the towel to dry as we talked about our upcoming college applications. My lifelong passion for drawing

and painting had only increased in the last year. Cove Haven
High School had one art teacher, Mrs. Avery, who taught everything from photography to mixed media to ceramics, and I'd
taken nearly all her classes. After watching a career path
presentation she'd put together last year, I'd dreamed of getting
into the Stamps School of Art and Design at the University of
Michigan. My parents had taken me to visit one Saturday, the
school sitting a mere two-and-a-half-hour drive from Cove
Haven but a world away. After the trip, I'd become laser-
focused on getting accepted. Meanwhile, Bailey was obsessed
with crime drama on TV and often talked about becoming a
prosecuting attorney, despite her underwhelming grades. I bit
my tongue and let her dream, knowing her parents weren't
supportive of her college aspirations. Mr. Maddox was the
assistant manager at a car dealership one town over and often
pressured Bailey to work the dealership's front desk after graduation instead of accruing student loans. Regardless of where
Bailey and I ended up going, this was likely to be the last year
we lived in the same place, at least for a while.

When the nail polish had dried, we clipped the necklaces
around our necks, admiring the way they looked on each other.
Then we laid back and enjoyed the afternoon. But Bailey's
news about making the cheerleading squad weighed like an
anchor in my gut. Our friendship had always been a soft place
to land—safe, secure, and sewn up tight. But that day on the
beach, I feared things were about to change. I'd spent enough
time observing Mikayla, Liz, and Zoe from a distance and knew
they were bad news.

A cloud passed overhead, blocking out the sun and turning
the lake black. Propping myself up on my elbows, I stared out at
the dark, undulating currents, unable to shake the sinking
feeling that my friendship with Bailey was heading into murky
waters.

FOUR

NOW

The chains weighed in my pocket, and it felt more like I was carrying a national secret than some tarnished necklaces. I was still in disbelief at the reappearance of Bailey's long-missing pendant, and every little noise caused me to flinch and scan my surroundings as I headed toward Willa's thrift shop. Whoever dropped it there might know more about the night Bailey died. Maybe it was the same person who'd texted the strange tip to Hannah. Or the person who'd caused Bailey's death. I couldn't focus on anything else until I knew who it was. An occasional person or two passed me on the sidewalk, and I wondered if anyone noticed anything unusual on my face. I silently debated whether to take the discovery to the police, but the police had never given much significance to Bailey's missing necklace. I couldn't imagine them caring that it had reappeared so long after her death. My molars ground together as I tried to imagine who could have kept the necklace all these years. I hoped the answer waited for me at the thrift shop, and I walked a little faster.

Footsteps skittered behind me. I turned around, confused when no one was there. But a woman and two kids whizzed past, riding identical bikes and wearing matching helmets, the kind rented from my friend Dan's local bike shop.

"Slow down!" a little girl screamed to her brother. I watched them ride away, jealous of the carefree day I pictured ahead of them. When I was growing up, this sleepy lakeside town had barely been on the map, only drawing a modest number of seasonal visitors. Now the Chicagoans and Detroiters had discovered the hidden gem of Cove Haven's beaches. Even so, the town had retained its claustrophobic feel. The difference between the locals and the vacationers remained obvious. I liked to think I was a summer visitor now, but I wasn't so sure. Faces from my past materialized everywhere I went— storekeepers, neighbors, parents of classmates—still fraught with lingering suspicion, as if to say, "Isn't that Brooke Webber, the dead prom queen's former best friend? Surely, she bears some responsibility." In the few days since I'd returned, I'd made a habit of averting my eyes, lifting my chin, and hurrying away from the weighty stares.

I continued down the sidewalk, turning a corner. A shadow flitted in the corner of my vision, and I whipped around again. The sensation of someone watching me bristled across my skin. My gaze skimmed across the yards, the manicured shrubs, and mature trees. The houses were further apart on this street. Some had boats or RVs parked in the driveways. Whoever it was must have slipped behind a line of hedges or an oversized vehicle. Or maybe I was merely paranoid. A woman emerged from the flowerbed of a nearby house and smiled at me when she caught me staring. I hadn't seen her kneeling there amid the colorful pansies and shoots of lavender. I gave a quick wave, embarrassed. My feet pushed forward as I silently scolded myself for my overactive imagination.

My breathing had returned to normal by the next block, when I heard it again, the pitter-patter of footsteps behind me. I flipped around to find a different woman approaching from behind.

"Brooke Webber? Is that you?" She flashed a pretty smile as she strode toward me, touching her chest. "It's Zoe from high school."

I stood tall, fighting the urge to run and hide. Her appearance had altered since high school, but she was easily recognizable. I'd remembered Zoe as a mean girl who wore garish red lipstick and had too many teeth in her mouth. But she'd grown into her teeth, her makeup was tastefully done, and subtle caramel highlights added depth to her dark hair. Zoe and her friend Liz were the quietly vengeful girls on the cheerleading squad who, along with their leader, Mikayla, had befriended Bailey, had given her the social status I hadn't been able to provide.

Unlike the two-faced cheerleader I'd known in high school, the woman before me exuded a genuine warmth, and I wondered if the horrible ordeal of Bailey's death had changed her for the better.

"Hi, Zoe." I froze, unsure what to expect.

She lunged forward and hugged me. "It's been so long. You look terrific."

I stepped back, shaking off my surprise at the friendly reception and looking down at my body. Since the divorce, I'd done my best to stay in shape, despite never having lost the ten pounds of baby weight I'd gained while pregnant with Ruthie. Still, I often got compliments on my thick eyelashes and my new hairstyle, dyed slightly darker than my natural color and cut just below my shoulders. All things considered, I was more comfortable with myself now than I'd ever been in high school.

"You look great too."

She waved her shiny fingernails in the air. "My husband and I run a chain of health food stores, so that helps."

"That's right. I heard that." Mom had mentioned Zoe's

specialty grocery stores a few years back. "So you still live in town?"

"Yes. A different house now. We're right on the beach."

I looked around, wondering why she was walking down this street nowhere near the beach.

As if reading my mind, she said, "I was returning a book to a friend who lives around the corner when I saw you and thought I'd chase you down."

"I'm glad you did."

"Where are you headed?"

"Oh. Nowhere in particular. Just out for a walk." Heat prickled up my neck at the lie, at the discovery in my pocket.

Zoe nodded, seeming to accept my explanation at face value. She continued talking about her boys, ages twelve and fourteen, and how they were obsessed with baseball. She inquired about my life, and I told her about Ruthie, my position as an exhibit director at the Detroit Institute of Arts, and how I was back to fix up Mom's house. We talked easily for a few minutes before I realized she was a genuinely nice person, someone who'd matured since high school. Maybe even someone I could be friends with. She gave me her number in case I needed help with anything while I was in town, and by the time we said goodbye I'd almost forgotten how much I'd despised her in high school.

Once Zoe was out of sight, I touched the piece of jewelry in my pocket and continued toward the thrift shop. A more painful past came hurtling back at me as I neared the place I usually avoided, or at least allowed a wide berth: the old train station, which sat in front of the site of the fateful prom night bonfire. The massive stone building had long since been abandoned, and its current appearance did nothing to hide that fact. Thick, green moss grew across wide swaths of the roof, several stones had fallen off the exterior, and vines climbed up everything that remained. Even the tracks running behind the station had become obsolete, having been converted into a ten-mile walking and jogging trail a dozen years before. The wooden bridge loomed on the horizon, an unwanted reminder of Bailey's last moments on earth. Someone had staked a massive sign into the ground in the forefront of the abandoned station. Red-and-black lettering against a white backdrop announced, "Future home of The Train Station, a 120-room state-of-the-art luxury hotel and restaurant. Call Harsons Real Estate Group for more information." A Chicago phone number and address followed in smaller print.

I tore my eyes from the sign and kept walking, unsure how I felt about the planned development, and shaking unwanted memories from my head. A pale-yellow ramshackle house came into view about a half-block down. It was the only other building on this desolate stretch of road. Turquoise letters hung above a door painted the same color. *The Treasure Cove.* I hadn't been inside the place in over two decades, and I wondered again how the thrift shop was still standing, much less making a profit.

As I approached the entrance, a cat darted in front of me and leaped into the overgrown bushes. Tall weeds reached through the cracks of two cement front steps, scratching my ankles. Tentatively, I grasped the door handle, bells jingling above my head along with the creak of hinges. The musty smell hit my nose first as I stepped past rows of hanging clothes, stacks of records and CDs, and sets of mismatched china displayed on dusty glass shelves. Another cat jumped off an old wooden chest and stretched in front of me.

"Is someone here?" A woman's raspy voice reached my ears from somewhere in the back.

"Hi. It's Brooke Webber. I'm not sure if you remember me. Judy's daughter."

The old lady hobbled through a darkened doorway and stopped behind a glass counter. "Ahh. Yes. I see you now." She removed the reading glasses from her face, revealing a wandering eye on one side. We stood there for a minute, taking each other in.

When I was younger, Willa Jones had put the fear of God in me. Her wayward eye always seemed to be watching me even when it wasn't. She'd appeared ancient, even decades ago when she'd probably only been in her forties. Judging by the way my heart was slamming against my ribs, I realized she still scared me now. Her coarse, gray hair was clipped back from her face, and her skin was marked with sunspots and deep frown lines. Her stable eye stared directly through me.

"The dead commune with me from time to time." Willa's body swayed as she closed her eyelids, suddenly popping them open. "Don't worry about your mom. She's doing fine."

I glanced at my feet, unsure how to respond. "Okay. Thank you." I almost asked how Dad was doing. And Bailey. But there was no point encouraging Willa's delusions.

Willa, who lived on the second floor of her unusual second-hand shop, had a long-standing reputation as a woman who was off her rocker, who'd crossed the line from eccentric to being completely unhinged. Willa had never abided by social norms or attended church on Sunday, which in a small town like Cove Haven was an open invitation for suspicion and scorn. Growing up, the kids in our neighborhood called her Willa the Witch and regularly threw eggs at her windows, and toilet-papered her trees. She had never fought back with anything more than a stony, one-eyed glare. Instead, she had retreated into solitude and surrounded herself with cats, of which I could see at least five now in various corners of the cramped store.

She peered down her crooked nose at me. "Are you here to drop off some of your mom's things?"

"No. I'm not here about that." I'd already donated many of her clothes and knick-knacks to a nearby charity in preparation for repainting the walls and refinishing the floors. The contractor I'd hired was set to begin work next Monday.

The woman shook her head and continued speaking as if I hadn't answered. "Because my space is running low. My garage out back is bursting at the seams. That's what those horrible devils next door don't understand. I have valuables here that cannot be moved. There is no price on my home. My memories. Other people's memories."

"Do you mean the developers?"

"Those vultures tried to pay me to leave, but I won't ever leave. They'll have to build that monstrosity around me. Even when I'm dead and gone, I'll still be here. I curse the new hotel." Her voice had increased in volume.

"I'm glad you didn't let them bully you into selling."

She pinned her colorless lips together, apparently satisfied that I understood her side of things. "What brings you here, then?"

I touched the chain in my pocket and pulled it out. "A woman bought this necklace from you a few days ago."

Willa squinted at the chain. "Did she?"

"Yes. She has long, black hair. Maybe in her late twenties. She's visiting from out of town." I gulped back the desperation that pulled at my voice.

Willa's lips puckered. "Ah, yes. She bought that chain and an old postcard. My cats didn't like her."

"Do you remember who brought the necklace into the shop originally?"

Willa threw her head back. "Ha! No. I can't remember who brought in tidbits and shiny things weeks, months, or years ago."

I could feel my shoulders fall, the hope for an easy answer slipping from my grasp. "Are you sure?"

She picked up the chain, letting it swing from her finger. "Sometimes my cats return my lost memories to me. They communicate with me in my dreams."

I followed her gaze toward a black cat perched on a stack of dusty magazines and licking its paw. "Oh." I looked away as any remaining hope drained out of me. Willa closed her grip around the necklace and thrust it toward me. As I tucked it back into my pocket, I willed her to piece the past together, to recall anything about the long-missing relic she'd sold to Hannah, but she was fully entranced by the movements of the feline. My fingers touched the grimy counter. "Well. If you—or your cats— remember anything about who brought this necklace to you, can you let me know? I'm staying at my mom's house for a few weeks."

Willa's focus snapped back to me. "I don't leave my house much. But, yes, I will find a way to contact you if the memory returns."

"Thank you." I couldn't help wondering if her means of communication required me to put tin foil on my head. I reached down to pet a striped cat, but it skittered away from my hand before I touched its fur. Straightening up, I glanced back toward Willa, but she'd already disappeared into the back room. I let myself outside, disappointment weighing down my limbs. Now that I was a mom myself, I had greater empathy for the old woman whom we used to call a witch. She'd suffered her own fair share of tragedy.

Because Bailey wasn't the only person to die on the tracks behind the station. Fourteen months before her death, in March of my junior year, Willa's son Jasper threw himself in front of a speeding train about a mile away from where I now stood. Unlike Bailey, Jasper's death had never been questioned as anything other than suicide. He'd been acting erratically in the days preceding his death, giving away his prized guitar to a music teacher at school. A note was found in his bedroom stating that he was sorry for hurting anyone, but he couldn't go on living in a world that wasn't big enough for him. I hadn't known him well, but I'd thought about him over the years—his dark brooding eyes, his downward gaze—and wished I'd known him better, wished I could have said something to change his mind, to let him know there were treatments for depression, that he could have a different life once he moved away from his strange mother, who clearly had plenty of mental issues of her own. Some people blamed Jasper for Bailey's death, saying she must have gotten the idea from him. But I'd never felt that way.

I hung my head as I left the store, unsure where to go next. My hope for an easy answer had been derailed, the thrift store leading me to a dead end. I couldn't let Hannah find out she'd given me Bailey's necklace. She could use the information to spread lies and throw suspicion my way, a thorny path I'd already traveled through years earlier and didn't wish to return to. I'd hide the necklace. I'd keep my eye on the podcaster and listen to her theories. But I'd keep my distance from her too.

FIVE

THEN

September 2002

The shrill ring of the lunch bell cut through the cinderblock hallways of Cove Haven High School. It was the second day of school, and I lugged my backpack to the cafeteria, finding the empty table where Bailey, Lacey, Dan, and I sat yesterday. A minute later, Dan joined me with our other friend, Henry, a quick-witted kid who everyone liked.

"Hey, guys."

"What's up?" They threw down their things and raced to get in line for pizza slices. As I removed my lunch and water bottle from my backpack, Lacey plopped down in the chair next to me, setting her brown bag lunch and a book on the table. I'd learned not to take it personally when Lacey preferred reading over talking to me, which was much of the time. The chair on the other side of me sat open, and I pulled it closer, saving it for Bailey.

A second later, Bailey walked through the double doors with Liz, Zoe, and Mikayla flanking her, all four wearing their purple-and-black cheerleading uniforms. She stopped mid-laugh when she saw me staring and waited for the other girls to sit at their usual table by the windows. I exhaled. For a second, I thought Bailey was going to ditch me. She headed toward me, wearing more makeup than she'd had on when we walked to school this morning. Or maybe I hadn't noticed.

"Hey."

"Hi." I waited for her to sit down, but she only stood there, looking from me to the windows. "I, uh..." She stopped talking, shifting her weight. "Mikayla asked me to sit with them, and I think it would be kind of rude if I said no."

I stared at her. Somehow her words weren't surprising, yet I felt as if she'd tasered me with a stun gun. "Oh."

"They kind of expect the cheerleaders to sit together, I think." She glanced at Lacey, who was already absorbed in the pages of whatever YA thriller she was reading. "I'm sorry."

"Yeah. It's okay." Heat needled across my cheeks as my stomach folded. It was the same visceral reaction I'd had when Andy Nichols broke up with me at the Cove Haven Carnival the summer before ninth grade. Although Bailey hadn't said it directly, I knew I'd just been dumped.

"Maybe we can hang out this weekend, though. Like we planned."

"Yeah." I thought of the plans we'd made yesterday for her to sleep over at my house on Friday night and watch a scary movie. "My mom said she'd order pizza for us."

"Cool."

Bailey hesitated again, then turned and strode to the long table on the far side of the cafeteria, where Mikayla and Liz waved, and Zoe smiled at her with her toothy grin. Spike Newson and Trevor Baker, two stars of Cove Haven's football team, sat at the other end of the table with a few other boys wearing their varsity jackets.

"She seems different." Lacey's voice jolted me from my spiraling thoughts.

"Yeah." I pulled out my sandwich, finding I'd lost my appetite.

"Then again, I guess I switched tables last year too." She nodded toward two boys and a girl who sat in the corner with textbooks spread out next to their lunches. "They only talk about coding."

Bailey and I had sometimes referred to the group at the nearby table as the computer nerds because they spent so much time in the computer lab writing code or doing something similar, none of which we understood. Jasper Jones used to sit there too. And Lacey. But after Jasper's suicide, the dynamics at the table must have changed.

"I think you made a good choice."

Lacey smiled and set down her book as Dan and Henry returned with their pizza slices and drinks. "Where's Bailey?" Dan asked.

I tilted my head toward the windows. "She's eating over there now. With the cheerleaders."

"Seriously?"

"Yeah."

Henry shook his head, smiling. "Wow. That's a bitch move if I've ever seen one."

The rest of us couldn't help chuckling at that.

I picked up Dad's sweater from the couch, folded it, and set it on the stairs, tidying up before Bailey got here. The first week at school had left me exhausted, but I was excited for our sleepover. I couldn't wait to fill Bailey in on all the funny things that had happened in my classes. We'd both been half asleep when we'd walked to school this morning, but she'd confirmed she'd be over at six o'clock.

The clock on our living room wall read 5:40 p.m. when a

light knock sounded on the door. Bailey was early, probably just as anxious as me to get together.

I pulled open the door, where Bailey stood, wearing jeans and an unbuttoned flannel shirt with a T-shirt underneath.

"Hi. You're early."

She nodded and glanced over her shoulder. That's when I noticed her lips pulling downward, and that she didn't have her pillow or the overnight bag she usually brought. "I'm really sorry, but I have to cancel for tonight. I didn't realize I have cheer practice tomorrow morning. It's to get ready for the football game next weekend."

"Can't we just go to bed a little earlier? I don't care." Dishes clanged from the kitchen as I waited for Bailey's response.

She glanced over her shoulder toward her house. "My mom said I can't do both. She wants me to get plenty of sleep because it's been a long week."

"Oh." I crossed my arms in front of me, not sure whether to call Bailey out on her bullshit. Mrs. Maddox was a high-functioning alcoholic who was addicted to soap operas and could care less how much sleep Bailey got. But I didn't want to make things worse.

Bailey pushed a piece of her sandy blonde hair away from her eyes. "Can we reschedule another time when things are less hectic? I'm really sorry."

"Yeah. Fine."

"Thanks for understanding." She started to leave but turned back to face me, pulling up the chain on her neck to reveal the small puzzle piece. "I really like this necklace you gave me. I've been wearing it every day."

My hand reflexively reached for the identical necklace around my neck. "That's good. I like mine too."

Bailey offered a sad glance that seemed to say, "I'm sorry," before cutting across the yard to her front door. Mom poked her head into the foyer and said, "Is Bailey here already?"

I shook my head, motioning toward the front door. "She had to cancel because of cheerleading practice."

"Ah." Mom's eyelids lowered. "Dad and I will watch a movie with you. We can still order the pizza."

"Okay." I forced a smile, but the bright glow of my earlier anticipation had been doused in black paint.

It was still light out an hour and a half later and, after eating pizza with my parents, I decided to make the best of the quiet night. I hooked our dog, Rufus, to his leash, following our usual thirty-minute route through the neighborhood, across Main Street, and down the pathway along the beach. The summer tourists were mostly gone by now, so I freed Rufus and let him swim in the lake, which was his favorite thing to do. I loved watching him bob through the water and circle back, tail wagging wildly as he re-emerged on the beach, shaking, water flying off him in all directions. We repeated the exercise several times, and my spirits had lifted by the time the sun sank behind the lake and we headed home.

The shadows grew longer as I strolled along Main Street, keeping Rufus close to me as an occasional car passed and laughter and conversation drifted from the nearby restaurants— The Chicken Shack and Joe's Diner. That's when the high-pitched babble of Bailey's laugh met my ears. I turned my head toward the giggles, feeling as if someone had knocked the wind out of me.

Bailey emerged from the backseat of a car on the opposite side of the street. She smoothed down her hair and followed Liz, Zoe, and Mikayla into Joe's Diner. She'd changed her clothes since I'd seen her on my doorstep, now wearing a black mini-skirt and a white sleeveless shirt, her wavy hair flowing down her back as she disappeared into the diner.

It took a minute to catch my breath as I pulled Rufus into the shadows, sinking my fingers into his damp fur. His saucer eyes looked up at me, confused by the pause in our walk. Bailey had lied to me. And it wasn't just that she was too tired to hang out. She wanted to be with them instead. We were next-door neighbors who'd been best friends since kindergarten, we spent entire summers building sandcastle towns on the beach, we knew each other's dreams and secrets, we braided each other's hair, we shared our crushes with each other, and the details of our first kisses, we made up silly dance routines, we stayed up until three in the morning laughing about the dumb things our parents said, and in seventh grade, we embarrassed ourselves in front of the entire middle school singing "Hakuna Matata" in the school talent show. Nothing ever seemed bad when Bailey was by my side because I could be myself, and it was easy. But now, she preferred these other girls over me. A part of me understood why. They were the confident, shiny trendsetters who told the rest of the school what was cool and what wasn't. And maybe it was only natural for her to be attracted to that power, to want something different in her final year of high school.

I jiggled the leash and pulled Rufus along the sidewalk, traveling a block further north so as not to have to pass the diner. Tears built behind my eyes as I jogged the rest of the way home. I reminded myself that Bailey was allowed to have other friends just like I had other friends. We would likely be living in different cities next year anyway. Maybe I was overreacting. Still, she'd lied to me and ditched me again. *A bitch move*, as Henry would have said.

I let myself in through the front door, hoping to slip past my parents and hide in my room. But Dad paused the movie, stretching his arms over his head.

Mom glanced at me from the living room couch. "Did you have a nice walk?"

I unclipped Rufus from his leash, not looking up. "Yeah. I guess." My voice hitched with emotion.

"What's wrong?" Mom sat up straighter.

I couldn't stop my face from crumpling and the tears from leaking out. "I saw Bailey with her new cheerleader friends. She lied to me about the sleepover."

Mom rubbed my back. "Oh, dear."

Dad joined us in the foyer now, looking uncomfortable. He placed two large hands on my shoulders, demanding eye contact. "Keep your chin up, Brooke. Never give her the satisfaction of seeing you cry. If Bailey turns out like either one of her parents, you're better off without her."

Mom tilted her head. "Gary!"

"It's just an observation."

I nodded along with Dad's words, familiar with his refrain to keep my chin up and his belief that crying was a trait reserved for failures. It was advice he'd given me and Derek many times before. Prior to going to trade school and becoming an electrician, Dad had spent two years in the army, where he'd learned never to show weakness to his enemy.

With the back of my hand, I wiped the wetness from my cheeks, pulling myself together and hardening my emotions. "I'm going to bed."

"She'll come around." Mom offered a sad smile, then hugged me.

Dad squeezed my shoulder. "Good night, sweetheart."

I retreated to my bedroom, shocked by the sight of my puffy eyes in the mirror and ashamed I'd let Bailey get to me. The silver necklace peeked out from beneath my shirt, and it suddenly felt toxic, as if it were burning my skin. I unclasped the necklace, removed it from my neck, and buried it in the bottom of my jewelry box.

SIX

NOW

I cut down Main Street, heading back toward Drips Café, which seemed a less depressing destination than sitting alone in an empty house. Bailey's memory pulsed through me as if the discovery of the necklace had unleashed her spirit. Somehow, I felt her with me, prodding me along in the search for answers. Someone in town had set Hannah into action because they knew Bailey's death hadn't been a suicide. But who was it? Dozens of potential anonymous tipsters raced through my mind, but not one more likely than any other.

The return trip was taking longer, my feet moving more slowly after the disappointing encounter with Willa. Along the sidewalks, a small crew of people in orange vests hung colorful flags that said "Cove Haven Harvest Festival" from the lamp-posts. The Harvest Festival was an annual mid-June celebration intended to honor the area's farmers but, from what I could remember, had become more about marching bands, horses, and promoting local businesses. The last one I'd attended had been twenty-one years earlier, Bailey and I scraping spoonfuls of frozen lemonade from flimsy cups as we viewed the parade with the kind of detachment only bored teenagers could muster.

I did a double take at the storefronts along Main Street, finding them more well-maintained than I remembered, their bold signs, shiny windows, and contrasting exterior walls reminiscent of an Edward Hopper painting. But while some change was to be expected, what shocked me even more was how much had remained the same. Landmarks like Joe's Diner, Molly's donut shop, The Chicken Shack, and the Rotary Club appeared to have been preserved in a time capsule. Even the kitschy dime store still stood under the same rusted metal sign I remembered as a child, with a familiar handwritten piece of cardboard taped to the window, alerting fishermen "Night Crawlers Sold Here," just as it had decades earlier. The small-town charm was ingrained in Cove Haven's DNA, and probably part of what drew the tourists from their hectic lives in the cities and suburbs.

I approached Drips Café slowly, peering through the window toward the table where Hannah had been sitting, and finding it empty. Breathing easier, I ducked through the door, where a half-dozen people languished at small tables around the coffee shop, and the line at the counter had disappeared.

"Back already?" Gabe, the owner of Drips, asked with a smile. He was a towering man with a reddish beard. I thought he'd be better suited as a lumberjack if he wasn't so charming. I'd met him three days ago, my first morning back in town, explaining I'd be here all summer fixing up my mom's house and would probably need somewhere else to hang out while the work was being done. "You found the perfect spot," he'd said with a wink. "I won't even charge you rent." Then he told me how he'd visited Cove Haven on a summer weekend getaway five years earlier and never left, a line I'd heard him repeat to at least three other patrons in the last few days.

I smiled at him. "Just a water, please."

"You got it."

I grabbed a seat at the counter, the same counter where

Bailey and I used to sit and drink chocolate sodas and root beer floats. In a previous life, Drips Café had been an ice cream shop called Scoops, where Bailey had worked the summer before our senior year and where she regularly passed me and Derek free ice cream cones when the manager's back was turned. My chest swelled at the memory.

Gabe set a cardboard cup filled with water in front of me. "I saw you talking to that podcaster earlier."

"Yeah." I tightened my jaw, reluctant to tell him about my personal connection to the prom queen of Cove Haven. My brief conversations with Gabe had been enjoyable precisely because he had no ties to my past.

He continued. "Hannah's been in here the last few afternoons and then this morning. She seems nice enough. Probably going to piss off a lot of people in town, though."

"I was thinking the same thing. She's trying to monetize one of Cove Haven's biggest tragedies."

Gabe shook his head. "Money, money, money. That's what it's all about, unfortunately."

I nodded toward the cup of water. "Speaking of which, how much for the water?"

He waved me off. "No charge. Not for you, anyway."

Gabe held my gaze a moment too long, and an odd sensation traveled through me. Was he flirting just a little? It had been so long since I'd dated anyone other than Shane. I didn't even know the signs anymore.

Before I had the chance to say anything stupid, the door swooshed open, and a familiar face headed toward me. It was one I was happy to see. "Lacey?" I leaned back on the stool to face her. "It's Brooke."

"Oh my gosh!" She stepped forward and hugged me, her hair carrying the faint scent of musty paper and flowery perfume. "I heard you were in town. I was going to stop by and say hi."

Lacey was now the head librarian at the Cove Haven Public Library, located several blocks from the coffee shop. She had attended Mom's visitation at the funeral home six months ago. Ruthie had been with me then—and even Shane—along with so many other townspeople showing up to pay their respects. I'd observed Lacey from afar, thinking how she'd grown into herself, more confident in her chosen calling in life. But Lacey and I hadn't had much chance to talk that day. And before that, I hadn't seen her since she'd visited for a weekend during my freshman year of college. We'd promised to meet up again, but new friends and classes got in the way, and we never made it happen.

"This is why I love small towns," Gabe said, looking between us. "Everyone knows each other."

"That's also a reason to hate small towns." I pulled away from Lacey, who giggled and shook her head at my response.

"It's so great to have you back, Brooke. Even if it's just for a couple of months."

"Thanks." I patted the stool next to me, and Lacey sat down. "How are things at the library?"

"Pretty good, except for the lack of funding. But we have a day camp starting in two weeks, and it's completely full. That's the summer tourist effect." She leaned in closer as her smile faded. "Did you hear about the podcaster?"

"Yeah. I met her this morning." I caught the flash of concern on Lacey's face and glanced away, leaving out the part about the necklace. "I didn't tell her who I was."

Lacey nodded. "Good. But she's going to find out. She's been hanging out at the library and going through materials from back then—old maps and yearbooks and the like. She's using the meeting room to record her episodes. I mean, what does she think she's going to solve? The police determined it was a suicide back when real evidence was available."

I murmured my agreement, deciding to keep my doubts

about the cause of Bailey's death to myself as long as Gabe was nearby. "She probably views it as a sensational story she can make money on. That's what we were just saying."

Gabe stepped closer, peering down at us. "Wait. Did you know the prom queen?"

I wrapped my fingers around the cardboard cup of water, measuring my words. "Yeah. Bailey was a close friend."

"She was Brooke's best friend for a while," Lacey said, offering another concerned look.

Gabe's eyes grew wide, the hint of a frown showing through his unruly beard. "Oh. Wow. I'm so sorry. I always kind of thought of it as more of an urban myth. It's so sad to think someone so young really died that way, much less one of your friends."

"I've never really gotten over it, to be honest."

Lacey shifted her weight. "Me neither."

"I'm sorry." Gabe tapped his thick fingers on the counter. "Hannah shouldn't be stirring up something that should be left alone." He released a long, low whistle, shaking his head and staring out the far window as Lacey and I sat in silence. A few seconds later, he returned to himself. "Can I get you a drink, Lacey?"

Lacey ordered a coffee, and Gabe went to retrieve it as we drifted toward other subjects, including my plans for sprucing up Mom's house and how much I already missed Ruthie. Lacey told me she was divorced and owned a small house in a neighborhood about a mile north of town. She was planning for a visit from her sister, Maeve, over the Harvest Festival weekend and was looking forward to a couple of days off from the library.

I remembered how quiet and mousy Lacey had been in high school, with her head always in a book. But she'd been there for me during senior year when Bailey had ditched me for her new group of friends. Lacey had accepted me as is, never requiring anything of me other than occasionally needing to tell me about an especially good book she'd read.

Lacey checked her phone and said she had to return to the library. We promised each other we'd meet for dinner soon.

A trim man with slicked-back hair held the door open for Lacey as she left. His pressed black pants, button-down shirt, and polished leather shoes stuck out in the casual and beachy surroundings. Another heavier-set man dressed in similar clothes followed behind him, dark sunglasses shielding his face.

"We can run the numbers here and call the office from the site," the first one said to the other. His voice was too loud for the small coffee shop, and a few people turned to stare.

"A large shaken cold brew with oat milk," the second man said to Gabe, who nodded as the other man gave his order.

I turned away, noting the BMW parked outside with an Illinois plate. I wondered if these were the developers of The Train Station hotel, the men Willa had referred to as vultures and devils.

They continued talking loudly to each other about things like price per square foot and possible easements as Gabe set their drinks on the counter. I stole a few glances at them until the one with the sunglasses caught me staring and turned away. Maybe I wasn't being as stealthy as I imagined.

"I have to take this," the same man said to his colleague. He pressed his phone to his ear and scurried out the door, with his colleague following behind him.

Just as I decided to tell Gabe more about my complicated history with Bailey, a large group filed into the café, talking about needing caffeine before going out on their boat, and immediately placing their orders. I'd lost my chance for a private conversation.

Hopping off the stool, I nodded goodbye to Gabe, who acknowledged me with a wink. He seemed like a nice guy who was easy to be around, although I didn't feel any sort of romantic attraction to him. I'd heard that the most enduring relationships often began as friendships, so I promised myself to stay open-minded as I left the coffee shop.

The two businessmen stood near the BMW, the broad-shouldered man still absorbed in his phone call. I stepped toward them, gathering my courage to ask a few questions about the hotel. "Excuse me," I said to the one who wasn't on the call. "Are you with Harsons Real Estate Group?"

He shrugged. "Is it that obvious?"

"Kind of."

The man chuckled, holding out his hand. "Michael Harsons." He nodded toward the car. "That's my partner, Jonathan."

I shook Michael's hand as Jonathan turned his back toward me and continued barking responses into the phone. "We've gotta go," Jonathan said, ducking into the driver's seat.

"I was just wondering when you're breaking ground on the hotel?" I asked Michael, who remained outside the car.

"All set for July 14th. Just five weeks away. The information is on our website." He raised his hand. "Sorry. We're running late."

"Can you leave Willa alone? The old woman in the yellow house. She's not well."

He paused, making a face. "We don't have much of a choice. She lives in the middle of what should have been an outdoor pool. She's caused a lot of headaches."

"Michael! Let's go." Jonathan yelled through a crack in the window as he started the ignition.

Michael gave a nod and slipped into the passenger seat.

I watched the car idle by the curb, unsure what to think. The men were brusque and made a poor first impression, but they were also in a rush. Their BMW careened through a U-turn as I pulled out my phone to text Ruthie a message. I wanted to tell her to have a great day and that I loved her. But as

I started typing, the car slowed next to me, motor humming. My gaze lifted toward it, catching Jonathan looking at me through the driver's side window, the black sunglasses still covering his eyes. The moment I caught him staring, he gunned the car forward, leaving me in a cloud of dust and fumes. A warning pricked over my scalp as I watched them disappear around the bend. I'd discounted Willa when she referred to the real estate developers as "the devils," but now it occurred to me that maybe she hadn't been completely wrong. Something about the men felt off. Jonathan in particular. The way he'd dodged me, only to stare from behind his sunglasses, engine revving, left a sour swirl in my stomach. I shook off the strange encounter, turning my attention back to my text and hoping I wouldn't run into them again.

SEVEN

NOW

I leaned back in the wicker chair, taking in the crisscrossing string of white lights above my head and the well-kept flower garden bordering the wooden fence. Dan, one of my oldest friends, and his wife, Maggie, had invited me over for dinner. I sat across from them on their back deck, nibbling at chips and guacamole and sipping a cold beer. Their six-year-old twins, Olivia and Marci, played in a sandbox nearby, occasionally wandering the perimeter of the yard for sticks, rocks, or flowers to add to their creations.

"How has it been? Coming back to Cove Haven, I mean," Maggie asked as she tucked her brunette curls behind her ear. She had an impish quality about her, but she was easygoing and down to earth. I'd taken an immediate liking to her the first time we'd met at their wedding over ten years earlier.

"It's been weird," I said. "So much has changed. And at the same time, so many places look exactly the same." I couldn't help thinking of Mom's house, the familiar nooks and crannies that were now empty, and that I'd soon be resurfacing or painting a more modern color, before passing it all on to a new owner.

Dan folded his hands, leaning forward. "I felt the same way when we moved back."

There'd been barely over a hundred people in our 2003 high school class, and it wouldn't have even been that big except our school drew from a few even tinier towns surrounding Cove Haven. Dan and I had been two of only nineteen people to pursue a college education. Most had stayed near Cove Haven to learn a trade, work the family farm, or survive a minimum-wage job, while a few others had joined the military. After graduating from Western Michigan, Dan had gone on a wilderness outing to Oregon, where he'd met Maggie. They'd gotten married a couple of years later and eventually moved back to Cove Haven when an opportunity arose for them to open a sports rental shop on Main Street.

I scooted my chair closer to the table, preparing to share the secret I'd been carrying all day. "I went over to The Treasure Cove this morning. It was such a sense of déjà vu."

Dan tipped his head back. "Oh, no. Was wacky Willa there?"

"Oh, yes. She told me her cats talk to her in her dreams."

Maggie slammed down her beer bottle and laughed. "That poor, poor woman. Those developers must have their hands full."

A look of bemused confusion stretched across Dan's face. "Why did you go there?"

I froze for a second, reconsidering whether my discovery of the necklace this morning was too big to share. On the other hand, there were few people in this town I trusted more than Dan. I'd known him since kindergarten. He was my date at senior prom the night Bailey died, although we had agreed to go as friends.

"There's a podcaster in town, Hannah Mead."

"I heard." Dan shook his head, he and Maggie sharing a look of disgust.

"She was at Drips this morning. I didn't tell her who I was, but she told me she's looking into Bailey's death because someone texted her an anonymous tip that it wasn't suicide."

Dan squinted, skeptical. "Anyone could have done that, even someone who never knew Bailey."

"Yeah. But..." I unzipped the pocket of my hoodie and closed my fingers around the cheap chain, pulling it into the dimming daylight and placing it on the table. "Hannah was wearing this."

They leaned forward, staring at the piece of jewelry I'd laid in front of them.

"Wait. Is that..." Dan started to say but lost his voice. "It can't be."

"It's Bailey's necklace. The one she was wearing that night. The one that was missing from her body when she died. The chain is different, but this is the pendant. I'm sure of it. I have the other half, and they fit together perfectly. There's a dot of nail polish in the same shade of purple that's on the back of my necklace. We painted our initials on the back the day I gave it to her." I paused, realizing my voice had become frantic.

Maggie's skin grew paler in the waning light.

"But how?" Dan asked, rubbing his forehead.

"I have no idea. But Hannah said she bought the necklace a couple of days ago at The Treasure Cove. Meaning someone in town probably had it all these years and recently donated it. Maybe the same person who sent the text to Hannah."

Dan placed his hands on top of his head. "Holy crap. Who dropped it off there?"

"That's the frustrating thing. Willa couldn't remember who brought it in. She said she'd let me know if her cats remembered."

"Oh, dear." Maggie closed her eyes and made a face. "Why would anyone drop that necklace at a thrift store?"

I stared at the mismatched necklace. "Maybe by mistake.

Maybe they didn't know who it belonged to. Or maybe it was mixed in with a bunch of other things."

"Or maybe Bailey was murdered like we've always suspected." Dan took a swig of his beer as I recalled dozens of hushed conversations we'd had after Bailey's death, meeting on the beach late at night to try to make sense of what happened, following long, twisting theories that had no proof to back them up. "Maybe someone thought enough time had passed that they were in the clear."

That thought had crossed my mind too. But another more troubling option had been weighing down my thoughts. The timing of the necklace seemed especially coincidental with my return to Cove Haven. Almost as if someone had been waiting for me to come back, had wanted me to see it, maybe acting on the likelihood I'd drop some of Mom's old belongings at the thrift shop. Except, Hannah had visited the store before me. I kept the paranoid theory to myself.

Dan grunted. "I mean, not many people knew about the necklace. It was really only you who thought it meant something that Bailey wasn't wearing it when she died."

I nodded, remembering how, a few days after Bailey's death, I'd been the first to realize that the necklace she'd been wearing that night was missing. And I'd only known that because I'd asked Mrs. Maddox if she would consider giving me the necklace back. Bailey's mom told me the necklace was never recovered. "Bailey must have taken it off at the bonfire or thrown it away somewhere," she'd said. "The search was very thorough."

She was correct that the search for Bailey's remains had been exhaustive. I'd seen the authorities combing the tracks with their metal detectors and plastic bags, some even using tweezers to collect the tiniest bone fragments or bits of the rhinestone tiara. Some items had been recovered up to a quarter-mile away because of the force of the impact. They'd been looking for a note too, but never found one, concluding that

Bailey must have been too distressed at that moment to think of writing one.

Amateur searchers took up the hunt in the days and weeks that followed for any sliver of overlooked evidence—note, necklace, or otherwise. But as far as I'd heard, nothing more besides a tooth fragment was ever found.

Like Mrs. Maddox, the police never gave much weight to my revelation about the missing necklace. They'd already decided that Bailey had caused her own death, probably imitating the suicide of Jasper Jones fourteen months earlier, and were quick to discard any information that didn't fit their theory. They leaned into the idea that Bailey had been depressed in the months prior to her death, a change in behavior her friends, family members, and teachers all claimed to have noticed, but only in retrospect. It wasn't too unlikely that she'd tossed the necklace that probably reminded her of a lost friendship into a nearby garbage can or some overgrown shrubs. Either that, or the necklace had gotten caught in the wheels and carried further down the tracks, before getting spit out again, never to be found. The police's explanations for the missing necklace had been plausible, and so my concern that someone may have stolen the necklace had fallen on deaf ears. Even worse, my introduction of the news of Bailey's missing necklace sparked rumors among the locals that I must have stolen it back, implying I'd done something even worse to her. I quickly learned to keep my mouth shut, holing up in my bedroom, and counting the days until I could leave for art school.

I pointed at the recovered relic. "Someone replaced the chain."

Maggie leaned back and hugged her thin arms around herself. "This is so creepy."

"I ran into Zoe as I was walking over there. She was... nice."

Dan nodded. "Yeah. She's not too bad. I see her around once in a while. Her older kid is a star baseball player."

"Who else from back then still lives in town?"

Dan stared off into the night. "I guess I don't know everyone, for sure. Maggie and I hang out with a different crowd now."

"We see Lacey every now and then," Maggie said.

Dan cleared his throat. "Trevor lives in one of those run-down places up on Route 16. He runs a mechanic shop that's seen better days. He and Mikayla got divorced a long time ago."

"Is Mikayla that rude woman who works at The Chicken Shack?" Maggie asked.

"Yeah. Her life is a mess. She has a ton of kids and still lives with her mom."

I closed my eyes, remembering Mikayla as someone who'd intimidated me with her confidence, her thick mascara and glossy lips, and her loud voice. Then in one night, she'd transformed into the jilted prom queen who wasn't. But Mikayla should have had the last laugh, as far as Zoe and Liz were concerned. She'd married the prom king in the end. Apparently, that hadn't gone as planned either. "Man. It's funny how things turn out."

A conspiratorial smile pulled at Dan's lips. "My dad always told me you never want to peak in high school. I think he was on to something."

"No kidding. Thankfully, you and I were total nerds back then."

"Here, here!" He raised his beer bottle and took another swig, and it was a relief to see the mood had lightened a tiny bit.

"What about Liz? And Spike?" I asked. "Where are they?"

"Liz is a hairdresser at a salon on the outskirts of town." Dan nodded toward his wife. "She cuts Maggie's hair."

Maggie nodded. "I see her every two months or so. My hair is pretty basic, but she does a good job. Tells lots of funny stories. I guess she was a lifeguard at the public beach for many summers. You wouldn't believe some of the stuff she saw."

"Huh." I couldn't reconcile Maggie's description with the memory of the Liz I'd known in high school, the one who'd always had her nose in the air and who'd used Bailey for her own benefit. "I guess people grow up at some point." I gripped my beer, taking another sip. "What about Spike?"

"Who's Spike?" Maggie asked.

"He was Bailey's date the night of prom," I said, leaving out the part about how she'd all but ignored him.

Dan picked at the label on his bottle. "Spike's family moved to Milwaukee after we graduated, remember? I think he went to a community college somewhere over there too. As far as I know, that's where he still lives."

"That's right." I'd pushed so many memories of Cove Haven out of my mind in the intervening years that I was thankful Dan was nearby to retrieve some of them for me.

Maggie sighed, a faraway look in her eyes. "The thing is, anyone could have dropped that necklace off at the thrift store. Even someone who just found it in the woods."

"Yeah. I was thinking the same thing," I said. "It really doesn't prove anything."

Dan ran his fingers through his thinning hair. "I always wondered about Spike, though. He and his family were so quick to leave town and never come back."

"Weren't we all quick to leave town and never come back?" I asked.

A dry chuckle escaped Dan's mouth. "Yeah. I guess. Except here we are."

I felt my weight sink into my chair.

We continued to test theories about various people who could have wanted to harm Bailey or take her necklace, and possible motives, from revenge to self-defense. Finally, Maggie edged forward and said, "Hey. Guys? I hate to be the one to tell you this—and please don't take this the wrong way—but isn't it more likely that Bailey died the way the police said she did? I mean, it sounds like she'd been depressed about not being able to go to college. She'd ditched Brooke." Maggie paused, frowning. "And she ditched you, too, Dan. Then her new friends weren't the people she thought they were. And it sounds like her parents weren't the greatest. Maybe she felt like she was out of options."

I sat back, unclenching my jaw and remembering that this was the problem with questioning Bailey's death. It never led anywhere, never reached any satisfying destination. Time and time again, suicide surfaced as the most logical option, though never sealed with any certainty. Unanswered questions always poked through, creating a gaping hole like a final chapter ripped from a book.

But now the necklace lay before me like a piece of my former best friend rising from the dead, restoring a few pages of that missing chapter. The necklace had landed in front of me for a reason. It seemed obvious that someone in this town—likely one of my former high school classmates—knew more than they were saying, and I was determined to find out who it was. And as much as I didn't want to revisit the most painful time of my life, to kick up the dust of old rumors, I had to follow the necklace wherever it led me.

EIGHT

THEN

October 2002

A fall chill prickled against my skin, and I kicked at a tuft of grass. I looked at my watch again, then at the blackened windows of Bailey's house. First hour started in seven minutes, and my English teacher, Ms. Parsons, was a stickler for punctuality. Tired of waiting for Bailey to join me, I turned from her front porch and headed toward school alone.

"Brooke, wait!" Bailey's voice reached me from behind. She exited her house and jogged to meet me, swinging her backpack over one shoulder.

I strode forward, already angry at myself for waiting as long as I did. "We're going to be late."

"Relax. Five years from now, it won't matter if you were late for first hour." She chuckled. "Five days from now, it won't matter."

"It matters to me. I don't like being late for things, especially Ms. Parsons' class."

"Okay."

She trotted beside me, but I refused to look at her. I'd never confronted her about the night she'd ditched our sleepover to go to the diner with her new friends, but I had distanced myself, making a point not to invite her over again or attend any of the football games where she cheered.

She peered over her shoulder at me. "The only class I care about anymore is drama."

Bailey wanted me to ask her what was so great about Mr. Sampson's drama class, but I wasn't playing.

Bailey kept pace with me, still looking in my direction. "I saw your mural in the hallway, Brooke. It's really good."

"Thanks." My six-foot-long painting of the Cove Haven lighthouse holding steadfast amid violent Lake Michigan waters as a storm swept through had been selected from all of Mrs. Avery's students to adorn the front wall of the school. I'd been proud of the way I'd layered the white and gray paint to create movement in the waves.

"I bet you're going to be a famous artist someday."

I shrugged, pretending I didn't care what she thought.

She plucked at the loose strap of her backpack. "Hey. Do you want to know a secret?" The tone of her voice had changed to something playful and mischievous.

I kept my eyes straight ahead, but I could see Bailey was trying hard to connect. My curiosity got the better of me. "Sure."

"I think Trevor is cute."

An involuntary grimace pulled down my mouth. "You and half the girls in the school."

"Ha."

"I thought Trevor and Zoe were together. Or is it Mikayla now?"

She waved me off. "Zoe is old news. He's dating Mikayla, but I doubt it will last. I caught him staring at me yesterday." We took a few more steps before she spoke again. "Do you think I should tell one of his friends how I feel?"

I slowed my pace and looked at her, checking to see if she'd lost her mind. "No. I think you should be careful."

"What does that mean?"

"It means those girls would chop off your head and feed it to the sharks if one of them even dreamt you were messing with her man."

Bailey crossed her arms in front of her chest, frowning. "Don't be so dramatic, Brooke. This is why I don't tell you things."

I wasn't sure what "things" Bailey wasn't telling me, but I'd felt the chasm opening between us recently, and her words stung. Now my blunt advice had likely made things worse. I debated closing the gap by sharing my crush on Will Tuttle, a serious, long-haired boy in three of my classes whose dad worked at the marina, but I suspected she wouldn't approve.

The bell rang in the distance, sending a jolt of panic through me as I envisioned Ms. Parsons' pinched features reprimanding me in front of the class. "I've gotta go." I sprinted toward school, leaving Bailey behind.

Seven hours later, the final bell of the school day had rung, releasing a horde of teenagers onto the school grounds. I flanked the exterior brick wall, cutting past a group of freshmen to take the quickest path home.

Mikayla's shrill voice cut through the air, making me pause. "Oh my God, Bailey. Spike is so into you. It's not even funny."

I stopped short of turning the corner, ducking behind a tall shrub.

"Do you like him?" It was Liz who asked the question, her gravelly voice easily identifiable. "You guys would make such a cute couple."

"Yeah. I'm not sure." Bailey paused. "He's funny and everything, but…"

"Ooh. She likes someone else. Who is it?"

Still hidden behind the bush, I held my breath, hoping she wouldn't admit to liking Trevor in front of Trevor's current girlfriend. My instinct was to protect her, and I fought the urge to jump out from my hiding place and clamp my hand over her mouth.

"No one," Bailey said. "I'm just not sure about Spike."

"Give him a chance, at least."

"Yeah. Maybe."

One of the girls coughed, and it sounded too close.

I stepped back, pressing my back against the wall, hoping they didn't wander in this direction. But a few seconds later, the voices faded. I peeked around the branches finding them further away, backs facing me. Zoe and Liz stopped to do a little dance and Bailey threw her head back in laughter. I stayed there for a minute, jealousy booming in my chest as I watched Bailey walk toward the football field with her new friends.

NINE

NOW

The night after my dinner with Dan and Maggie, I lay on the couch watching a low-budget thriller about a mother who realizes her son may have murdered his prep-school classmate. Derek had canceled Mom's cable weeks earlier, and this was the best programming I could get via the old-school antennae. The consignment company had arrived this afternoon with a large moving truck and removed the pieces of furniture they could resell. The tattered couch I now sat on, the worn coffee table in front of me, and the outdated TV were a few items that remained, along with my bed upstairs. With most of the furniture gone, it would be easier for the construction crew to begin removing the dated wallpaper and worn carpeting on Monday.

I pushed Ruthie's name on my phone, reading through our recent texts. I'd been sending her daily messages, telling her I wished she was here, that I was sure she'd love the beach, the dime store, the putt-putt golf course, and the soft-serve ice cream place nearby. I'd gone through the closets in the basement this morning, putting together a box of board games that I thought Ruthie would like and trying not to think of the last time I played them, which had most likely been with Bailey.

I miss you! I typed. *Did you have fun at camp today?* I added a bunch of tent emojis even though that wasn't the type of camping she was doing. Ruthie had a big appreciation for emojis.

Yes! Her response was followed by five smiley faces. *Did you have fun today?*

I couldn't help but chuckle at that. An hour of directing furniture removal, followed by several hours of cleaning out hard-to-reach cupboards and moth-bitten closets, hadn't been my idea of fun. My body felt like a twisted heap of broken bones.

> *Not exactly fun, but I made some progress on the house. I can't wait to see you again!*

> *Me too. Dad and I are going to see a movie now.*

> *Have a good time!*

My heart hurt. In a parallel universe, maybe we were all still together, and I was grabbing my purse and going to the movie with them. I banished the vision from my mind, reminding myself it wasn't productive. Shane and his girlfriend, Mandy, had already moved in together. I wanted to ask if Mandy was going to the movie too but stopped myself. I hated that I still had feelings for my ex-husband, while he had no trouble moving on. In his own words, he'd found someone who wasn't as 'emotionally unstable' as me. It had been over a year since the divorce, and while Shane and I had our differences, I'd never doubted his devotion as a dad.

Ruthie sent three hearts back. I closed my eyes and hugged my phone to my chest. I watched the movie for another hour, and when I couldn't keep my eyes open any longer, I climbed

the creaky stairs to bed. Before turning in for the night, I
checked the closet for the locked metal box that held the necklaces. I'd moved it in there, along with a few stacks of clothes,
before the consignment company had carried away my empty
dresser. The box sat exactly where I'd left it. I turned off the
lights, climbed into bed, and went to sleep.

Something creaked, waking me from my dreams. I froze as the
bright numbers of my alarm clock glowed through the darkness:
3:14 a.m. I sat up, tilting my ear toward the doorway and
listening for the noise again. A floorboard groaned from somewhere downstairs. Was it a footstep? My pulse accelerated. The
old house made strange noises, and I told myself not to freak
out. We'd never locked our doors when I was growing up. No
one in Cove Haven did. But those were different times. The
town had doubled in size since then. People didn't necessarily
know their neighbors anymore. I thought back to earlier in the
day, retracing my steps after I'd gotten home from my quick trip
to the café. I pictured myself locking the front door, but I
couldn't remember if I'd secured the back lock, the one off the
laundry room that led to the backyard and the detached garage.
Oh, no. That's the way I'd come in.

The clap of something wooden caused my heart to lurch.
What was that? A cupboard closing? A door? Or was it the
wind banging a loose shutter? My hand fumbled through the
darkness, finding the phone on my nightstand. I debated
whether to call 911, but was afraid of looking like a fool if it was
only the wind or the constant bumble and grind of the ancient
refrigerator downstairs. I pressed 9, then 1, then slipped my legs
out from beneath the sheets, slowly rising to my feet. I paused,
waiting for another creak or bump to urge me to hit the final

digit. For several seconds, there were only a few gusts of wind blowing against the window. Maybe it was nothing. I couldn't imagine why anyone would want to break into a house that had just been cleared of eighty percent of its contents.

Suddenly, Bailey's necklace glinted in my mind, along with the idea that someone had brought it out of years of hiding specifically for me to see. *Oh my God.* Was someone after me? My heart raced, but I gritted my teeth, wishing I hadn't watched that creepy movie before going to sleep. It had set me on edge.

I wouldn't be able to sleep until I made sure I was alone. I inched toward the bedroom door, carefully turning the door-knob and opening the door to the shadowy hallway. Pulling in a breath of courage, I careened toward the light switch across the hall and flicked it on. I braced myself for an armed intruder to be standing directly in front of me, maybe one of the locals who believed the rumors that I'd killed my friend and had been waiting years to get payback. Instead, the overhead light illuminated an empty corridor stretching toward the stairs. I slumped forward, arms dropping to my sides.

Drawing air into my lungs, I forced my bare feet forward until I reached the top step. Below me, beyond the flight of stairs, the small foyer sat empty, the lock on the front door secured. I paused, listening. Again, I heard nothing except the light whistle of the wind outside and the low hum of the refrigerator turning on in the kitchen. I made my way down the steps with my finger still positioned over the 1 on my phone. At last, I reached the foyer, keeping my back against the wobbly banister and peering into the empty dining room and the kitchen beyond. The lighting was poor, and I could barely discern the outlines of cabinets, appliances, and counters. Nothing appeared out of place. I scooted the other way, peering into the living room. Just as I reached to turn on the light—BAM!—

something crashed against the window. I screamed and jumped backward, covering my face. A second later, something more delicate, like fingernails, scratched the glass. Lowering my hand from my eyes, I studied the windowpane, realizing it was only a tree branch making the noise. An overgrown oak tree grew on that side of the house, and a gust of wind had caused a branch to hit the window. That must have been the loud noise I'd heard when I was upstairs too.

I rubbed my palms on my pajama shorts and took a confident step forward, turning on the lights in the living room, and finding everything exactly as I'd left it. I shook my head at my paranoia, making a mental note to trim the tree branches. One more item on the to-do list, but at least it was work I could complete myself. I did a quick tour of the other rooms, checking the closets and bathrooms for anything suspicious, ultimately returning to the conclusion that it was only me in the house. I pushed the thought of a stalker from my mind, reminding myself that the idea that someone would target me twenty years after Bailey's death was ridiculous. Then, I deleted the two dialed digits from my phone and went to the kitchen to make some chamomile tea. I turned on every available light, eager to rid the jitters from my body. In the harsh light of the kitchen, I could see, again, that everything was just as I'd left it. I grabbed a mug and then headed toward the small pantry in the laundry room to find the tea. That's when I noticed the handle of the back door, its brass fixtures shining back at me. A fresh jolt of fear speared through me as I realized my previous worry had been correct: I'd left the door unlocked.

My head swung around in all directions, but I saw nothing. Heard nothing. Lunging forward, I turned the lock, exhaling at the sound of the click. I reminded myself that I'd already checked the whole house, and the noise I'd heard was merely the wind moving a tree branch. Even so, my nerves rattled through me. The town was small, and many people likely knew I was back staying in my old house. As much as I tried, I couldn't erase the thought that someone was trying to scare me. I skipped the tea, left the lights on, and returned to bed with my eyes wide open.

TEN

THEN

November 2002

It was three minutes before midnight on a Saturday night in early November. I sat at my bedroom desk, dipping my brush into the inky paint and adding a dab of black to achieve a darker hue. After suffering through last night's football game, where Trevor and Mikayla were announced homecoming king and queen at halftime, I'd happily skipped tonight's homecoming dance. Will Tuttle hadn't asked me—or anyone else—to be his date, and Dan, Henry, and Lacey hadn't wanted to go. My bedroom window faced the front of the house, and with my tiny desk light tilted downward and the full moon outside, the last few dead leaves clinging to the branches of the oak tree were visible as they rustled in the wind. I flicked my brush across the canvas, practicing the technique of painting a scene through a window at night. The effect of the glass was proving to be a challenge. Three weeks ago, I submitted my application and portfolio to Stamps School of Art, along with inquiries to various organizations offering financial aid. Now I kept busy with plenty of new projects in case the school asked for additional pieces while I waited for a response.

The moon hung low in the night sky, and I studied its shape behind the wispy clouds. But as I stared through the glass, flashing lights marred the soft lighting. I stood up, shocked to find a police cruiser easing to a halt in Bailey's driveway. Beneath the pulsing lights, a thick-necked, grim-faced officer in his early twenties emerged from the driver's seat and opened the back door. He took Bailey's arm as she stumbled out of the backseat, her lacey, black dress slightly askew. My brush fell from my hand, landing on the canvas and ruining my painting. Suddenly my project didn't matter. Bailey was in some kind of trouble.

I threw on a hoodie and shoved my feet into a pair of sneakers, running past the bedroom where my parents slept and taking the steps two at a time. I slipped out the front door. One house over, Mr. Maddox flipped on the porch light and stepped outside just as I reached the edge of our yard, crouching behind a line of boxwood bushes to avoid being seen.

The officer supported Bailey's weight as she slumped forward, crying and saying, "I'm sorry."

Mr. Maddox scowled. "What the hell is going on here?"

"Evening, sir. I'm Officer Warner. I pulled over your daughter for driving under the influence. We got the other passengers in the car home first, but now I need to take her in for processing. She's a minor, so I'll need a parent or legal guardian present."

Bailey's dad threw his head back. "Oh, for the love of—"

"Oh my God! Is everyone okay?" Mrs. Maddox stepped next to her husband, her bathrobe cinched tightly around her ample midsection.

I spied through the leafy hedges, my feet sinking into the ground as the scene unfolded. Bailey and I had stolen a beer a couple of times last year from her mom's stash in the garage, secretly sipping the sour, bubbly liquid from a tumbler and making faces. But we'd been sitting on the beach, not consuming much, and walking home—definitely not driving. Bailey had been going to so many parties these last few months, especially after football games, and while she might not have tried to exclude me, it just wasn't my idea of fun. I preferred hanging out at Joe's Diner or Scoops and talking with one or two people, usually Dan and Lacey. Sometimes Henry or one of my friends from art class. That was what Bailey used to like to do too.

Officer Warner spoke again. "Everyone is okay, but unfortunately, this will go on her record and there will be a fine. She may have her license suspended and will probably have to do some community service. A judge will decide all of that. We'll go over this down at the station."

Mr. Maddox glared at his daughter. "What have you done?"

"I'm sorry." Bailey slurred her words, head slumped downward. "There was a bonfire after the dance, and some people needed a ride home."

"And you were drinking?" Mrs. Maddox's voice was louder now, and I wondered if she saw the irony of criticizing her daughter for copying her own behavior.

The officer stepped forward. "Okay, let's all take a breath. If you folks want to get your clothes on and meet me at the station. Or one of you can ride in the back with her. We can get her back home with you yet tonight."

"We'll meet you there. Where's the car?" Mr. Maddox asked. "That was from the dealership. Not for you to drive into a ditch!"

Officer Warner raised his hand. "It's over on Main Street. They were partying in the woods behind the train station, and we got a call about a car swerving down the road. Thankfully, no one went into a ditch."

I held my breath, crouching lower. I wouldn't be able to talk to Bailey tonight, but this was bad, something Bailey would never have done if she'd been with me. I wouldn't have let her. She was in trouble because of those girls.

———————

On Monday morning before school, I waited outside Bailey's house. I'd tried to see her the day before, but her dad told me she wasn't allowed any visitors. Now she slunk through the front door, looking like she'd been to hell and back. She wore her hair in a severe ponytail which only accentuated the purple hollows under her eyes and the red cracks in her chapped lips.

"Are you okay?" I asked, touching her arm.

Bailey's eyes flickered toward me, then refocused ahead. "Yeah. It's been a long weekend." She began walking in the direction of our school, and for once, I had to pick up my pace to keep up.

"I saw you getting out of the police car. I heard about the DUI."

She frowned. "I'm sure the whole school knows by now."

"Why did you drive? Why didn't you just walk home?"

"Because some of the other girls live further out. They needed rides home. And Trevor too."

"Didn't they see you drinking?"

Bailey hoisted her backpack further up on her shoulder and kept walking.

"They're not your friends, Bailey. They're using you because you have a car."

"Thanks." Her voice was cold and sharp.

"I'm trying to help."

"It's not working." A streak of clear liquid ran down Bailey's cheek, and she wiped it away. "Anyway, they are my friends. I made a mistake. That's it."

"I'm here for you, you know. I'm still your friend."

"I know. It's just that I'm really into cheerleading right now. I'm sorry that it's taking up so much time. It must be hard for you."

"Yeah." I could see that Bailey was in a bad place, so I swallowed back about a hundred other comments about how she'd been acting like a different person and how Dan and Henry had started keeping tally of what they called her "bitch moves." It wasn't only me who'd noticed the change.

Things got weirder once we reached school. Liz, Zoe, and Mikayla met Bailey outside the front doors with dramatic hugs and reassuring squeals of everlasting friendship. The scene nauseated me, and I found it all a little too hard to watch, so I headed straight to first hour. It wasn't until I was in my seat that I heard the whispers of what they'd done to Willa's house a few minutes before getting pulled over. And I wondered what kind of horrible people would leave burning bags of dog poop outside the door of a mother whose son had killed himself less than a year earlier.

ELEVEN

NOW

The house felt less scary in the morning light. I'd managed a couple more hours of sleep after returning to bed and convincing myself the origins of the banging noises were harmless. Still, I hadn't gotten enough rest. I stifled a yawn and eyed Mom's old coffee maker on the counter. It had been spitting out bitter dregs of coffee the last few days, and I couldn't do it again. The smooth coffee from Drips was addictive, and it was calling my name. Gabe was pleasant to be around. Given the upheaval of my recent divorce, a platonic male friendship with potential was enough for me right now. With that thought, I went upstairs, pulled on some jeans and a T-shirt, and brushed my teeth. Then I looked in the bathroom mirror and applied makeup to cover the circles under my eyes and some light pink gloss to my lips. Satisfied I wouldn't scare Gabe away, I grabbed my purse and headed out the front door, making sure to lock it behind me.

I stepped outside where a layer of clouds blocked the sun, sketching the landscape in shades of charcoal. As I took in the gloomy morning, my gaze snagged on something out of place—a woman standing across the street and scowling in my direction. I nearly tripped over myself at the sight of her.

The podcaster, Hannah Mead, marched toward me, arms crossed in front of her waif-like frame. She wore a crop top that showed off her impossibly thin stomach and belly button ring. "Hi, Brooke. Remember me from the café a couple of days ago?"

I froze.

She squinted, her eyes flattening into suspicious lines. "Why didn't you tell me who you were? Did you think I wouldn't look up Brooke Webber's address and find you staying at your childhood home?"

"Good morning, Hannah." I took a step toward her, raising my chin. "I prefer to keep my distance from someone trying to make money off sensationalizing my friend's death. I'm sure you understand."

"I only want to get to the truth."

I stared right back at her. "Most people believe they got to the truth twenty years ago. I've managed to avoid this town since then. All I want to do is fix up my mom's house and get the hell out of Cove Haven as soon as possible. Without any drama or people flinging false accusations at me."

"I'm sorry about your mom." Hannah wiped her palm on her jeans and glanced away before refocusing on me. "I came across the obituary when I was researching."

The sincerity of her condolences caught me by surprise, and I toned down my defensive attitude, softening my voice. "Thanks."

Hannah edged closer, her face suddenly flush with sincerity. "But Bailey was your best friend. Don't you want to make sure the police got it right back then? Their investigation, if you can call it that, left something to be desired. Don't you want to help me re-examine the events of that night and make sure the full truth is exposed?"

"It's already been done. Bailey decided she couldn't deal with her life and jumped in front of the train. End of story." I stepped forward, obeying my gut instinct to get away from her. But my words had sounded hollow even to my own ears.

She jutted in front of me as I started walking past her. "Why did you want that cheap necklace I was wearing so badly? It wasn't really for your daughter, was it?"

My feet stopped again. Hannah was smart. She'd figured it out.

Hannah continued. "Yesterday, I did a closer examination of a 2003 photo in the *Cove Haven Caller*. It was of the cheerleaders. Bailey was wearing the necklace, and the pendant looked exactly like the one I gave you. Did I buy Bailey's necklace from the thrift shop? Or yours?"

"I've kept my half all these years." I paused, registering the shock on her face. "I couldn't believe it when I saw it on your neck."

Hannah's mouth gaped, but no sound came out. She looked toward the gloomy sky, then back at me. "Did you turn it over to the police?"

"No. And I'm not going to. They'll just say she took it off at the bonfire, and then months or years later, someone found it. They've always said it didn't prove anything, and you know what? They were probably right. I'm going to send it to her mom. Or maybe I'll keep it. I haven't decided yet."

"What are the odds of the necklace resurfacing just as you came back to town?"

"I don't know." I fidgeted with my watch to avoid her stare. Of course, I'd been wondering the same thing. Armchair detectives had postured over the years that I'd stolen back Bailey's necklace after the bonfire, that our broken friendship was a motive for murder. Since rediscovering the necklace, I'd been paranoid that someone was watching me, sending me a threat in a roundabout way. Perhaps the same person who had sent the cryptic text to Hannah. The noises that had awakened me last night still clattered through my mind. But I refused to admit any of this to her. "The necklace could have been gathering dust in the thrift shop for years for all I know."

"Yeah, but there must be more to the story. Who found it? Who brought it into the thrift store?" Something undiscernible flickered in Hannah's eyes. "I went to question Willa, and she said you'd already been there."

I dropped my gaze.

"I'd like to ask you to be a special guest on my podcast, so you can tell your side of the story."

The spark of excitement in Hannah's voice ignited a new flame of anger inside me. "Don't you have any shame? Any compassion for the people who knew Bailey? There's no big unsolved mystery here. Trust me. I've been through every detail of that night a thousand times. Why don't you leave us alone and move on to something else?"

"I'm sorry you feel that way. I've already been lectured by the police chief, Justin Warner, about all the harm I'm doing to the people in the town. How a story like this hurts tourism and scares people."

I recognized the name Warner, the same officer who'd pulled Bailey over for the DUI. A few months later, he'd also worked the scene after Bailey's death. He'd interviewed me once the next morning, then I'd returned a day or two later to tell him about the missing necklace. But he'd been a young officer then, merely following the orders of his superiors.

Hannah kept talking. "I don't see my podcast as hurting anyone, though. I'm helping someone who doesn't have a voice. She was your best friend. Some people even blamed you for her death. Don't you want the full truth to come out? And now with this necklace. It's giving us another piece of the story."

Although part of me had thought the same thing, I didn't want to show my cards to Hannah. I wasn't sure if I trusted her to do the right thing. "I'm sorry, Hannah. I'm going to pass. Go interview Trevor Baker. Or Zoe, Liz, and Mikayla. They know just as much as me. Maybe more."

"I tried to talk to Trevor yesterday. It didn't go well."

"Oh yeah?"

"He was very confrontational. He wouldn't answer a single question. Liz told me to go fly a kite, in so many words. And Mikayla's mom slammed the door in my face as soon as I told her who I was."

"I guess we all feel the same way."

"I have an interview with Zoe later this morning, though. She said she remembered a few things from the bonfire that I might like to know."

I shrugged, pretending I could care less.

"Okay, I hate to do this, Brooke, but my next episode is going to be about you. I can make things look bad for you. You know, stir up all the old rumors, mention your odd behavior in the coffee shop. Or you can join me as a guest and tell your side of the story. I bet everyone would like to know more about your relationship with Bailey and where you were after the dance."

"No."

"Why not?"

"Because I've already relived it too many times."

"Not the way I'm doing it." Hannah paused. "I'm staying at the Sandcastle Motel if you change your mind. Room 208. I'm recording tomorrow at 3 p.m. at the library. I want to help you."

"I don't need your help."

"Like I said, let me know if you change your mind." Hannah dug into her purse and shoved a card toward me with her name, phone number, and podcast information. "You should really reconsider."

I took it, suddenly wondering what she would say in her next episode. Panic rose in me as I remembered the whispers that followed me that summer after Bailey died, the suspicious glances, and clucks of disapproval, suggesting I was somehow responsible, that I should have been a better friend. And they were right. Now I stood in place, feeling like a cornered animal with nowhere to run. I kept my face still, but a cold dread seeped through my veins as Hannah walked away.

TWELVE

NOW

I did my best to brush off my encounter with Hannah, instead focusing on the gathering clouds as I arrived at Drips a few minutes later. Gabe's eyes brightened when he saw me, and I waved hello and got in line behind an older couple to place my order. I watched him work, admiring the animated way he greeted the other patrons as if their coffee order was the most important thing in his world.

"Hi, Brooke," he said as I reached the front of the line. "What can I get you?"

"Morning." I placed my order as he punched it into his screen.

"Anything exciting happening with you today?" he asked.

I told him about my scheduled meeting with Eric, the contractor I'd hired, as three more people filled in behind me, waiting to order. I moved out of the way, gazing around the airy café, pausing at a man sitting near the window. He was one of the real estate developers, the dodgy man named Jonathan who'd been talking on the phone the other day, the one who'd given me an uncomfortable look before speeding away. He'd dressed more casually today, in a polo shirt and a Chicago Cub's baseball cap with the brim pulled low. He caught me staring, and I turned away, embarrassed. But there'd been something familiar about his face, the curve of his brow. When I glanced back a few seconds later, he was pushing his way out the door.

Gabe called my name, holding up a cardboard cup.

"Do you know that guy?" I asked, pointing toward the door.

"John, I think. Not the friendliest guy in the world, but he's become kind of a regular."

"He's one of the developers of the new hotel."

Gabe nodded. "Yeah. I heard him talking about it the other day with his colleague. Sounds like it's going to be nice."

Someone coughed behind me, and I realized the line had grown. "I'll let you go."

Gabe greeted the next people to order as I carried my coffee out the door. I sipped my drink while I strolled, thankful for the energy boost. Still, Hannah's veiled threat circled through my thoughts. There wasn't much she could say on her podcast that hadn't been said about me before. Except, the other day, I'd pretended to be someone else as I secretly bought the necklace from her, which could look bad. If I cooperated, I could control the narrative and downplay any fault of my own in Bailey's death.

"Is that Brooke?"

A voice yanked me from my thoughts. I looked up to find a slovenly woman with a mop of over-processed hair. She wore a stained T-shirt that accentuated a generous bulge around her middle. A towheaded baby of about a year old was propped on one hip, and a little boy with cornsilk hair and a smudge of dirt on his face stomped next to her. I had no idea who the woman was.

She leaned toward me. "Don't act like you don't know who I am. It's me, Mikayla. From high school."

Holy shit. I tried to hide my shock at the dramatic transformation from the attractive, athletic, and confident cheerleader, and girlfriend of the star football player, to the person who stood before me. I felt disoriented, as if viewing my memories in a funhouse mirror. I widened my stance and studied her face, recognizing something familiar in the pale color of her eyes from twenty years earlier but not much else. "Oh, my gosh. Sorry. Hi."

"I heard you were in town. I'm surprised you came back."

I nodded. "Me too. I'll be around for a few weeks." I explained how Mom passed away six months ago, and I'd returned to fix up the house and put it on the market before my leave of absence at the art museum ended in August.

"So, you're an artist?" Mikayla let out a huff. "That figures."

"Kind of. I procure exhibits for—"

"I'm the assistant manager at The Chicken Shack," she interrupted me. "It's a pretty good gig."

"Maybe I'll stop in sometime."

The baby on Mikayla's hip let out a high-pitched squeal.

"Are these your kids?" I asked.

She jiggled the baby. "This is my granddaughter. I've got five kids too." She nodded toward the little boy. "He's the youngest of mine."

I looked at my coffee, trying to hide my shock. Mikayla had always struck me as one of the least maternal people on the planet. I'd been surprised when Dan had mentioned her slew of kids. But five kids and one grandchild by the age of thirty-eight? I tried to do the math, wondering if it was even possible. She must have gotten pregnant soon after I left for college.

"How many do you have?" she asked as if it were a competition.

"My daughter Ruthie is eight. She's with her dad right now."

"Only one? That's a shame." She made a face like she'd gulped a spoonful of paint thinner, apparently judging me harshly for my lack of procreation.

"Yes. Just Ruthie." Mikayla's comment poked at a raw nerve. Although my goal in life had never been to have as many kids as possible, I had hoped to have two children, to give Ruthie a sibling just as I'd had growing up. It was unlikely to happen now that Shane had left me, a painful realization I'd been trying not to think about. I squeezed my coffee cup, struggling to reconcile the disheveled woman standing before me with the popular teenager from my high school days. The only similarities remaining were her poison-laced words and the judgmental stare she fixed on me.

"You looked better when your hair was longer," Mikayla said, speaking with the same kind of casual cruelty I remembered from high school and cementing my suspicion that she was still a bully.

I'd had enough of her scrutiny and battled the urge to tell her what I really thought of her. I'd never fought back against her mean-spirited jabs when I was in high school, but I was stronger now, more self-assured. I cleared my throat, having learned a thing or two in the last twenty years. "I heard you and Trevor got married. That's so great." Mikayla's face flinched, and I smiled. A twinge of guilt sparked through me for the cheap shot, but she deserved it.

She tossed her head back. "I left Trevor's lazy ass last year. I still see him every week, though, because of the kids and grandbaby."

"Oh, that's rough."

Mikayla's toe tapped the ground as something hardened in her face. "There's a podcaster who came around yesterday asking about you. And about Bailey."

"I know. She cornered me too."

"Mom slammed the door on her, but I think I might talk to her." A devious tone stretched through Mikayla's voice.

"Why?"

"People will always wonder if I pushed Bailey in front of

that train just because she stole the prom queen title from me.
But I wasn't even mad at her. I was mad at Liz and Zoe. If I
were going to kill someone that night, it would have been one of
them."

I remembered the storm brewing in Mikayla's eyes as she
watched Bailey wearing the crown and dancing with Trevor in
front of the school, cameras flashing. I wasn't sure I believed her
about not harboring resentment against Bailey.

She motioned at me with her free hand. "You're the more
likely suspect. I mean, look at you."

"What?" I shifted my weight, realizing I'd been staring at a
nearby treetop, its leaves whipping in the wind.

"I forgot how secretive you are, Brooke. Brooding Brooke.
That's what we used to call you. Some things never change,
huh?"

"I don't know what you're talking about."

"Sure you do. Everything was so vague about your whereabouts after the prom. Only your mom vouched for you."
Mikayla heaved out a throaty laugh. "For whatever that's
worth."

I tightened my fingers around my cup, fighting the urge to
throw my coffee in her face. "Bailey was my best friend."

"No, she wasn't." Something dangerous glittered in Mikayla's eyes as she ignored the writhing baby in her arms and
fastened her stare on me. "Bailey thought you were sad. That's
the truth. I'm going to tell that lady I'll be on her podcast
because I'm tired of people thinking I did something. You were
the only one with a motive."

My molars clenched together, heat gathering in my face.
The conversation had quickly spiraled downward. "It was so
nice to see you, Mikayla." I layered my voice with an over-the-
top sugary sweetness. "I have to meet with my contractor." My
feet pivoted as I strode away, leaving my former classmate
behind me and fearing the rumors that Mikayla's skewed

version of events was sure to kick up. I had no choice but to join forces with Hannah now. And I wanted to get to her first.

———

An hour later, I was back at Mom's house, meeting with Eric to discuss the particulars of the paint colors, wood stains, and countertops. After the meeting, my big task for the day was complete, and I felt somewhat accomplished. But the shadow of Bailey's death refused to leave my side, and my earlier run-ins with Hannah and Mikayla had set me on edge. Deciding to tackle the next hurdle straight on, I retrieved Hannah's card and entered her number into my phone. She answered on the first ring.

"Hi. It's Brooke."

"I was hoping I'd hear from you."

"I've been thinking about what you said, and I changed my mind. I want to help you." I paused, looking at my hand. "For Bailey. But I need to meet with you before anyone else."

"Of course. You're doing the right thing."

"Have you talked to anyone else?"

"Only Zoe on the phone. She didn't tell me anything I hadn't learned already through my research."

I released a breath.

"How about tomorrow morning at the library?" Hannah asked. "I have a meeting room reserved there all week."

"Yeah. The earlier, the better."

"The library opens at nine."

"Nine works."

"Great. I'll get my questions organized, and I'll see you then. Oh, and Brooke?"

"Yeah?"

"Bring the necklaces."

Before I could respond, she hung up. I felt like I was going to throw up. How had I gotten myself into this situation? Why did she need to see the necklaces? There was something about Hannah that was a little too pushy. Or maybe it was this claustrophobic town that was suffocating me. I got up from the couch and went outside, desperate for some air.

THIRTEEN

NOW

A few minutes after Hannah ended our phone call, I found myself outside Lakeside Bike and Boat Rentals, where a dozen bikes of various makes and sizes were lined up near the door. Beyond the bikes, kayaks and paddleboards rested on stands. Red buoys attached to the white clapboard siding added to the store's quaint beachside vibe. I'd stopped by Dan and Maggie's shop on my first day back in town, impressed by the airy, beachy space and the ease with which my friends ran it. The front door was propped open, and I ventured inside, where helmets and lifejackets lined the walls. Dan handed a man a clipboard, asking him to fill out the form for insurance purposes as two young girls tried on helmets.

He looked up, noticing me. "Hey, Brooke! Any progress on the home improvement projects?"

"Yeah, things are coming along. I just met with the contractor, and the work is still scheduled to start on Monday."

"Like I told you the other night, our guest bedroom is open. It's no fun to live through construction." Dan rubbed his forehead, chuckling. "Maggie and I almost killed each other when we had our bathroom redone."

"I appreciate the offer, but I think I can manage. I don't want to be in the way."

"You wouldn't be. There's plenty of room. Maggie and the girls would love it."

"Thanks, but I'm good for now," I said, although the idea of getting myself out of the creaking, empty house sounded appealing. "I'll let you know if things change."

"Fair enough," Dan said with a nod. "It's an open invitation."

I caught a flowery whiff of perfume as another woman entered the store. "Hey, Dan. Do you sell life vests here?"

"Liz! How's it going?" He motioned toward me as I turned around. "You remember Brooke?"

I faced the person behind me. Although her hair was now dyed an unnaturally bright shade of red and cut into an angled bob, her athletic frame, round hazel eyes, and the gravelly notes of her voice were familiar. It was Liz Rhemy, another one of the cheerleaders who'd stolen Bailey from me, who'd betrayed her trust.

The smile vanished from Liz's face as she took me in. "Oh. I heard you came back."

I laced my fingers together, wondering who she'd been talking to. "My mom passed away. I'm fixing up her house before we put it on the market."

She raised her eyebrows. "That sucks."

Unlike my run-in with Zoe yesterday, a shield of ice seemed to separate me and Liz. There was no indication that she'd let bygones be bygones. She turned her back to me, pretending to look at lifejackets as Dan offered me an apologetic shrug. I wasn't surprised by her cold reaction. Two days after Bailey had died, the school held an impromptu candle-lit vigil to honor her memory. I'd confronted Liz and Zoe on the sidewalk, accusing them—between breathless sobs—of causing Bailey's death and calling them selfish horrible people. I'd left for college two months later and had never apologized.

Dan stepped over to Liz. "We don't sell lifejackets here. I only have rentals. But you can try the sporting goods store out on Sandpiper Road."

"Ah. I thought you might say that. My boyfriend just bought a boat from his friend, and I wanted to check while I was walking by." Liz nodded toward Dan. "I've gotta run." She strode out of the store, making a point to look over my head.

Dan gave my arm a friendly nudge. "Sorry. Some people never get over things."

"That's okay. I probably deserved it." I wanted to tell Dan about my meeting with Hannah tomorrow, but the man with the two little girls now waited by the counter for him to return.

He eyed them. "I'll catch you later, Brooke."

"Sounds good." I exited the store and decided to hit the beach, hoping I didn't run into anyone else from high school.

The next morning was Thursday. I paced the kitchen, preparing myself to meet with Hannah. Last night's sleep had been restless, which only increased my anxiety over the podcast interview. The old house's banging and knocking noises had awoken me again, but I chose to ignore them this time, reminding myself it was only the tree branch hitting the window. I'd forgotten to cut it back yesterday. I looked at my watch. 8:20 a.m. I still had time to grab a coffee from the café and make it to the library by nine.

As I rounded the corner to the foyer, a pop of white from beneath the console table caught my eye. Thinking it was a rogue piece of mail, I stepped toward it, picking it up. But when I unfolded the paper and read the words, the air left my lungs.

WELCOME BACK TO COVE HAVEN, BROOKE.

The words themselves weren't threatening, but the unsigned note had an ominous vibe. I glanced over my shoulder, then back to the note. Someone had scrawled the message in all caps as if trying to disguise their handwriting. I spun around, looking into the living room and back into the kitchen, wondering who wrote it. How had it gotten inside the house? My gaze paused on the mail slot in the front door. Someone must have slipped it through the opening during the night, causing the paper to flutter to the side and land under the table. I planted my feet on the floor and told myself not to freak out. At least no one had entered the house as I'd feared the night before. Still, if the note had been meant as a genuine welcome-back message, the person who wrote it would have signed their name.

I wondered who would be immature enough to do this. Liz's face flashed in my mind, followed by Mikayla's. While Liz had given me the cold shoulder at the bike shop yesterday, Dan hadn't had a problem with her, and she'd been eager to get on her way. On the other hand, Mikayla seemed to have some kind of personal vendetta against me despite us having had very few interactions in high school. The whispers over Bailey's death had followed her too, and unlike me, she'd never moved away and started fresh somewhere else. Now it seemed she'd decided I was to blame for her troubles. I folded the note back up and tucked it inside my pocket. Some people never grew up.

Still, I had no proof the note was from Mikayla. The noises from the other night had scared me enough to prevent me from sleeping. Now the thought of some unknown person lurking around my house at night, possibly inside, was more than I could handle. The offer of Dan's empty guest bedroom floated into my mind like a lifesaver. I lifted my phone, deciding to accept his invitation.

FOURTEEN

THEN

December 2002

A thin layer of snow crunched beneath my boots as I approached our house, where Dad strung Christmas lights around the hedges under the front windows, his warm breath steaming the frigid air.

"Ooh. Looks good," I said, giving him a thumbs-up.

"Thanks, hon." He lowered the tangle of lights in his hand. "There's an envelope inside you might want to open."

"Really?"

His eyes mirrored the sparkling lights as he gave a nod.

I ran inside, dropping my bag on the floor and spotting a large, white envelope on the table near the door. It was from the Stamps School of Art and Design. Dan had heard last week that he'd gotten into Western, and Lacey had gotten into a small school called Alma, where she planned to earn her undergraduate degree before pursuing a graduate degree in library science. But I still hadn't heard anything. My fingers shook as I ripped the envelope open, finding the top words. "Dear Ms. Webber, Congratulations! We are pleased to accept you into..."

"AAAAHHHH!!!!" I screamed, jumping up and down and not bothering to read the rest. "I got in!"

Dad stepped through the open doorway, pulling me into a hug. "You're really going places. You deserve it."

Mom ran downstairs and clapped as tears formed in the corners of her eyes. "We're so proud of you, Brooke. This is just wonderful."

After a few minutes spent celebrating and rereading the acceptance letter, I went back outside to help Dad finish stringing the lights, feeling a little like I was levitating off the ground. The sound of heavy footsteps drew my eyes toward the sidewalk, where Bailey moped toward home, a thick winter coat adding bulk to her thin frame.

Dad waved. "Hey, Bailey. Brooke has some good news."

"I got into Stamps!" I yelled as Bailey looked at me.

"Good job, Brooke. That's great. I knew you would." Bailey smiled from the yard next door, but she didn't come over to hug me. She shoved her hands in her pockets, something weighing down her features.

"Any word from State? Or Western?" I asked, suddenly aware that I might have been pouring salt on an open wound.

Bailey glanced away and gave a slight shake of her head. Then she hurried into her house without saying good night.

———

The next morning as we walked to school, Bailey told me in an emotionless voice that she'd been rejected by all four of the in-state schools where she'd sent applications. She was failing two of her classes, and her grades had fallen below a C average this year. But the DUI was the nail in the coffin. "My parents didn't want me to leave Cove Haven, anyway. Dad wants me to work at the dealership."

The bright lights of the Millbrook Chevrolet dealership

seared my memory, along with the unfriendly woman named Shirley, who worked the front desk. Last year, Bailey and I had spent hours in my bedroom impersonating Shirley's permanent scowl and throaty voice before collapsing into giggles. In a cruel twist of fate, Bailey would soon be working alongside the unpleasant woman or maybe replacing her. I hoped the position wouldn't kill my friend's spirit the way it must have done to Shirley.

I squeezed Bailey's arm, telling her everything would turn out for the best. But even as I said the words, I wasn't sure I believed them.

FIFTEEN

NOW

With a coffee cup in hand, I waited by the library's front doors. A young mother played pattycake with her toddler nearby. At precisely nine o'clock, Lacey approached from inside and unlocked the entrance.

Her eyebrows lifted when she saw me. "Hi! I wasn't expecting to see you here."

"I wasn't expecting to be here." I leaned closer to her, whispering, "The podcaster got to me. I figured it's better to get everything out in the open, so she doesn't spread false rumors about anyone."

"Maybe you're right. Plus, the sooner she gets her story, the sooner she'll leave town and free up our meeting room." Lacey gestured toward the two glass-walled rooms in the far corner. "We're going to need those spaces for the day camp. Hannah hangs out in Room One. Go make yourself comfortable." Lacey retrieved an armful of books from the book return box and loaded them onto a shelf with wheels. Her chin-length hair was pulled back with a purple fabric headband, and her clothes were casual but professional. She moved methodically, taking pride in her work. I felt a little bad that someone as capable as Lacey had ended up back in Cove Haven, although she didn't seem to harbor the same resentment against the town as I did. At Mom's funeral, she'd confided that she'd never earned her master's degree in library science as she'd originally planned to after graduating from Alma. The Cove Haven Library was one of a few that didn't require that qualification to run the place. She'd jumped at the chance to return and improve the bare-bones space, and I could see by the look of the library—the framed black-and-white architectural photos on the walls, the rows of neatly stacked books, the trendy chalkboard labels above the shelves, and the colorful and cozy kids' corner—that she had done a fantastic job.

I sat down in Meeting Room One and tried not to overthink the impending interview. A minute later, Hannah rushed through the door, two large bags slung over her shoulder. She wore a prairie-style top with her ripped jeans, and her wet hair was slicked to her head. "Hi, Brooke. Sorry to keep you waiting. My morning swim ran a little long today."

"That's okay. Where do you swim?"

"In the lake. I did a triathlon last year, and I'm trying to keep in shape for the next one."

"Wow. That's great." I studied Hannah's smooth skin and the intensity in her dark eyes. It was clear, once again, that despite her casual demeanor, she was no slacker. Lake Michigan was still frigid in early June, not a welcoming place for the faint of heart. She positioned a microphone between us and plugged it into her laptop. Then she typed some keys, presumably pulling up files or questions she wanted to ask.

She explained that the interview would be more like a casual conversation that she would later edit for the next podcast episode, centered around me as Bailey's best friend. "Did you bring the necklaces?"

I nodded, digging into my purse and pulling out the small

bag. I removed the two mismatched chains with the interlocking pendants and set them on the table between us.

Hannah's eyes grew large as she lifted the necklaces, popping the puzzle pieces apart and then back together. "This was really Bailey's necklace."

"Yeah. Not only do they fit, but there is matching purple nail polish on the back. We painted our initials with it the day I gave her the necklace."

Hannah held up a hand. "Okay. Wait. I'm starting the interview now, and we can go over all of this again." She hit the record button and introduced herself, and then me. She asked me several questions about my life in Cove Haven and my relationship with Bailey—how we'd met, what we did for fun, and where Bailey lived in relation to me. I answered everything easily and honestly. Then she said, "Do you remember when your friendship with Bailey first started to go south?"

I told her about the day on the beach when I gave Bailey the necklace for her seventeenth birthday. It was the same day Bailey told me she'd made the cheerleading squad. Soon after, she started acting differently toward me, sitting with the other girls at lunch, cancelling our plans at the last minute, and ignoring me in the hallways if the other girls were around.

"So, your best friend since kindergarten ditched you for the popular crowd?"

"Basically, yes."

"Ouch."

"Thankfully, I had other friends."

"Still, that must have hurt. Did Bailey ever invite you to any of the parties?"

"No. Not that I can remember. I think she knew I wouldn't go."

"But she still wore the necklace you gave her?"

"Usually. Yes."

"And she was wearing it the night of prom?"

"Yes."

Hannah clucked, shaking her head and recounting how the necklace was missing from Bailey's remains after her death. The conversation turned to Bailey's DUI and slipping grades, which contributed to her college rejections. "Did you notice that Bailey was depressed in the weeks leading up to senior prom?"

"I knew she was making bad decisions, skipping class, and drinking more than she had before. She loved watching crime dramas like *Law and Order* on TV and always wanted to be a prosecuting attorney. It must have been hard for her to watch that dream slip away."

"Were you surprised when Bailey was crowned prom queen? It's my understanding that Mikayla was expected to win."

"Everyone was surprised. Especially Bailey."

"Was Bailey acting strangely at the bonfire?"

I pressed my palms on the table, thinking back. "I'm sure she was upset by what those girls did to her. I wasn't at the bonfire."

"Where were you?"

"I went to a diner in town, Joe's Diner, with two of my friends, Dan and Lacey. We got some food, and then we went home. I heard about Bailey's death the next morning."

"What time did you get home?"

"Around eleven, I think."

"And did anyone see you?"

"Yes. My mom. She stayed up to wait for me."

"Your mom was your alibi?" Hannah's voice grew louder, slightly incredulous. "An alibi like that doesn't always hold much water."

"I was a teenager who lived with my parents, so I'm not sure who else could vouch for me. Besides, there was no crime, so I didn't really need an alibi in the first place."

"So, you believe Bailey killed herself that night?"

I stared at my hands for a second, choosing my words carefully. Back then, I'd been almost relieved at the ruling of suicide and had convinced myself to accept it as fact, even though the determination had felt a little too swift, a little too convenient. But the sudden reappearance of Bailey's necklace had me rethinking everything. "I don't know for sure, but I always thought suicide was a plausible explanation."

"And what do you think happened to the necklace?"

"I don't know. I can't explain it."

"How long have you been back in Cove Haven?"

"About a week." I explained about my mom's recent death and the house sale.

"And had you often visited Cove Haven before that?"

"No. Not since I left for college, except for the funeral six months ago. And I came back for a few days when my dad died about seven years ago. Mom always traveled to us because she knew I didn't like it here. It's a small town, and people like to gossip about things they know nothing about." My voice came out a little sharper than I intended, but Hannah didn't react. Instead, she quickly explained how she'd purchased a necklace a few days ago at the local thrift shop to use as a prop for her podcast because she thought it looked similar to the necklace Bailey had been wearing the night she died, not realizing it was the actual necklace. She described how I'd approached her at the café and offered to buy it from her. "It strikes me as very strange that this necklace that has been missing for twenty years suddenly reappears as soon as you return to town for more than a couple of days."

"Yes. Me too."

"Some people in town say you must have dropped the necklace at the thrift shop when you arrived."

I tipped back in my chair, stunned. Of all the things I expected Hannah to say, this accusation hadn't made the list. "What people? Who said that?"

Hannah only stared at me, waiting for me to say more.

I shook my head. "No one even knows about the necklace reappearing, except for you and a couple of close friends. And why would I drop it at the thrift shop only to buy it from you?"

"Some killers like to brag. Show off because they think they're smarter than everybody else." She shrugged. "Or it could have been a ploy to make it look like Bailey's necklace has been out of your possession all this time."

"It wasn't me. None of this makes any sense." I squeezed my eyes closed, seeing spots. "Can we cut this? You're twisting everything around."

Hannah raised her eyebrows. "Maybe. But I feel obligated to turn the necklace over to the police."

My mouth went dry at Hannah's betrayal. "They won't care. They never did."

Hannah shrugged. "Even so. It might be evidence."

"Like I said, I have nothing to hide." I swiped the necklaces from the table, pocketing my half and sliding Bailey's half toward Hannah. "I'd like it back after they tell you they don't want it. Bailey's death is a closed case." I stood up to leave but paused to glare at Hannah. "This kind of lying bullshit is exactly why I didn't want to talk to you." I squeezed the handle of my purse and turned toward the door.

"Brooke, wait! Let's switch gears."

"Forget it."

"Wait! Please." Hannah jumped up from her chair. "Don't go. I found a new lead. Something I wanted to show you. I'm turning off the microphone." She made an exaggerated gesture to hit a button.

I hesitated.

"Trust me. You're going to want to see this." She'd dropped her overly dramatic manner of speaking and pointed to her laptop.

Curiosity getting the better of me, I let my weight fall back into the chair, watching Hannah's fingers clacking away at the keys. She paused and slid her chair closer, pivoting the screen toward me.

"How familiar are you with Harsons Real Estate Group in Chicago?"

"Not familiar at all. I only know they're developing the old train station into a hotel."

The corners of Hannah's mouth twitched as she pointed at the screen. "And do you recognize either of these co-owners?"

I leaned forward, seeing the two men who frequented Drips Café.

"Read the names under their photos."

The first name was Michael Harsons. I recognized him as the man I'd chatted with briefly the other day as his friend barked at him to get into the car. And the name under the second photo said Jonathan Newson.

"Look at Jonathan's picture," Hanna said, waiting for me to put the pieces together.

I studied the black-and-white headshot, the kind with soft lighting and crisp edges, clearly taken by a professional photographer. My eyes flicked back to the last name: Newson. "Holy crap." Although the broad-shouldered man with the thinning hair barely resembled the lanky jock I remembered from high school, I could now see it in the deep set of his eyes and his heavy brow. "It's Spike Newson."

Hannah leaned back, smiling. "Bailey's rejected prom date has returned to town. I couldn't believe it when I made the connection either."

"He's been avoiding me at Drips. I've seen him there twice, and he darts away, always wearing sunglasses or a hat. Even when he's inside."

"Yep. He seems to be working undercover on the new hotel. But why be so secretive? Unless he has something to hide." She picked up a pen and tapped it on the table. "And isn't it convenient that they're tearing the bridge down?"

I looked from Hannah to the picture on the laptop, still shocked by the revelation about the developer's identity. Hannah was correct. Why would Spike be so secretive about his return? Then again, I understood why he'd want to avoid confrontation and whispers. But it was quite a coincidence that the hotel development plans included tearing down the bridge that Bailey jumped from. The memory of its existence would be erased. I wasn't sure if that was good or bad.

"What if Spike had the necklace all this time?" I spoke under my breath, asking the question to myself just as much as to Hannah, and remembering how Dan had always been suspicious of Spike.

Hannah lifted her chin. "I need to talk to Spike. Or I guess we should call him Jonathan now."

"He agreed to let you interview him?"

Hannah laughed. "No. But I'm hoping you can help me."

"Why would I do that?"

"Because I sense you still have questions about the night Bailey died."

I laced my fingers together, neither confirming nor denying her statement. "Cut the part about my mom's alibi not being reliable and the lie about me planting the necklace in the thrift shop from your podcast, and I'll help you."

"I don't know. That's two big cuts." Hannah pinched her lips together, her face taking on a pained expression. "Will you talk to Trevor Baker too? Just a few questions that I'll send you."

There was nothing I wanted to do less than drive out to the boonies and ask the former prom king, Trevor, a bunch of questions about the night Bailey died. Then again, Trevor could potentially fill in some blanks and lead me closer to the truth. I suspected Mikayla was the one who'd left that unsettling note at my house. Maybe Trevor could confirm my suspicions about his ex-wife. "Okay. Fine. I'll give it a shot."

Hannah tilted her head, pretending to think about it. "Then we have a deal," she said a little too quickly. She scribbled down two addresses on a piece of paper and handed it to me. One was for Trevor on a country road off Route 16, and one was for Jonathan, who was staying at what I assumed was a rental property across from the beach. "I'll send you the questions soon," Hannah said, the upbeat cadence having returned to her voice.

As I turned to leave, I had a funny feeling she'd played me once again.

SIXTEEN

NOW

I propped my sunglasses on top of my head and compared the address on the paper with the black, lacquered numbers nailed to the side of the house. 853 Lakeside Drive. The bungalow featured a red door and white trim around the windows. Yellow flowers bloomed in a manicured flowerbed that ran in front of the porch. It was the quintessential American beach house. Jonathan Newson had good taste. A clothesline ran along the side of the house, probably meant for hanging beach towels to dry. But the line sat empty. I wasn't surprised, as it was hard to imagine the abrasive man I'd observed at the café as someone who enjoyed much time at the beach.

I pressed my heels into the porch's wooden floor and knocked four times, holding my breath and unsure why I was doing this. But if Hannah wasn't allowing me to remain anonymous in this town, I wouldn't let Jonathan get away with it either. Several seconds passed, and I debated whether to bail out or knock again. Having already taken the time to memorize Hannah's questions and walk over here, I set my jaw, my knuckles hitting the door three more times.

A few seconds passed with no movement, except for two

bikers speeding past behind me. Just as I stepped back to leave, the door clicked and creaked open. The man I now knew was Jonathan Newson filled the opening, a surprised expression replacing the frown on his face.

"Hi, Spike," I said before he could close the door. "It's Brooke Webber from high school. We've seen each other at Drips a couple of times now."

He looked over his shoulder as if considering running. Apparently realizing it was too late to hide, he turned to face me, his manicured fingers rubbing his forehead. "Shit. Sorry. Hi. I go by Jonathan now."

"Yeah. I saw that on your company's website."

Jonathan's phone rang from inside his pocket. He pulled it out, hit a button, and returned it to his pocket. It was surreal processing the sight of the adult businessman I remembered as a popular, athletic, and slightly obnoxious teenager, and someone whose social circle, save for Bailey, probably would never have intersected with mine. His polo shirt and linen shorts were perfectly fitted to his frame, which had filled out since high school. And while his hairline had also receded slightly, a clear portrait of the person I'd known as Spike came into focus.

"Sorry if I'm interrupting you. I just hoped we could chat for a second."

"Yeah, okay. I only have about five minutes." Anxiety creased Jonathan's face. He'd dropped the bullish attitude I'd witnessed at the café, and now had the look of a dental patient who was resigned to getting his procedure over with as quickly as possible. He motioned toward two wicker chairs on the front porch, where we sat, perched uncomfortably on the edges as we stared out at the picturesque street. The sun had broken through the clouds, burning them away, and the beach and lake stretched out beyond the park across the way. If not for the circumstances, it would have been a perfect summer's day.

"You still live here?" he asked, confusion straining his voice.

"No. I've barely been back in twenty years. My mom died six months ago. I'm fixing up her house and selling it."

"Oh. I'm sorry." He fidgeted with his fingers, the chairs creaking beneath us.

"Then I'll go back to Ferndale, where I live. I'm an exhibit director at the Detroit Institute of Arts."

His head lifted. "Yeah? Good for you."

I continued. "So you just decided to come back after twenty years to make money off the site of one of Cove Haven's biggest tragedies?"

He leaned his head back, eyelids flickering. "It's not like that. I swear."

"What is it like, then?"

"It's the real estate business. This property just fell into my lap."

I suppressed a laugh. "Don't take this the wrong way, but that's a little hard to believe."

"It's true." He wiped his palms on his shorts, turning toward me with a solemn face. "One day last year, I was researching distressed properties at the office back in Chicago, and I came across the Cove Haven train station listed on a tax sale website. I couldn't believe it. There are so few opportunities for development near the waterfront anymore. We've been looking to build a hotel in one of the towns along Lake Michigan, but the prices for buildings we found in New Buffalo, Union Pier, and Saugatuck were too high. The train station was a steal. I mean *that* place! What were the odds?" He tipped his face toward the sky and let out a sad kind of chuckle. "As much as I didn't want to come back here, it was almost like the universe was giving me a chance to make something good out of something bad, if that makes sense."

I shifted my weight, not answering.

"I saw all the new development happening here, the restaurants and rental properties, and I had an idea for a hotel called

The Train Station. It would preserve some of the old building's history and provide a unique place for tourists to stay. I drove my business partner over to check it out, still not really believing it would amount to anything. Turns out he loved the town and the property, and the numbers made sense. So, we bought the old building and some of the surrounding land."

"Why are you hiding your identity, then?"

Jonathan traced his finger along his jawline. "My legal name has always been Jonathan. Spike was a stupid nickname."

"That's not what I meant. You've been dodging me, wearing sunglasses inside."

"Probably for the same reason you haven't been back here in twenty years. Because the memories of Bailey's death are painful, and so are the rumors that follow people like us."

It wasn't what I'd expected him to say.

Jonathan leaned forward, letting the sunlight hit him. His eyes glistened with a watery sheen, and I could see Bailey's death still affected him. "I had such a crush on her back then." He stared at his hands. "I know she didn't feel the same. I wish I hadn't been such a jerk that night."

"What do you mean?" I asked, although I remembered the way he tore the fairy lights off the wall in the hallway outside the gym, ripping the paper decorations along with them before storming off.

"I don't know. I was pissed about her and Trevor kissing on the dance floor in front of everyone. I don't even think she liked him, but it was embarrassing, and I left. Maybe if I'd been at the bonfire, things would have been different. I would have insisted on walking her home."

The news about Bailey's missing necklace having resurfaced balanced on my tongue, but I wasn't ready to share it, still didn't know what it meant, if anything. Or if Jonathan was responsible.

"I second-guess my actions that night all the time," I said. "But it doesn't serve a purpose. We had no way of knowing."

He sighed and ran his fingers through his hair as if he didn't entirely believe me.

"Does anyone else know you're here?" I asked.

"I don't think so. Only Justin Warner, the police chief. He recognized me a few months back when I was touring the property with an appraiser." Jonathan paused, cracking his knuckles. "Anyway, I told him I wanted to keep my involvement in the hotel project a secret, and he agreed that it was better for the town not to stir things up again. Aside from him, I haven't had any contact with anyone. My business partner has been the public face for any local building issues." Jonathan's phone buzzed from his pocket, and he silenced it. I noticed the thick gold band on his ring finger.

"You married now?" I asked.

"Yeah. My wife and kids are driving over to stay with me this weekend. You?"

"I got divorced last year. My daughter, Ruthie, is eight. She's with her dad for the summer."

"Too bad. I bet she'd like the beach."

"Yeah." I looked at Jonathan again, realizing I might have pegged him wrong. Or maybe, like Zoe, he'd simply grown up. This introspective version of him was so different from the impulsive, self-absorbed jock I remembered. His evasiveness at the café had only been to protect himself from painful memories. "I'm not sure if you heard about Hannah Mead, the podcaster? She's in town investigating Bailey's death."

Jonathan squeezed his eyes closed and shook his head. "Why?"

"Because it's a sensational story." I looked toward the lake, watching the steady movement of the water. I had to share the discovery that would soon be made public on Hannah's podcast anyway. "And because Bailey's missing necklace has suddenly turned up."

"What? How is that possible?"

"I don't know. Hannah found it at the thrift shop. It got me thinking that maybe whoever took that necklace was the last person to see her. Maybe that person caused her death. As much as I hate to kick up old rumors, I think it's more important to get to the truth. Hannah is looking into the possibilities on her podcast. And she wanted me to ask you if she could interview you."

"No. No way."

"You can control the narrative that way."

"Absolutely not." Jonathan slapped the side of the chair, his voice turning steely. "I've been visiting this town for months and have kept a low profile. This new hotel will be my biggest professional achievement. It might be the largest profit margin our company has ever made on a single project. A stupid podcast about Bailey's death could ruin it, especially if people start whispering that I was involved. I put that night behind me a long time ago, and so should you."

The tone of his voice warned me that his mind was made up and not to ask again. I scrambled to remember Hannah's other questions before he kicked me off the porch. "What about the bridge? Why are you tearing that down?"

"That's not our decision. The bridge is on municipal property. Last I heard, the county was pushing to have it torn down because it's a safety hazard. Besides, it's no longer needed because the train stopped running years ago."

"Oh." Everything he said made sense. Admittedly, more sense than trying to destroy some fictional evidence left over from twenty years earlier.

"Anything else you want to clear up?" He held a palm in the air. "Wait. Let me save you the trouble of asking. No, I didn't push Bailey from the bridge. My ego was bruised that night, for sure, and I've never denied that. I went home and sulked in my bedroom until I fell asleep. Like I said before, I wish I'd been with her. Maybe I could have stopped her."

I swiped a loose strand of hair out of my eyes. Jonathan's words sounded genuine, but I didn't know him well enough to be sure.

"And the necklace?"

"I have no idea. It's weird that it suddenly turned up, but I can't imagine it means anything. Someone could have found it after the fact in the garbage or in the grass and probably didn't even realize whose it was." He grunted, squaring his shoulders at me. "Tell this podcaster I don't want any part of whatever she's doing. And if she so much as mentions my name in connection with Bailey's death, I'll sue her for slander. That's a promise."

A droplet of spit hit my face with his final words, and I caught another flash of the boy named Spike, the one with the temper who destroyed the decorations in the hallway after Trevor kissed Bailey during the royal dance. A swirl of suspicion traveled through me at how vehemently he was trying to avoid any mention on Hannah's podcast. Then again, I suppose I'd had a similar reaction. I slid forward in my chair. "I understand. And I'll tell her."

Jonathan's phone rang again. He stood up this time, turning his back to me and taking the call.

Recognizing my cue to leave, I walked down the porch steps and toward the beach. Despite Jonathan's angst about being interviewed, I tended to believe him and would tell Hannah exactly what he'd said.

The problem was, I wasn't sure if she'd listen.

SEVENTEEN

THEN

March 2003

It was one of the first warm days of spring when Bailey and I walked to school on Monday morning, barely talking. I'd been making the ten-minute journey alone most mornings because Bailey was usually late. She'd decided school didn't matter anymore, except for socializing. And she could do that any time of day. I'd gotten used to the solitary walks and had taken to silently documenting the change of seasons, sketching the emerging daffodils and flittering songbirds in my mind as I headed to and from school.

Now Bailey's foot splashed into a puddle. She released a squeal that only emphasized the wedge of silence between us. I was about to make some dumb comment about the weather when a police cruiser rumbled behind us, lurching to a stop when it reached us. Officer Warner, the same policeman who'd pulled Bailey over for the DUI four months earlier, lowered his window and peered out.

"Hi, ladies. Do you have a minute?"

Bailey and I looked at each other. Fear flashed across her face, and I couldn't help wondering what she'd done now.

"Sure," I said at the same time Bailey said, "Okay."

He turned off the ignition and stepped out of the car. "I'm looking into some damage to Willa Jones's house. Someone spray-painted some nasty words on her front porch over the weekend."

My heart sank. Poor Willa. She'd lost her son just a year ago. Now some horrible people wouldn't stop harassing her just because she was a little eccentric. That's how bullies worked. They picked up the scent of weakness and targeted the most vulnerable. Bailey seemed willing to do anything to please her new friends, and I hoped she hadn't been involved.

Bailey shook her head. "It wasn't me."

A hint of a smile pulled at the corner of the officer's mouth. "Of course not. I didn't think it was you. I just thought one of you might have thoughts on who it might have been."

"I don't know," Bailey said.

"Me neither," I added, although if Bailey hadn't been standing next to me, I might have suggested the group of people she'd been hanging around with the last few months.

The officer hitched his thumb in his pocket. "Do you mind if I ask what you were doing Saturday night?"

Bailey looked at me, hesitating. "I was at Mikayla Michaels' house with some other girls. We didn't leave."

"I went to Joe's Diner with a couple of friends. Then we walked on the beach. I was home by eleven."

"Which friends?"

"Dan Tanner, Henry Kresge, and Lacey Dunn."

He nodded. "Well, do me a favor. If you hear anyone talking at school or bragging about tagging Willa's house, will you call me at this number?" He handed us each a business card with his name and number at the station. "All tips are anonymous. People think this kind of thing is harmless, but it's not."

I pinched the card in my fingers, nodding.

"Who would do such a cruel thing?" Bailey lowered her eyelids, frowning. "People are messed up."

Bailey seemed genuinely disturbed, and I suddenly felt guilty for suspecting her. Maybe she'd never been involved in harassing Willa, this time or previously. The Bailey I knew wouldn't have sunk that low. Not even for those girls.

I refocused on the officer. "We'll let you know if we hear anything."

"Thanks. Have a good week at school. Study hard." He was only five or six years older than us, his cheeks still plump with baby fat, but the tone of his voice suggested he was a wise old sage, and we were mere children.

"We will."

As Officer Warner closed himself inside his car and drove away, we looked at each other, rolling our eyes and giggling. "Study hard." Bailey lowered her voice, imitating the officer.

"He's like six months older than us." We laughed the rest of the way to school, and for a few minutes, it felt like old times again.

EIGHTEEN

NOW

On Friday morning, the dryer buzzed, and I opened the door, piling my warm clothes into a laundry basket. I was almost done packing for my temporary move to Dan and Maggie's house, thankful I'd made it through the night without any unsettling noises yanking me from my sleep or creepy notes appearing beneath the mail slot. Even so, I couldn't bear to spend another night alone in the empty house. And this way, I'd be out of the way when Eric showed up with his crew in a few days to begin renovations.

As I dumped my clothes on the living room floor to begin folding, a text buzzed through from Hannah.

> *Your episode just dropped. I made the cuts, but you still need to meet with Trevor. There are lots of episodes to go. I can always put the cuts back in.*

My stomach turned as I set down the basket. I'd driven out to Trevor's address yesterday, but he hadn't been home. I needed to try harder. Not only did I not want Hannah broadcasting lies about me, but I had a hunch Trevor knew things about our prom night that I didn't.

I stretched out my legs, deciding to get it over with and listen to the latest episode of *All the Dark Corners*. Hannah's voice chirped through my earbuds, "Welcome back to season eight of *All the Dark Corners Podcast*, where we're delving into the mystery of the mysterious death of the Prom Queen of Cove Haven. This is episode two: *Not So Best Friend, Brooke*." I huffed at the title of the episode but forced myself to keep listening, unsure of what Hannah had in store. Hannah gave some background about my friendship with Bailey and added some of her own commentary about the nickname, Brooding Brooke, that some of the popular kids had given me. She said many remembered me rubbing my acceptance to art school in Bailey's face and that I'd stopped wearing our matching necklace long before Bailey had. I wondered who had given Hannah that information as Mikayla's sneering lips surfaced in my mind. The rest of the episode consisted of my interview from a couple of days earlier, with lies and twisted facts omitted. Although I cringed at the sound of my own voice, the entire forty-minute episode, overall, wasn't too bad. Hannah left some questions open but didn't portray me as a murderer, which I took as a win.

An hour later, I parked near the curb outside of Dan and Maggie's place, relieved to be out of the empty house. Dan practically bounded through the front door to greet me. "Maggie is at the shop until two. Let me get your bags." He headed straight to the trunk, heaving my largest suitcase out, and grabbing two smaller bags with his other hand.

After getting situated in a small but bright guest bedroom, I joined Dan on the back porch as little Olivia and Marci ran through a sprinkler on the lawn, shrieking and jumping each time they passed through the water.

"Guess what I found out?" I leaned forward, sharing that The Train Station hotel was being built by none other than Spike Newson, AKA Jonathan Newson.

"What the...?"

"Look up Harsons Realty Group website."

Dan took out his phone and scrolled to the site, finding Jonathan's photo. "How did none of us know this before?"

"I don't know. Hannah figured it out. She might be a little pushy and annoying, but she's good at what she does."

Dan's eyes held a dazed look. "Man. This is too much."

I told Dan about my agreement with Hannah to talk to Jonathan and Trevor to convince them to be on her podcast.

"Spike—or I guess I should say, Jonathan—seems to have matured since high school. I don't think his motives for returning to Cove Haven were anything more than an enticing real estate deal." I'd already told Hannah the same, along with his legal threats. She'd only said, "Hmm. I'm not sure."

Dan raised an eyebrow. "How did it go with Trevor?"

"I don't know. I drove all the way out to his house. If you can call it that." I swallowed against my dry throat, remembering how I'd left Jonathan's quaint front porch and walked back to my car. Then I'd followed my GPS for fifteen minutes, traveling east on Route 16, and slowing when I reached the dirt road leading to Trevor's address. The pothole-filled road led me to a dilapidated house with white siding stained so badly it looked as if it had been dipped in green paint. A dog resembling a coyote was chained to the front post and barked frantically as I knocked on the front door. No lights were on inside, and no cars sat in the gravel driveway. Everything about the place gave me a bad vibe, so I high-tailed it out of there before Trevor stomped outside with a rifle and shot me for trespassing. My concerns for the mangy dog multiplied as I drove away, also stirring up

nostalgia for Rufus. My retriever mix had been such a loyal
friend when I needed him the most, and I hadn't owned another
dog since because of Shane's allergies. A vision of surprising
Ruthie with a puppy bounded through my mind, but I put the
idea on hold. Instead, I left an anonymous tip with the nearest
Humane Society as soon as I got home, requesting a welfare
check for the dog attached to the tether with no access to water
or shade.

Dan's brow furrowed. "Jeez. Be careful. Trevor is a heavy
drinker too. I can go with you next time."

"Thanks. I might take you up on that." I looked around the
well-kept yard, the laughing children, and the strings of lights
overhead. It was the first time in a few days that I felt somewhat
at peace. I'd already told Dan about the noises in the night, the
weird note that said, *Welcome back to Cove Haven, Brooke.*

"You okay?" he asked, maybe having noticed the competing
emotions on my face.

"Yeah. It's just that this town brings back so many memories. And I haven't been sleeping well, like I said."

Dan cracked his knuckles, a distant look in his eyes. "That
note was so strange. Who would do that?"

"I don't know." We sat quietly for a second, then I told him
about my run-in with Mikayla and how I suspected her. He
didn't disagree, although he also thought Willa was just as likely
due to our recent encounter and the eccentric woman's odd
means of communication. We listened to the latest podcast
episode, with Dan shaking his head and rolling his eyes in
certain places where Hannah had stretched the truth. "You
never rubbed your acceptance to art school in Bailey's face. This
is bullshit."

Dan still had my back. The thought bolstered me as we
listened to the rest, with Dan assuring me that it wasn't
that bad.

"Anyway, it's nice to be here." I paused, shifting my chair to keep the sun out of my eyes. "Can I take you and Maggie out to The Fish tomorrow night?" I asked, naming the upscale seafood restaurant that had recently gone in near the marina. I'd been eager for any excuse to try it.

"That would be great. We have a regular Saturday night sitter. She lives across the street."

"Perfect."

"And if you don't mind me making an observation..."

I cocked my head.

"I think you should invite Gabe too." Dan winked. "Maggie said he keeps asking about you."

For the first time at the thought of Gabe, I felt the heat creep up my neck into my cheeks. "Yeah. Maybe I will."

The following night, we sat at a white-clothed table overlooking the marina. A wide array of watercraft, from colorful sailboats to looming yachts, bobbed in the water beyond the picture window, some of their captains looking just as wind-worn as their boats. At Dan and Maggie's urging, I'd gotten the courage to walk over to Drips and ask Gabe if he'd like to join the three of us for dinner. He'd accepted without hesitation. Now he sat next to me, smelling faintly of oaky cologne. His beard was neatly trimmed, and he'd swapped his usual graphic T-shirts and apron for a button-down shirt.

"To new friends." Gabe's eyes crinkled as he raised his glass.

"To new friends, and old," Dan added, smiling at me.

"Cheers." We all clinked glasses.

The dinner proceeded with two shared appetizers, four delicious entrées, and no lack of conversation. We talked about the happenings at the sports rental shop and the café. I filled them in on the renovation plans for Mom's house. And, of course, we talked about Hannah Mead's podcast and the recent discoveries of Bailey's necklace, Spike Newson's new identity, and the mysterious note that someone had slipped through my door.

Maggie caught my gaze, her eyes shining with something mischievous. "So, Brooke. Can you give me any dirt on Dan's high school girlfriends?"

Dan almost spit out his drink, his eyes bulging at his wife. "Why would you ask that?"

"Because you never tell me anything. I want to know if you used to make out in the backseat of your car with one of these women we run into in town."

I angled myself toward Dan, thinking back. "You didn't really have any girlfriends, did you?"

"Oooh!" Gabe shook his head, smiling.

Dan held up a finger. "Not true. I dated Crissy Metcloff for three weeks in ninth grade."

"Oh, yeah. I forgot about that."

Maggie frowned. "But what about the one you lost your virginity to? You wouldn't even tell me her name."

"Oh my God!" Dan buried his face in hands. "Maggie, please stop. Those were private conversations."

I leaned back in my chair, having no idea who Maggie was referring to. "This is all news to me."

Dan's face reddened by the second, and I got the feeling he might have told his wife a little white lie. Maybe it had happened early on in their relationship to make himself seem cooler than he'd actually been in his high school days.

"Hey! Let's give the guy a break." Gabe winked at me, and a knowing look conveyed he'd had the same thought. "I didn't lose my virginity until I was thirty-seven. You're making me feel bad."

We all laughed at Gabe's joke, then Dan turned the conversation to the new boat tour service that carried passengers on a two-hour ride along the coast to look at all the fancy waterfront houses while they ate appetizers and drank cocktails.

By the time the meal ended, we were too stuffed to order dessert. Although Gabe tried to steal the bill from me, I insisted on paying it. Gabe asked if we'd heard about the concert at the new venue in the park, and I realized it was the same park that sat across from Jonathan Newson's rental house. The night was still young, so we decided to walk over and enjoy the music. We exited the restaurant into a steady stream of people bustling along the sidewalk leading to the marina.

"Brooke! Dan!" A voice called from across the street, and I looked up to see Lacey waving at us. A toy poodle on a nylon leash circled her ankles.

"Hi, Lacey!"

She crossed the street and introduced us to her dog.

Maggie looked back at the restaurant. "Brooke just treated us to a delicious meal."

"How nice. Good to see you, Gabe." She eyed him, flashing me a sly grin at the realization that we were possibly a couple. "I've been meaning to try this place."

"You'll come with us next time," I said.

Gabe motioned between us. "See. More small-town magic. You don't even have to make plans. You just run into friends everywhere."

I giggled at Gabe's relentless nostalgia for small towns, knowing from my experiences that one could just as easily be trapped with their enemies, but decided to keep my mouth shut. He didn't need a full view of my cynicism just yet.

Maggie asked Lacey to come to the concert with us, and she agreed to join us for a while but had to get up early for a morning event for preschoolers at the library. The music floated through the summer air as we approached, acoustic guitar, drums, and a female lead singer with a haunting voice performing a cover of an old Sheryl Crow song. I felt a warm pressure on my back and realized Gabe had slung his arm around me. I turned toward him, surprised.

He only smiled. "I don't want you to get cold."

I relaxed my shoulders and leaned into his touch.

There were more people than I expected in the park. Some had blankets spread out, drinking wine or beer or letting kids dance. We squeezed between groups of people, getting closer to the stage where a crowd stood and clapped. I noticed two uniformed police officers posted on the periphery. One of them looked familiar, and I realized it was Justin Warner, the same barrel-chested police officer who'd pulled Bailey over that fall night twenty years earlier, resulting in her DUI, one of the first incidents contributing to her downward spiral.

I blinked away the memory and continued scanning the crowd, my gaze snagging on another familiar face. Jonathan stood near a tree, a woman in a flowery sundress next to him, and two kids jumping up and down. I motioned toward the others and pointed. "There's Spike."

Dan followed my line of vision, his mouth twisting. "He actually looks pretty good."

"Holy cow." Lacey gawked at me, holding her little dog to her chest. "He has a family?" She peered around the crowd some more, nodding toward a small hill to the right. "And there's Hannah."

Hannah stood alone, bobbing her head to the beat and looking as if she was legitimately enjoying herself. I had to give her some credit for making the most of her time in Cove Haven.

Maggie turned back, waving to someone. "Hi, Liz." Liz's shock of red hair stood out from the crowd a few rows behind us, her body leaning against a burly man whom I assumed was her boyfriend as she stood on her tiptoes, straining to wave back. She lowered her arm as soon as she caught sight of me.

We went back to enjoying the music as more people packed

in around us. It seemed the entire town had gathered for the concert.

After the third or fourth song, Lacey thanked us for letting her hang out but said the loud music was stressing out her dog and she should go. The rest of us stayed for another hour before heading home. It was the most fun I'd had in months, at least with people other than Ruthie.

We walked in the direction of Dan and Maggie's house, and Gabe peeled off near the café. He lived in a rented apartment three blocks in the other direction. "Thank you for a lovely evening," he said to the group but squeezed my hand. "Next time, I'll pick up the tab."

"Sounds good," Dan responded, and we all laughed.

Twenty minutes later, I sunk into the bed in the guest bedroom, but my body was still wired from the night's events. As I changed from my scratchy sundress into soft pajamas, I realized I needed to charge my phone, which was still in my purse. I peered into the opening of my bag and spotted a piece of folded, white paper resting on my phone. I grabbed it, thinking it was the receipt from the restaurant. But the paper was too thick, too square, just like the one slipped through the mail slot. A jolt of terror tore through me.

Fingers trembling, I unfolded it and read the words.

YOU ARE A LIAR.

NINETEEN

NOW

I crept down the hallway, the note crunched inside my sweaty palm. Given the previous note and the unlikely discovery of Bailey's necklace, this message felt threatening enough to show Dan and Maggie before turning in for the night. But when I reached their bedroom, the light beneath their door was already out. It was after midnight, and they got up early with the girls, so I decided not to disturb them. I tiptoed back to my bedroom, turned off the hall light, and carefully closed the door, thankful, at least, that I was staying with friends tonight and not all alone in Mom's empty house.

I studied the note again. *YOU ARE A LIAR.* The paper and handwriting appeared identical to the note slipped through the mail slot two days earlier. I'd pegged Mikayla for the first note, but now I wasn't so sure. I hadn't seen her at the concert. Then again, after the sun set and people packed in around us, I wouldn't have necessarily known if she had been one of the crowd.

For the next hour, I lay in bed, staring through the darkness toward the ceiling. Who would have slipped the message into my purse? I'd had my bag on me most of the day, meaning it could have been anyone. But I hadn't noticed the paper earlier, so I started with the people I knew who were at the concert. There was my immediate group, Dan, Maggie, and Gabe. Then Lacey joined us for about thirty minutes or so. I'd also seen Jonathan Newson with his wife and kids, and Liz with her boyfriend. Chief Warner had been standing near his partner, keeping tabs on the crowd. And Hannah was there alone, dancing on the hill. I wondered how many other people from my high school class still lived here, or returned to visit, and whether I would recognize any of them if they passed me on the street or in a crowded park.

It was clear that whatever was happening with these notes was somehow related to the night of senior prom and Bailey's death and was likely connected to the reappearance of the necklace and the anonymous text that had ignited Hannah's investigation. Someone was harassing me because they believed I'd lied about something. But as my thoughts looped back over the night Bailey died, I still had no idea who it was.

I awoke on Sunday morning disoriented as memories from the night before fogged my brain. A girl shrieked from downstairs, followed by dishes clattering and Dan's laughter. I remembered I was at Dan and Maggie's house. The white piece of paper sat on my nightstand. I threw on some clothes and folded the note in my pocket.

Once downstairs, I accepted a cup of steaming coffee from Maggie. After a few minutes of listening to them chat about the store schedule and setting the girls up with cartoons in the living room, I set the note on the kitchen table between us.

"I found this in my purse last night. I didn't want to wake you."

"Oh, my gosh!" Maggie's eyeballs popped as she read the words.

"Who would do that? Why is someone harassing you?" The volume of Dan's voice had increased, and the girls looked over from the living room.

"I don't know," I said. "I've been thinking about it all night."

Maggie picked at her cuticles. "We should take this to the police, along with the other note. This isn't something to ignore."

"Yeah. I thought that at first, too. But—"

Maggie leaned forward. "But what?"

"This note is calling me a liar."

Dan shook his head. "So?"

"What if the police believe it?"

"Did you?" he asked.

"Did I lie about Bailey's death?"

"Yeah."

"No. Of course not." I could feel the emotion rushing to my face, the hot tears building behind my eyes. "I wouldn't."

Dan reached across the table and squeezed my hand. "I know you didn't. That's why you have nothing to worry about."

I knew Dan was right, but the lack of sleep had clouded my thoughts, preventing me from making clear decisions. I missed Ruthie so much. I just wanted to return to my normal life and my job at the museum, but I was trapped in Cove Haven for several more weeks.

Maggie stood, her chair scraping backward. "I'm calling the police."

———

A strange sense of déjà vu flickered through me as Chief Warner sat across from me in the bare-bones room with the cinderblock walls and fluorescent lighting. It was the same room where he had questioned me the morning after Bailey's death. The memory caused a puddle of acid to collect in the bottom of my stomach, and I was thankful that Dan and Maggie had dropped the girls with a neighbor and were now sitting next to me.

He dipped his head toward me. "Hi, Brooke." He pointed to himself. "Justin Warner. Nice to see you again. I'm sorry about your mom."

"Thank you. It's nice to see you." In truth, it wasn't nice to see him. Although the past twenty years appeared to have treated the police chief kindly, his presence just inches away from me in the sterile room was an unwanted shock. Flashbacks of the night Bailey got her DUI pulsed through me, followed by the grim investigation after her death.

"Will you be moving back into the house?"

"Oh." I almost laughed at the absurdity of it, but I realized he was posing a serious question. "No. I live in Ferndale with my daughter. I'll be putting Mom's house on the market."

"I see. A nice place like that will sell quickly, I'm sure." He tapped his knuckles on the table. "Tell me more about why we're here."

I slid the notes across the table to him, explaining how and when I'd come across each one. He frowned as he took the notes from me, studying them. He said Hannah had stopped by two days earlier to show him Bailey's necklace which she'd purchased from the thrift store. He hadn't been sure what to make of it. "To be honest, Brooke, I thought maybe you brought the necklace back to town." He held up his hand in a defensive gesture. "Not that that would mean anything. Only that you had the matching one, so it could have been yours."

I nearly fell off my chair as I remembered Hannah's comment that people were saying that it was me who had sold the necklace to the thrift shop. "It wasn't me. I've only ever had my half of the pendant. I haven't seen Bailey's necklace since that night. Until I saw Hannah wearing it at Drips Café." I looked toward Dan and Maggie, whose faces increased in pallor under the harsh lighting.

The police chief dipped his head. "I believe you, Brooke. Hannah told me you had the other half, and that Willa had no memory of how or when the necklace appeared in her store. But as I told Hannah, the existence of this necklace doesn't prove any wrongdoing. We always suspected the necklace had been carried further down the tracks by the train that night. Those tracks were converted into a walking trail a dozen years ago. Someone probably found the broken necklace as they strolled along the edge of the trail, replaced the chain, and dropped it at the thrift store at some point. It could have been found last week or ten years ago."

I lowered my eyelashes, realizing his explanation was just as plausible as mine. Maybe more so.

He continued. "I bagged Bailey's necklace so I can return it to the family. It's the right thing to do."

I nodded, silently acknowledging that I'd planned to do the same thing with the pendant, sooner or later. Still, his explanation for the reappearance of the necklace didn't explain the notes, and I pointed to them. "What about the notes?"

Chief Warner tapped his thick fingers on the table. "They are sure troubling, aren't they?" He rubbed his forehead, his gaze bouncing between the notes and me. "You are a liar." He read the note out loud. "Any idea what that refers to?"

My stomach folded as I wondered what he and the others thought of me. "I have no idea."

"If you had to guess."

My gaze skittered to Dan, who only looked at his hands. Chief Warner stared at me, waiting for an answer. "I guess it might refer to Bailey's death. Some people in this town still think—" I clenched my teeth, unable to finish the sentence.

"They think you caused her death, one way or another."

I nodded.

"That's a shame." He sighed, holding the paper further from his eyes, then picking up the other one and rereading it. "Nothing written in these messages is a direct threat, so there's no need to panic. Looks like someone isn't happy that you're back in town, and this is their way of letting you know."

I stared at the wall, having already determined that much on my own.

"I'll increase the police presence on Astor Way," he said, referring to Dan and Maggie's street. "We'll dust these notes for fingerprints in the meantime. Of course, that only helps if we have a match in our database. But call me immediately if anything else happens—any more notes, anyone following you."

"I'll definitely let you know if anything else happens." I stood and thanked the police chief for his time. Dan and Maggie ushered me back to their car, saying how much better they felt. Although it was a relief to share my fears about the notes with the authorities, a sour taste formed in my mouth. The person playing these games was smart. And whoever it was, I suspected my fifteen-minute meeting with a small-town policeman wasn't going to stop them from following me.

TWENTY

NOW

A few hours later, I sat in my car outside Dan's house. My keys weighed in my palm as I prepared to return to the address of the former prom king, Trevor Baker, and question him. Hannah had texted me an hour earlier, reminding me she'd done me a favor by cutting the unwanted segments from my podcast. Now I had to live up to my end of the bargain. So far, I'd only met with Jonathan. I squeezed my keys, questioning Hannah's true motivation for creating her Prom Queen of Cove Haven series. At times she seemed more hellbent on stirring up controversy, probably as a ploy to attract more listeners, than she did on getting to the truth. As I spun the key ring around my index finger, wondering if Hannah was taking advantage of me, the metal object slipped out of my hand and flew into the air, sliding into the tiny space between the seat and the door. I opened the door and shoved my hand down, but my arm wouldn't fit. I reached beneath the front of the seat, but the keys were a few inches out of reach.

"Seriously!" I flopped back into the seat, seeing red when I closed my eyes. Why couldn't anything be easy? Once again, it felt like the universe was ganging up on me, conspiring to make my life difficult. I slammed my hands against the steering wheel and yelled several obscenities. A white-haired woman walking a dog across the street paused to gape at me. I turned away and tipped my head back, inhaling oxygen through my nose and exhaling through my mouth. I needed to calm down, count my blessings, and be the kind of mother that Ruthie deserved, not one who flipped out because she dropped her keys. My lack of sleep was making every obstacle feel much bigger than it was.

I stepped out of the car, glancing toward Dan and Maggie's charming cottage-like house, thankful they weren't home to witness my mini tantrum. Although Dan had offered to go with me to talk to Trevor, I knew he had his store to look after, so I told him I felt fine going alone. After stretching out my arms and legs, I got down on all fours and managed to use a stick lying nearby to dig out the keys from beneath the front seat, determining to start my day over.

The route to Trevor's house took me in the direction of Cove Haven High School. I'd been avoiding my former school, but I also dreaded talking to Trevor. To buy myself a few more minutes, I tightened my grip on the wheel and made the turn, following the sidewalk Bailey and I traipsed over nearly every day for twelve years. I slowed as I neared the worn-brick building, which appeared just as I remembered it, save for a few dark stains running across the bricks and a bold sign with crisp purple-and-black lettering. School was out for summer, and the courtyard sat empty of students, but it held some new plantings —a couple of saplings and two beds of colorful flowers that battled an equal number of weeds for space. A shiny metal bike rack had been installed along the side wall just below the window of Mrs. Avery's old classroom.

An unexpected wave of wistfulness rushed through me. I wondered what my art teacher was doing now. I'd kept in touch with her during my first two years of college, but then our emails stopped. Did she still teach here? Was she even alive? Mrs. Avery had changed the course of my life, and guilt bubbled through me at my failure to keep in touch. I looked away from the window, my vision pausing on the green expanse of the football field in the distance, the field where Bailey spent so much time at cheerleading practice, shouting up to the rickety bleachers with a perma-smile on her face. I wondered what she'd be like now if she were alive. Would we still be friends? Would she be running the car dealership by now? Or would she have realized she was meant for something else and applied to junior college to pursue her dreams? I hoped she wouldn't have turned out like Mikayla. No. I knew she wouldn't have. I swallowed a gulp of sadness. I'd never know what Bailey could have become. But with all the strange happenings since I'd returned to town, I was more certain than ever that someone I knew had murdered my friend.

I absorbed the surreal scene of my former high school for another few seconds before my foot touched the accelerator, and I continued on my way. Several minutes later, my tires crunched over the gravel as I pulled outside Trevor's house. This time, I was too exhausted to feel any anxiety, almost like I was floating above myself, looking down. A man who vaguely resembled the Trevor I remembered from twenty years ago sat in a plastic chair near the front stoop, a beer can in his hand and a collection of empty beer cans beside him. His mangy dog barked wildly. The poor creature was secured to a nearby tree, but it was a small relief to see the dog now had access to shade and a bowl of water. I cut the ignition and exited my car, offering a half-hearted wave.

"Hi, Trevor. I'm sorry to show up unannounced." We stared at each other for a second, and through his greasy hair and sagging jowls, I caught a glimpse of the handsome athlete I remembered from high school. His bicep flexed as he squeezed the aluminum can, but a beer gut bulged beneath his dirty T-shirt. I touched my chest when he didn't speak. "It's Brooke Webber from high school."

A flicker of recognition shone in his eyes as he snapped his fingers and pointed at me, a sly smile on his lips. "No shit. I remember you." He struggled to stand, but I motioned for him to stay seated. It was clear he'd already consumed more than a few beers, and I found it troubling that people as flawed as he and Mikayla were already grandparents. "What are you doing here?" he asked, over the barking dog, then yelled, "Leo! Quiet!" The dog whimpered and lay down. "Wanna beer?"

"Oh, no. Thank you." I lowered myself onto the cement steps nearby, deciding to start with the question that affected me directly before mentioning Hannah's podcast. I told him how I was back in town for the summer and how Bailey's necklace had suddenly reappeared. Then said, "Someone has been leaving me threatening notes."

Trevor shrugged. "I don't know nothin' about any notes. I spend my time either here or at the shop. I'm a mechanic at the M&E Auto Shop about two miles down the road."

"Cool." I tried not to stare at the pile of empty cans next to him, and couldn't help wondering about the reliability of his work.

"And I had no idea you were in town."

"I didn't think it was you." Mikayla's pinched face popped into my mind. "The notes started happening after I ran into Mikayla the other day. And I wondered if she mentioned anything to you."

"She's a cold-hearted bitch, so I wouldn't put it past her." He coughed out a laugh and shook his head. "But we don't talk anymore unless we have to for the kids." He cleared his throat and spit into the tall grass.

Hannah had scolded me for failing to record my conversation with Jonathan, so I positioned my phone face-up on the step, hiding it behind my leg. With a quick flick of my finger, I

pressed record, thankful the dog had quieted down. I'd memo-
rized Hannah's questions and now tried to recall them, struggling to find a natural segue into the conversation. "I just drove
by the high school. It's so strange being back here after so long.
Do you ever think about prom night? About Bailey?"

"Try not to." Trevor took a swig of beer, staring toward some
trees in the distance.

"Yeah. Same." I scratched an itch on my elbow. "But I
remember how angry Mikayla was that she didn't win prom
queen and that you'd kissed Bailey on the dance floor."

"Well, Mikayla did win." He narrowed his eyes. "We just
didn't know it."

"Right. But my point is that maybe when you were married,
Mikayla told you she did something that night. You know, to get
revenge."

"Nah. She never said nothin' like that. Mikayla was pissed
at me, for sure. I had to promise her we'd get married to make
her stop crying. It was the only thing that calmed her down."
He gulped the last of his beer and crunched the can in his palm.

"Bailey had a big crush on you our senior year."

He twisted his lips to the side. "I don't think so."

"It's true. She told me."

"Sure didn't act like it."

"What do you mean?"

"When we were dancing on that stage, I asked her if she
wanted to sneak away later and hang out in my truck for a
while. She made a face and said no. Didn't even consider it."

"Maybe she was scared of Mikayla."

"Mikayla wouldn't have known. I'd done it plenty of times
before. No girl from Cove Haven High had ever shut me down
like that until Bailey. She musta been into some other dude."

I hid my eyeroll. Trevor had been so high on himself back
then, so coddled by the people around him. How typical for
him to assume the only reason Bailey would deny his advances

was if she was involved with someone else. "If she was into someone else, it wasn't Spike," I said, one of the few things I was sure about from that night.

"Yeah." Trevor chuckled. "It sure as hell wasn't him."

I stilled myself for a moment, pushing aside Trevor's narcissism and turning over the notion that Bailey could have had a secret love interest. Her words from all those years ago cut through me, *"This is why I don't tell you things, Brooke."* I wondered how much she hadn't told me as I refocused on Trevor. "Did you ever mention this to the police?"

"Nah. It never came up, and it was only a feeling. Plus, I didn't really want the whole town to know I was trying to cheat on my girlfriend."

His explanation made sense, and I nodded, mentally retrieving the next question on Hannah's list.

"Do you keep in touch with Spike?"

"Nah. His family moved somewhere outside of Milwaukee as soon as we graduated. Never heard from him again."

"That's too bad." I tapped my toe on the ground, wondering if I should tell him about the new Spike, Jonathan Newson, the developer of The Train Station hotel. But remembering how desperately Jonathan wanted to keep his identity hidden, I decided against it. "Where did you and Mikayla go after prom? You weren't at the bonfire?" I almost said, *with the rest of them,* but bit my tongue.

Trevor lowered his beer, peering down his nose at me. "Wait a second. Why are you asking all these questions about prom night?"

"I don't know. First, Bailey's necklace appeared. Then the notes. I thought you might be able to help me figure out what's going on."

"Are you working with that podcaster who came around the other day? She told me *she* found the necklace." A tendon strained in Trevor's neck. "'Cause I don't want no part of that.

Plus, she called the Humane Society on me." He glared at his dog. "Leo lives like a damn king."

I hesitated, looking back and forth from the malnourished dog to Trevor and thinking too long about my words.

Trevor tipped his head back and made a pained noise. "You busybodies don't know when to leave things alone, do you? I mean, you should be the one answering these questions."

"Huh?"

"Your best friend leaves you cold, then ends up dead with the necklace you gave her missing. Even a dumbass like me can figure out the rest."

"You're wrong. And Hannah is trying to get to the truth."

He lurched from his chair, nostrils flaring. "Tell that bitch she's not welcome here. She better go back to wherever she came from before she gets what's coming to her. And you can go along with her."

Something in the air had shifted. I stood, brushing the dirt off the back of my jeans and eager to get away from the man who had suddenly become unhinged. The increased volume of Trevor's voice caused the dog to bark again. I debated whether to make a smart remark about the sad state of Trevor's life, but he looked so tragic standing there, drunk at two in the afternoon. He was only thirty-eight, and it seemed his best years were already behind him.

Trevor lumbered closer, an unsettling grin spreading across his thin lips. He reached into his back pocket and pulled out a small object, flipping it open. My heart somersaulted at the sight of the switchblade just inches from my chest. Its razor-sharp edge jutted toward me, reflecting in the sun. "Get off my property, or there's no telling what I might do."

I took a clumsy step backward as fear pulsed through me. My pity for Trevor had been premature. I was alone with a dangerous man in a location where no one would hear my screams. My instinct told me to run, and I obeyed, hurrying toward my car and ducking into the driver's seat. Dust spewed behind the back window as I hit the accelerator and sped down the dirt road, nailing every pothole. I only allowed myself to exhale once his face was no longer visible in my rearview mirror.

TWENTY-ONE

THEN

April 2003

I matched the speed of the car in front of me as we traveled along the highway toward home. Lacey reclined in the passenger seat, streetlights flickering across her face. She appeared a thousand times more relaxed now that the poetry reading was over. My parents had lent me the car to drive Lacey to the amateur poets' event at a café in Saugatuck, an artsy town about thirty minutes to the south.

I swatted her arm. "Yours was the best one. I mean, so good!"

She hugged her notebook to her chest. "Thanks. I was nervous. I did what Mr. Sampson said and pretended everyone was naked."

"Ha!" I smiled, recalling the touching poem Lacey had written about a tree sprouting from a seedling into a mighty oak, watching the world change around it while providing constant shelter, shade, and oxygen to the birds, squirrels, and humans. The oak stood steadfast as the forests around it were cleared, the meadows filled with houses, and the waterways littered with plastic and oil spills. But still, the tree remained, a symbol of what was and what could be. Until one day, someone told the tree that it was next. The tree feared it would die and began to feel sick. Its wood rotted inside itself. Its green buds no longer appeared in the spring. It didn't want to exist in the damaged world surrounding it. The tree gave up and shed its branches, its trunk splintering in the wind. A man chopped it into firewood and burned its remains in a fire. The tree was gone, and no one remembered it except for a robin who returned to nest in its branches, and even she wasn't sure the tree had ever existed. There wasn't a dry eye in the café.

"I wish your mom and sister could have been there."

Lacey stared straight ahead. "It's fine. I read it to them earlier." Her mom worked long hours at a nearby motel and couldn't attend the event. Lacey told me once last year that her dad had abandoned them when Lacey was just a toddler. I wasn't sure where Maeve, the rosy-cheeked eight-year-old half-sister whom Lacey often looked after, came from. "Did you think the poem was about a tree?" Lacey asked.

"Yeah. And how humans are destroying the environment."

"Uh-huh. It was. But it was also about Jasper." Lacey's head turned toward me, the oncoming headlights illuminating her solemn eyes. "Jasper was the tree."

I gripped the steering wheel tighter, a swell of sorrow expanding in my chest. I'd never talked to Lacey much about Jasper. They were friends who sat together at lunch and analyzed computer stuff most of us didn't understand and books the rest of us hadn't read. It hadn't occurred to me to ask Lacey how she felt after Jasper's suicide or how she coped with missing him. It seemed unkind to raise such a painful subject, probably because I was more comfortable storing my own negative emotions safely away in a box.

"I didn't realize that about your poem, Lacey. I'm sorry. It was really beautiful." I moved over to the right lane to let a speeding car pass, recognizing how brilliant Lacey's poem actually was now that I was aware of the multiple layers of meaning.

"I helped him write songs sometimes. He played the guitar."

"He did?"

"Yeah. Not many people knew that. Jasper always dreamed of playing in a band."

It struck me again how I hadn't been a good friend to Lacey. Not to mention Jasper. I'd never been mean to him, but I also hadn't gone out of my way to be friendly. I'd never encouraged Lacey to share her memories with me. Most of what I knew about Jasper in high school came from Bailey, who'd been paired with him the winter of our junior year for a science fair project. "He's smart but kind of weird," she'd said, crinkling her nose. "Super intense. He already has like six ideas for our project, and he wanted to stay after school and go over each one in painful detail." I'd taken Bailey's comments at face value as they matched what I'd witnessed of Jasper from afar. He was a hyper-focused student who could be too quiet sometimes and too loud at others. There was something about Jasper that felt unpredictable, and maybe that's why I'd always kept a wide berth. With Willa the Witch as his mom, it was amazing that he made it to school at all.

"I'm sorry I didn't get to know him better." My gaze darted toward Lacey. It was a lame thing to say, but I couldn't think of the right words.

Lacey nodded. "You would have liked him." We continued silently along the highway for a minute. She fiddled with her fingers, suddenly speaking again. "Jasper's mom was horrible to him. She never hit him or anything, but she was mentally abusive. She told him that he was a loser who would never fit in and that he was destined for failure. I think after hearing it so many times, he must have believed her."

"Really?" I'd perceived Willa as being a bit out there in terms of societal norms, but I'd never pegged her as a mean person. Then again, no one could have known how she treated her son behind closed doors. "I'm so sorry that happened to him. That's horrible." As I put my turn signal on for the Cove Haven exit, Lacey's hand wiped tears from her face.

"How could a mom treat her own child that way?" Lacey's voice cracked as she asked the question. It had been over a year since Jasper's death, and I was shocked by the rawness of her pain.

"I don't know." I reached over and placed my hand on Lacey's, feeling the heat radiating from her skin.

She turned toward me again, anger hardening on her face. "Willa is the reason Jasper killed himself. I hope she burns in hell."

Lacey's statement sparked thoughts of the ongoing vandalism to Willa's house—the flaming bags of dog poop left on her front porch, the eggs, the spray paint. The word at school was that the most recent message written across Willa's siding said exactly what Lacey had just told me, *burn in hell*. I focused on the stop sign ahead to hide the sickening feeling surging through my core. It felt a little like someone had pushed me off the Main Street pier into the freezing waters of Lake Michigan. I couldn't shake the feeling that Lacey had been the one responsible for vandalizing Willa's house.

After dropping Lacey at her house with a hug and some encouraging words, I pulled into my driveway, picturing the business card Officer Warner had given me a few days earlier. It didn't feel right to go behind Lacey's back and rat her out, especially after she'd lost her friend. Maybe I'd encourage her to turn herself in the next time I caught her alone. As I debated the situation, a blackened figure moved through the shadows and drew my attention. I exited the car, realizing it was Bailey hurrying along the sidewalk toward her house.

"Bailey!" My voice caused her to jump.

"Oh. Hi, Brooke." The porch light illuminated her enough

for me to notice the smudged mascara, the stray hairs falling from her ponytail, and a rogue bra strap peeking out from her off-kilter shirt. "Were you out?" she asked.

"Yeah. I took Lacey to a poetry thing in Saugatuck. It was good."

"Cool."

"How about you?"

"Oh." She looked around as if searching for an answer. "I was just hanging out with a friend."

"Okay." I waited for her to say more, but she only folded her arms across her chest and glanced toward her front door. Her silence felt a little like she'd stuck me with a shiv. How could someone who used to tell me everything not feel comfortable sharing anything? I wanted to shake her, scream at her, and then confide in her about my suspicions about Lacey and the vandalism. But if I couldn't know Bailey's secrets, then she didn't deserve to know any of mine. So, I said good night and went inside.

TWENTY-TWO

NOW

On Monday morning, I pushed through the library's front door, breathing in the musty smell of the books. Lacey waved at me from behind the circulation desk.

"How are you?" I said as I approached.

"I'm fine." Her eyes darted toward the meeting room, where Hannah sat behind the glass wall with her laptop open. "Hannah keeps asking me if I'll be on her podcast. I don't want to do it."

It was clear the podcast was growing tiresome for everyone in town. Although I couldn't deny my own thirst for answers relating to Bailey's death, I didn't appreciate Hannah's pushy manner. Lacey had been nothing but accommodating to the podcaster, even confiding in me that she'd approved Hannah's daily use of the library's meeting room for hours on end, despite Hannah's lack of a library card.

"Don't let her pressure you," I said.

Lacey puckered her lips. "She's relentless."

"Maybe you can agree to talk to her but not have your interview aired."

Lacey bit her lip, considering. "Yeah. That's a good idea. I'm not trying to hide anything; I just don't want people to think I'm endorsing her podcast. There's something about it that doesn't feel right."

I nodded because I knew what she meant. "I'm actually going to see her now, and I'll mention it. Hopefully, it will be the last time I meet with her."

A girl stood behind me with an armful of books, so I headed to the meeting room to let Lacey do her job.

Hannah's eyes lifted as I approached, and she waved me inside. I closed the door, taking the seat across from her. "Can you leave Lacey alone? She's not cut out for podcast interviews."

She made a sour face. "Anyone can be on a podcast. Besides, I wouldn't have thought Lacey was cut out for vandalizing Willa Jones's house either."

My head dropped forward. Apparently, Hannah had left no stone unturned. "Lacey had her reasons for doing that. She made amends with Willa a long time ago."

"I know. I asked Willa about it, and she told me the same. But I'm not done researching the topic for a future episode about the possibility of a connection between Jasper's death and Bailey's death. Maybe something beyond a mere copycat suicide as has always been assumed."

"There's no connection there. I can pretty much guarantee it. Bailey and Jasper ran in completely different social circles."

"I'm going to look into it anyway." Hannah pushed her laptop a few inches away and stared at me, leaving me both impressed and annoyed by her stubbornness. "So? Did you meet with Trevor?"

"Um, yeah. He pulled a knife on me. I'm never going back there again, and neither should you."

Hannah rocked back in her chair. "Oh my gosh! Are you okay?"

"I'm fine. It was scary."

"Did you get anything from him?"

"Not too much. Except there was one thing he said that I'd never heard before. It's probably nothing, but—"

"What was it?"

I leaned forward, mildly ashamed at how eager I was to share the new information. "Trevor propositioned Bailey during the royal dance, and she flat-out denied him. He had a feeling that Bailey was interested in someone else. Not him, obviously."

"Wasn't Mikayla his girlfriend?"

"Yeah. It sounds like Trevor had a habit of cheating on her."

"Maybe Bailey just wasn't attracted to him."

I smirked. "Trevor said no girl at Cove Haven High had ever rejected his advances before."

"Oh, please!" Unlike me, Hannah made no effort to stop her eyes from rolling back in her head. "Someone's a little high on himself."

"No kidding. But he was kind of right, sadly. He was basically like a god back then."

Hannah made a face. "Jesus. What happened to him? Did you see his house?"

"Yeah. It's bad. And his poor dog." My mind wouldn't let me go to his menagerie of offspring, who likely lacked basic necessities. I forced away the thoughts and refocused. "I recorded our conversation like you wanted. You can listen for yourself."

I played the recording from my phone as Hannah leaned her ear toward it, a blank expression on her face as she jotted a couple of notes in her pink notebook. The recording ended with Trevor yelling for me and Hannah to get out of town and his final threat for me to get off his property.

The whites of Hannah's eyes showed at the threats. "Charming. Any other thoughts?"

"Kind of. Here's the thing. Bailey did have a crush on Trevor earlier in the school year. She told me."

"So..."

"So I was thinking about it last night. What would make her stop having a crush on Trevor?"

Hannah tilted her head. "Meeting someone else?"

"Yep."

"And then I remembered another thing. A few weeks before prom, I arrived home late and caught Bailey walking home alone. Her hair was a little messy, and her makeup was smudged like she'd been messing around with someone."

"Who?"

"I don't know. She wouldn't tell me. It could have been Spike, but I didn't think so at the time. She made it very clear she wasn't attracted to him. My point is that maybe Trevor was right. What if Bailey's secret love interest, whoever it was, met up with her after the bonfire? Maybe that was the real reason she stayed back when everyone else left. Maybe he took the necklace. Maybe they had a fight."

A realization shone in Hannah's eyes. "It's a new lead. One that's never been considered before."

"Possibly. Or, like all the other supposed leads, it could mean nothing."

Hannah leaned toward a stack of Cove Haven High School yearbooks on the side table. She grabbed the one from my senior year, 2003, and flipped it open between us. "Let's take a look and see who she might have been messing around with."

It felt like a fool's errand, but I hadn't looked at my high school yearbook in years, and curiosity got the better of me. My fingers flipped through the glossy pages, my eyes scanning over the small, square headshots of my former classmates.

Hannah said, "Look at every person in your senior class and read the names of anyone who might be a possibility."

I examined the faces on each page, most smiling but some looking more like mugshots. I read aloud the names of two or three boys who hung around Bailey's lunch table, although none of them stuck out for any particular reason. There'd been a wide distance between me and Bailey by the end of our senior year, and I didn't have a clue who I was looking for.

Hannah tapped her fingernail on the table. "Bailey felt comfortable telling you about her crush on Trevor but not comfortable telling you about the person she'd been hanging out with the night you saw her. She went to prom with Spike instead. Why?"

"I guess she wanted to keep it a secret." I flipped the page, my gaze snagging on a photo of the drama teacher, Mr. Sampson. It was a group photo of Bailey's third-hour class, Dramatic Arts. Bailey had lost interest in all her classes during her senior year except for that one. There were more than twenty students in the photo, but Bailey stood beside Mr. Sampson, the two of them practically touching shoulders. The rumors about the handsome, young drama teacher getting too close to a few of his female students came hurtling back to me. I remembered the whispers toward the end of junior year that Mr. Sampson had been hanging out with the ousted cheerleader, Sherri Stevens, outside of school and that he may have fathered her baby. A DNA test later proved that the gossip was untrue. The father was a nineteen-year-old from two towns over. Soon the Cove Haven High School rumor mill had turned to other topics.

I pointed to Mr. Sampson's face. "He was Bailey's drama teacher. It was the only class she made an effort to do well in. I didn't make the connection at the time, but there were rumors about him getting too close to female students. I guess I never really believed there was anything to them."

Hannah raised her eyebrows, scribbling. "That's a good thought. And it would explain why Bailey kept the relationship hidden. I'll look into it." She typed something into her laptop. "With this new tidbit, I have more than enough to record my next episode about the boys in Bailey's life—Spike, Trevor, and the drama teacher. One of them could be her mystery lover."

She clicked on something, eyes scanning back and forth. "Ha! Found him." She spun the screen to show me a photo of a fifty-something Mr. Sampson. He was a marketing director at a community theater in Grand Rapids. "I'll call him later."

"That's him. But just a reminder that you can't go on air and start accusing people of things they may or may not have done. Jonathan already threatened to sue you, and he wasn't joking. And like you heard on the recording, Trevor threatened you too. He said if you ever came near him again, you'd get what's coming to you. He's not joking around."

Hannah shook her head. "That was a little much. And what was that about me calling the Humane Society?"

"I'm the one who called, but I let him think it was you so he'd talk to me."

Hannah waved her hand in the air. "Fine. Whatever. I'm not scared of Trevor, and I'm not accusing anyone of anything. I only use first names or other generic identifiers so as not to ruin anyone's life. This is the way true crime podcasts work. We raise questions that have no clear answers and force people to ask themselves, 'what really happened?'"

I pulled a deep breath into my lungs. "I've been meaning to tell you something else."

"What?"

My fingernails dug into my knees as I realized I might regret what I was about to say. But participating in Hannah's podcast now felt too risky given the creepy notes someone had been leaving for me, threats that were likely to escalate the more I poked into other people's business. "Ever since I took that necklace from you, I've been getting threatening notes. They're anonymous," I said, describing the messages. "Someone slipped the first one through Mom's mail slot in the middle of the night and dropped the second one into my purse when I was at the outdoor concert on Saturday night. I turned them over to the police to check for fingerprints."

"Oh my gosh, Brooke! That's terrifying." She made a pouty face. "Are you okay?"

"I'm a little creeped out, to be honest. I want you to get to the truth behind Bailey's death more than anything, but I've done my part in helping you with your podcast. Now I'm going to fly under the radar and stay away from whoever this psychopath is that's harassing me."

"No, Brooke. Come on." Hannah's words were drawn-out, borderline whiney. "I need you more than ever."

"Why?"

She leaned closer to me, lowering her voice. "Don't you get it? What if it's all related? What if we're getting close to figuring something out? This person harassing you might be the same one who had Bailey's necklace. They probably heard you on my podcast. They know you're looking for answers and are trying to scare you away. Don't let them! You knew Bailey better than anyone."

I rested my head in my hands, trying to determine if there could be any truth to Hannah's theory. It had already occurred to me that the person who'd left the notes could have been the person who'd taken Bailey's necklace—or worse. The podcast would surely set them on edge even more than me returning to town.

"Okay, maybe you're right. I'll help you when I can, but don't mention my involvement on the podcast. I'm only talking to you because I want to get to the truth and I don't want this creepy note-writer to win."

"Got it."

"But my first priority is getting my mom's house sold and returning safely to my daughter in six weeks or less."

Hannah winked. "The daughter who likes jigsaw puzzles?"

"I might have lied about that."

"I never would have known." She lowered her eyelids, appearing simultaneously impressed and insulted.

My phone buzzed, and a message from the contractor popped on the screen.

We have an issue over at the house. A woman is standing inside and won't leave until she talks to you.

Who is it?

Willa Jones

TWENTY-THREE

NOW

I hurried toward the front door of my childhood home. Eric stood outside and shook his head. Another worker sat beside him, smiling.

My contractor thumbed toward the door. "Willa's in there. Apparently, she has something very important to tell you."

"I'm sorry for the disruption," I said. "I didn't know she was coming over."

Eric smirked. "I tried to get her to call you, but she said phones are the devil's device or something like that."

"That sounds about right. Just give me a couple of minutes, and I'll get her to leave."

"Sounds good." He stepped aside, unscrewing the cap of his water bottle.

The pungent smell of sawdust surrounded me as I entered. The construction crew had removed the worn wallpaper and carpeting and had started sanding the floors already. Willa hovered in the middle of the living room, pulling at a bundle of sage hanging from her neck.

"Hi, Willa."

"Brooke. You have arrived."

"I'm here."

She stared at me with her good eye as the other flickered toward the wall.

"What did you want to tell me?"

She stretched tall, slowly raising her arms into the air between us. "I have beckoned the spirits of memories past, present, and future. They have answered my chants, and I followed them here to share the message."

A mix of excitement and dread prickled through me. "Is this about the necklace?"

She touched her knotty fingers to her temples. "The memory was returned to me in my sleep." She spoke each word so slowly. It was all I could do not to grab her by the shoulders and shake the name out of her.

I stepped closer. "Who was it?"

"The man who provides recreation to weary travelers."

My molars ground against each other, and I wished she'd stop talking in riddles. But she'd said "man," so not Mikayla, who I still suspected of writing the notes. "Can you be more specific?"

"The nice man who owns a shop with bikes and kayaks. He comes by the shop from time to time."

"Dan?" I asked as my mouth went completely dry. *Dan? The person I considered my most loyal, lifelong friend?*

She pointed at me. "That's correct. Dan. I'd misplaced his name. He brought the necklace to me. It was mixed in with other treasures. That's probably why I lost the memory."

I blinked, feeling a little like she'd punched me in the stomach. Why did Dan have Bailey's necklace? Why had he feigned surprise when I showed it to him a few nights earlier? We'd had a long conversation about why it had suddenly reappeared and who could have dropped it at the thrift shop when it had been him all along. He lied. The floor seemed to tilt beneath my feet as I took a wider stance and found my voice. "When did he bring it in?"

"Maybe a week ago. Maybe two." Her stable eye honed in on me. "Most people don't understand that time is a false construct prone to shifting."

I massaged my forehead, wondering about the reliability of Willa's information. Then again, she had no reason to lie. My thoughts circled back to one to two weeks ago. I'd been in Cove Haven eleven days, so Dan must have dropped the necklace off right around the time I'd returned. Hannah must have purchased it just a day or two after it landed at Willa's store. What if Dan wanted to get the necklace out of his house before I arrived? But I never would have seen the necklace if it was hidden away somewhere. I remembered complaining to him a few days before I arrived about how much stuff I still had to clear out of Mom's house. Had he assumed I'd take at least a few of her things to the thrift shop? Had he wanted me to find the necklace on display? I couldn't wrap my head around the unlikely set of facts.

Willa studied my face, surely picking up on my fear. "Sometimes answers beget more questions."

I struggled for air. "Yes. That's true."

"I have spells for every ailment. Come see me if you need one."

"Everything okay in here?" Eric's booming voice made me jump. He poked his head through the doorway, raising his eyebrows at me.

"Everything is fine," I said, although nothing could have been further from the truth. "Can I drive you home, Willa? These men need to get back to work."

"If you insist."

I nodded because it was the fastest way to get Willa out of the house. My mind reeled with unwanted questions as I showed her to my car. I wondered again why Dan would have

Bailey's necklace. Had he held on to it for all these years? Was he the one who'd replaced the chain? Had he been with Bailey when she died? Or just after? If so, why hadn't he told anyone? I wouldn't let my thoughts go any further because the potential answers were too unsettling, too gruesome. Besides, it was completely possible that Willa was merely confused. Three minutes later, I dropped Willa back at the front door of The Treasure Cove thrift shop, watching in a daze as she pulled her shawl around herself and hobbled inside.

Turning my car around, I wondered where to go next. My home base was Dan's house, but I was too unnerved to face him. I had no idea what I would say. Hannah would surely gobble up this juicy piece of information, but sharing it with her too soon, before I had a chance to think things through, felt reckless. Lacey would listen, but she was at the library, where Hannah was likely to see me. I needed more time to process Willa's troubling revelation. Had she gotten it wrong? The Dan I knew wasn't a liar, much less a murderer. He was a steadfast friend, a loving husband to Maggie, and a doting father to Olivia and Marci. I struggled to grasp a thread of clarity, to find another explanation.

I slowed my car next to the old train station and parked, spotting Jonathan talking to another man on the far side of the building. My body was dead-weight, dragging along in slow motion as I exited the car and approached. He looked surprised to see me and said something to the other man, who turned and left to measure the distance from the building to a distant tree.

"Afternoon, Brooke." He gave a bemused smile. "Stopping by to accuse me of another crime?"

"No. I'm sorry to bother you like this. I just..." My head turned in the direction of Willa's house. "I wanted to ask you something about Bailey." I held up a hand. "It's not for the podcast. It's just for my own sanity."

Jonathan sighed, a layer of perspiration glazing his forehead. "Fine. Let's make it quick, though."

"On prom night, or even before that, did you get the feeling Bailey was involved with someone else? Romantically speaking."

"She practically made out with Trevor on the dance floor, so there was that."

"No. Not him. Was there someone else?"

"I have no idea." Jonathan adjusted his sunglasses. "When I asked her to prom, I wasn't expecting her to hesitate for so long before answering. She said yes, though. Eventually. I took it at face value. I mean, if she was interested in someone else, she could have just told me."

"Did you and Bailey go on any dates before that?"

"Only in a group with the others. Not alone. I asked her to go to the movies with me one night, and she said her parents wouldn't let her. But I got the feeling it was a cop-out."

"So you and Bailey never went on a date alone?" I paused, remembering the night of the poetry reading when I'd caught a disheveled Bailey returning to her house. "Or made out in the back of your car?"

Jonathan threw his head back and laughed. "Nope. Not even close." He chuckled again. "I dreamed about that, though."

A gust of wind blew my hair across my face, and I wrangled it behind my ear. Bailey had been with someone the night I went to Lacey's poetry reading, but it hadn't been Spike. This morning, I thought we'd been onto something when I realized Bailey's secret lover might have been Mr. Sampson. But now I couldn't help wondering if there'd been something going on between Dan and Bailey instead. As unlikely as that seemed, Dan was the one with Bailey's missing necklace in his possession. Dan, who had always felt more like a brother to Bailey and me than someone we'd kiss. I'd never noticed the slightest hint of anything between them other than them being frequently annoyed with each other. But had Dan been secretly attracted to Bailey? And her to him? It was a question I'd never considered before, and I suddenly felt sick, as if I'd just swallowed something toxic.

Like so many times before, my mind traveled back to the night of prom and the hours after the dance. I'd gone to Joe's Diner with Dan and Lacey. Henry was out of town that weekend with his parents for his grandpa's funeral. After devouring milkshakes and French fries, Dan, Lacey, and I parted ways around eleven to walk home, splitting off at the corner of Fourth and Cottage. Dan's parents said he arrived at 11:10 p.m., about the same time Lacey's mom and my parents confirmed we'd arrived at our houses. But what if Dan snuck out again to go to the bonfire just after the popular crowd scattered due to the rain? Maybe Bailey didn't walk home with the others because she was meeting Dan. *Stop it. Stop it.* My mind was a runaway train.

"Are you okay?"

I looked up, having forgotten Jonathan was standing next to me.

He offered a concerned smile. "Did I help you get your sanity back?"

I wiped my palms down the outside of my pants, snapping back to the present. "Yeah. Not really. But thanks for talking."

He glanced toward the old stone building. "I've got to get back to the surveyor."

I followed Jonathan's gaze toward the other man. "Okay."

He began to walk away but flipped back around. "Wait. If you don't mind me saying..." He paused, checking to see how far away the surveyor was, then refocusing on me. "It can help to talk to someone. You know, about everything that happened back then."

"I know. I have." If only he knew how many people I'd talked to about my guilt. My anger. I used to think all those therapy sessions had helped, but I'd recently realized that enlightened self-awareness only went so far.

Beyond Jonathan's shoulder, the rickety bridge loomed in the distance, a painful reminder of the past. I couldn't help noticing the juxtaposition of brightly clad joggers and young parents pushing strollers or walking dogs along the path where Bailey had once been crushed by the train. I assumed none of them knew the history. Surely, they wouldn't be bouncing along the path like that if they did.

"Take care, Brooke."

"Thanks. You too." Pulling my stare away, I turned and forced my feet toward my car. But when I reached the street, I realized I had no idea where to go.

TWENTY-FOUR

NOW

I drove toward the café and parked nearby, slumping over the steering wheel to collect my thoughts. Nothing felt more urgent than talking to Dan, but he was working at the bike shop. Hannah's name buzzed across my phone. My impulse was to ignore her, but then I'd only wonder why she'd called. I took a calming breath and answered, reminding myself not to show my hand. Hannah didn't need to know about Dan and the necklace just yet.

"Hi, Brooke. I left a message for Ron Sampson, the former drama teacher. He hasn't called me back yet."

"Okay." My shoulders tensed as the new information about Dan and the necklace sat on my tongue.

"So, we'll have to put that theory on hold." Hannah huffed. "I'll call him again tomorrow."

Willa's revelation expanded inside me, itching to burst forth. I pushed it down, still not fully trusting Hannah and her agenda.

"Brooke, I'm not too happy with you." Hannah's voice had hardened, sounding like a parent chastising a child. "Not happy at all."

"Why not?"

"I don't like being lied to."

"I didn't lie." The creepy note scrolled through my head. *YOU ARE A LIAR.*

"Really? Because you told me you were on a leave of absence from the museum to fix up your mom's house."

"That's right. I am."

"But when I called your workplace, someone named Cheryl told me that you're on a forced leave of absence because of an unfortunate incident with a patron."

My fingers tightened around the phone. "You called my work? Hannah! Why would you do that?"

"And when I cross-referenced the dates with local news articles, I found an interesting account of a museum visitor getting attacked by an exhibit director who worked there, the patron's bracelet torn right off her wrist. There's a pretty revealing video on YouTube too."

My breath rushed in and out. I felt like I was suffocating.

"Remind you of anything, Brooke?"

"No. It wasn't the same thing. That woman wouldn't stop touching the exhibit pieces. Those oil paintings were three hundred years old. I asked her not to touch the paintings, and when she refused, I batted her hand away. She made a huge scene, and things got blown out of proportion." I squeezed my eyelids shut, remembering how helpless the woman looked lying below me, the beads from her snapped bracelet rolling across the marble floor. She'd been older and frailer than I realized. I'd accidentally knocked her down and then tried to help her up as a disapproving crowd gathered, at least one of them aiming their phone at me.

"Do you have a problem with anger, Brooke? Does the rage simmer inside you? A slow boil until you can't take it anymore, and then you snap?"

"No!"

"Really? Because I found a bit of a pattern. Did you have a college roommate named Erin Cross?"

I clenched my fists, rage steaming through me. "Yes."

"That's what I thought. I found an interesting blog post written in the spring of 2004 by Erin, a student at the same art school you attended. It described how her roommate B. W. thought she'd left the room too dirty, so B. W. took Erin's fresh pot of brewed coffee and poured it all over her bed, then threw her clothes in the hallway. You are B. W., right? Brooke Webber. Sounds like you were the roommate from hell."

My molars ground into each other. I didn't know Erin kept a blog or that she'd written about the incident that led to the university moving me to a single room to live alone. There'd been a school-appointed moderator who heard us out and then decided we were incompatible. "Other things were going on there." I lifted my chin. "Erin was the awful roommate. Not me. She stole my idea for our end-of-term project." Our assignment had been to create a piece of art depicting a transformation. She'd been struggling with an idea, so I'd described mine to her —an urban landscape decomposing and turning back into a natural wilderness. She stole my concept—flat-out copied it— never mentioning her betrayal to me until I spotted her project on display in the school art gallery for the final exam.

Hannah clucked. "I would have liked to have known about your anger issues before our interview. It's relevant to the investigation into your best friend's death."

"I don't have anger issues." I pressed my palm into my eye socket, fighting the urge to scream, to jump out of my car and heave it over, Incredible Hulk style and then stomp over to the library and punch Hannah in her snarky face. Because yes, I did have anger issues, but I could control them now. I'd visited a therapist for years, every week, whether I wanted to or not. She taught me how to express myself in times of distress so I didn't hold everything inside until it exploded. The recent incident in the museum was a slip-up, just a blip on the radar. That same morning, I'd learned that Shane's new girlfriend, Mandy, had already moved in with him. Instead of letting myself be upset, I told myself it was fine, that it had nothing to do with me. I went on with my day. And then that woman kept ignoring the signs to stay twelve inches back from the artwork. The temporary exhibit she was viewing hadn't been equipped with the same electronic sensors installed in the larger rooms, the ones that beeped when people got too close. I asked her politely three times. She didn't seem to care that the oil on her fingers could ruin a centuries-old painting!

Hannah's lips smacked through my phone. "I'm going to have to add this information to a future episode. We'll let the listeners decide if your pattern of explosive anger is relevant."

I placed a hand against the dashboard, feeling like I was tumbling backward through time, back to the whispers about me after Bailey died, back to the people saying I hadn't been a good enough friend. Desperation rose in me, a primal panic. I had no defense. Except I did have one way to stop her. I had new information Hannah didn't have.

I sat up, hating myself for what I was about to do but realizing that Hannah had painted me into a corner once again. The quiver in my gut told me it was wrong, but my head knew I'd run out of options. This was the only way to save my reputation. "Wait, Hannah. I learned something important today, but I don't have all the facts yet. I'll tell you what it is if you don't mention the incident at the museum. Publicity about that could cost me my career. I have a daughter to think about. What I did was inexcusable, but I had one of the worst days of my life that day, even before the incident happened. I can explain it all to you later, when we're face-to-face."

"Hmm." I heard tapping from Hannah's end. "That's a big ask. What kind of important information did you learn?"

I ignored the guilt rippling through me, reminding myself

that Dan was the one who'd lied in the first place. "I found out who dropped the necklace at the thrift shop."

Hannah gasped. "Okay. You've got my attention. Who was it?"

"I need you to promise not to include it in your podcast until I have a chance to talk to the person Willa identified."

"Yeah. Yeah. I'll give you a chance to talk to them. Who was it?"

I lowered my voice to a loud whisper, feeling like I wanted to cry. "It was Dan. Dan brought it in about two weeks ago. Probably just a few days before you bought it."

"What the...? Are you serious?"

"That's what Willa told me. I still can't believe it. I don't know what it means. There must be an explanation."

"What if Dan and Bailey were secretly seeing each other?"

"No. That doesn't make sense," I said automatically, although I'd had the same thought just a few minutes earlier. "Why would they keep it a secret?"

"Because he wasn't part of the cool crowd. Maybe Bailey was embarrassed to be seen with him. No offense, but Bailey sounded like a real peach."

I heard the sarcasm in Hannah's voice but didn't respond. She wasn't wrong. Bailey had her moments, but she hadn't always been like that. Not until she started hanging out with those girls. I cleared my throat. "I still think Mr. Sampson makes more sense. Just let me talk to Dan and find out his explanation before you do anything."

Hannah released a drawn-out sigh as if my request was physically painful. "Okay. You have twenty-four hours."

TWENTY-FIVE

THEN

April 2003

I opened the foil and removed a cold piece of pizza. Dan sat next to me, slurping a can of Coke. Outside, rain battered the windows of the noisy cafeteria. Two boys a grade below us barged past, knocking the empty chair where Lacey usually sat as they hurried toward an open table.

"Our table feels weird without Lacey here," Henry said, biting into a sandwich.

Dan shook his head. "I still can't believe she did that to Jasper's mom."

I watched the raindrops snaking down the window. "Me neither."

After I'd gotten home on the night of the poetry reading, I threw the card Officer Warner had given me into my waste basket. I was almost certain Lacey was the vandal, but I didn't want to share my hunch with anyone. Lacey was already in so much pain, and I couldn't bring myself to snitch on her. I was glad I hadn't made the call because Lacey confessed to her mom two days later, and her mom had made her turn herself in to the police. Last Friday, she'd officially been identified as the vandal of Willa's house. The school was called too, and they had a meeting, deciding that because Lacey was an otherwise upstanding young citizen who had recently lost her best friend under tragic circumstances, her punishment would be a two-day suspension from school and an in-person apology to Willa Jones, along with fifty hours of community service. Apparently, Willa had agreed to the terms.

Today was the first day of Lacey's suspension. I was thankful for the quick resolution but could only imagine what other students were saying about her. I glanced toward the table of cheerleaders on the far side of the cafeteria, who all wore their purple-and-black uniforms, despite no sporting events that I knew of. Zoe leered toward me, then looked back at Liz, Mikayla, and Bailey, saying something before the group erupted in laughter. My hands gripped the edges of my chair if only to stop myself from marching toward Zoe and flinging her lunch tray to the floor. I wanted to take Bailey by the neck and squeeze some basic decency back into her.

"You okay, Brooke?" Dan tilted his head, lips pinched in concern.

"Yeah."

He followed my stare toward the table where Bailey sat. "What a bunch of two-faced wannabes."

Henry glanced over his shoulder to see what we were looking at. "Seriously. They suck."

I couldn't help giggling at that.

We made a pact not to look at them and eventually settled into a normal lunchtime conversation. A few minutes later, a palm pounded on a tabletop, drawing my attention. Trevor stood on a chair, hands cupped around his mouth. "Listen up!" he yelled.

The din of conversation quieted as everyone turned toward him.

Liz stood beside Trevor and waved. She wore her auburn hair in a high ponytail that bounced whenever she moved. "Attention, everyone. I'm Liz. Zoe and I are the heads of the senior prom committee."

"We know!" someone yelled from a distant table as a smattering of laughter echoed through the room.

Liz smiled, doing a poor job of hiding her annoyance. "In a minute, we're going to be passing out first-round voting slips for prom queen and prom king. Raise your hand if you're a senior, and we'll come around to give you a slip. Write your student ID number in the top right-hand corner and the names of three senior girls and three senior boys who you want to see on the royal court on the lines below. Then drop your slip into one of the drop boxes near the office. The three boys and three girls with the most votes will move on to the final vote in two weeks. And the winners of the final vote will be announced on prom night at the dance." Liz smiled, clearly expecting some applause, but only chatter rumbled through the cafeteria. "So seniors, raise your hands!"

Liz, Zoe, Mikayla, Bailey, and three other cheerleaders dispersed among the tables, each holding a stack of white paper squares. I hoped one of the nice cheerleaders, like my friend Libby, would find her way to our table, but she headed away from us.

Henry's arm shot up. "Right here! We're seniors. Woo-hoo! We need to vote."

My eyes connected with Dan's, and we doubled over laughing. Mikayla reached our table first, flashing a plastic smile. "Hi, guys!" Her voice was warm and bubbly as if we were friends. "Make sure you vote for me." She winked.

"And you for me." Henry smiled like a psychopath at Mikayla, who ignored him.

"We're voting for Brooke," Dan said without skipping a beat. "And Lacey."

Mikayla's eyes darted toward me, her mouth curving downward. "Good luck with that." She slapped down three pieces of paper and moved on to the next table.

I covered the papers, blocking Dan and Henry from grabbing their slips. "Please don't vote for me. It would be my worst nightmare. I mean, not that anyone else would vote for me."

Dan waved me off. "We won't. I just wanted to see the look on Mikayla's face."

Henry scowled in Mikayla's direction. "I don't care who wins as long as it's not her."

Bailey walked up behind Henry. "Hi, guys. I see you got your slips already."

"Yep."

She leaned toward me, the shiny silver of our friendship necklace catching my eye. I hadn't worn mine in months, and I wondered if she'd noticed. "I'm sorry to hear about Lacey. Is she okay?"

"Yeah. She's fine," I said.

Henry pointed at Bailey. "Let me guess, you want us to vote for you."

Bailey shrugged. "Mikayla's probably going to win, regardless. She and Trevor have already made everyone promise to vote for them so they can have the royal dance." She made a face and held up her voting slips. "I've got to go do this. See you guys later."

Dan, Henry, and I stared at each other. That was the most normal Bailey had acted with us in weeks. "I have an idea," Dan said. "How about we vote for Bailey and no one else? At least she has a shot of beating Mikayla."

"Seriously?" Henry asked. "She ditched us. Why would we do that?"

Dan shrugged. "It's the lesser of the two evils if you ask me."

Mikayla's cackle reached my ears from a few tables away, making me cringe.

"Dan's right," I said. "Bailey doesn't have much going for her right now. We can do this for her." No matter how much Bailey had hurt me recently, she'd been my friend for over twelve years. My loyalty to her ran deep, and her recent choices had left her in a bad place. I wrote down her name and folded my paper, watching as Dan and Henry did the same.

"I'll go campaign for her." Dan stepped toward a table of seniors behind us. "Vote for Bailey Maddox. She'd make a good prom queen." The kids at the table looked at him and shrugged, jotting down her name. He repeated the request at a few more tables as more kids shrugged and added Bailey's name to their sheet. There were no life-or-death issues on this ballot, and it seemed most people could care less whose names they added. The bell rang. I threw away my lunch bag and hurried down the hallway to drop my slip in the voting box, imagining the smile on Bailey's face when she made it to round two.

TWENTY-SIX

NOW

I hid in the shade of a tree across the street from Lakeside Bike and Boat Rentals. People moved inside, a blip of Dan's blue shirt flitting past the open door every couple of minutes. He exited, blinking into the sun. Two middle-aged women followed him, and he showed them to their bikes, pointing out the hand brakes and checking their helmets before he watched them pedal away.

He stood there for longer than necessary, hands on hips and staring into space as if in a trance. There was no sign of Maggie, and I presumed she was busy with the girls. The shop appeared empty. This was as good a time as any to confront him.

I stepped forward and waved. "Hi, Dan."

He snapped out of his stupor and smiled at me. "Hey, Brooke. I didn't see you hiding over there."

I shoved my hands into my pockets and crossed the street. "Everything okay?" I asked.

"Yeah. I was going to ask you the same thing."

I scratched an imaginary itch on the back of my neck, dreading the topic I had to address. "Actually, can I talk to you for a minute? In private?"

He tilted his head, looking both worried and confused. "Yeah. The store's empty right now. Let's go in there."

I followed him inside, and he closed the door. We sat side-by-side on a wooden bench positioned along the wall.

"I have to ask you something, and it's a little uncomfortable."

"Okay." Dan leaned forward tentatively as if preparing to let someone slap him in the face. "I'm ready."

I dug my fingernails into my arm, deciding to get it over with. "Willa Jones showed up at my old house today and said she remembered who dropped Bailey's necklace off at the thrift shop."

"Really?"

"Yeah. She said it was you."

Dan recoiled, stretching away from me. "What?"

"She said you dropped off the necklace about one or two weeks ago."

He shook his head, closing his eyes dramatically. "I think I would have remembered that."

"Willa said it was mixed in with other treasures."

"It wasn't me." Dan's eyes were wild. "Why would I have Bailey's necklace? That's literally crazy."

I softened my voice, struggling not to sound confrontational. "But why would she make that up?"

"I don't know." Dan shifted his weight, staring toward the window for an uncomfortable length of time. "Wait a second." He snapped his fingers. "I think I might know what happened."

"What?"

He stood up and walked behind the counter, pulling out a large canvas bin. "This is our lost-and-found. Willa was right. I dropped a box from the shop about two weeks ago. Maggie takes our lost-and-found bin over there two or three times a year when it gets full, but she was busy that day, so I did it. People are always leaving personal items in the store—hats, watches, jackets, jewelry, you name it. We figure the thrift shop is better than sending them to the landfill."

"So, the necklace was mixed in with the lost-and-found items?"

"It must have been."

"Didn't you look through it before taking it over? What if something of yours was in there?"

"I'm sure I took a quick look, but the necklace wasn't on my radar. I must not have noticed it or made the connection if I did."

I leaned back and crossed my ankles, realizing Dan's explanation made perfect sense. I felt stupid for imagining that he'd saved Bailey's necklace in his underwear drawer or under a loose floorboard all these years as a relic of some secret love affair. It was a relief to banish the fictional, creepy version of Dan from my imagination. But the new scenario still begged the question of who put the necklace in the lost-and-found box. I looked at the door. "Did any of the locals come into the store around then? Do you remember?"

Dan pressed his lips into a straight line. "Locals don't typically rent bikes unless they have friends or family in town. A few might take out kayaks in the warmer weather, I guess." He rubbed his chin. "Some of the things in the box were probably left over from ski rental season, which includes a lot of locals."

I leaned my head against the wall, realizing Willa's revelation was going nowhere. The lost-and-found box had been collecting stray belongings for several months before Dan dropped it at the thrift shop. Anyone could have dropped the necklace there, tourist, local, or otherwise.

I thanked Dan for going through everything with me and apologized if I'd sounded accusatory. He told me not to worry and that he'd let me know if he or Maggie remembered anything else about who had added things to the box.

I walked to the coffee shop, regretting my impulsive decision to tell Hannah about the necklace coming from Dan. I needed to update her on Dan's explanation before she said anything reckless on her podcast. But she'd promised me twenty-four hours, which left plenty of time to stop at Drips and try to enjoy a sliver of my afternoon before calling her back.

When I entered the café, it was as empty as I'd ever seen it. Gabe wiped down the front counter. "Hi, Brooke!" He stopped cleaning and tossed aside the dishrag. "I was getting worried I wouldn't see you today."

"I can't stay away, I guess."

Somewhere behind his beard, his lips curved into a smile. "What would you like? It's on me."

"Just ice water, please. I'm feeling a little dehydrated."

"You're a cheap date."

I couldn't help giggling as he turned toward the sink.

He handed me the water a minute later. "I was thinking we should hang out again."

I wasn't sure if he was asking me on a date or just a casual get-together, but I decided it didn't matter. I enjoyed Gabe's company and wouldn't mind seeing where our friendship led. "Sure. Let's do it," I said, trying not to sound too eager.

"I've been meaning to try that putt-putt golf place now that they've added the pirates."

"Oh my gosh. I haven't been there in decades." My mind tumbled back to the lazy weekends when Bailey and I would play the worn, bare-bones course together. We'd never dreamed of pirates. A single windmill on hole five and a water jump on hole eight had offered the biggest thrills. We made silly noises as the other one hit the ball to try to make each other mess up. Sometimes one of us had an extra dollar to buy a box of Sour Patch Kids from the shop. We'd share the candy on a nearby bench, watching the other families play and pretending to be sports announcers commentating on a serious round of golf.

"Someone bought the place and spruced it up. Are you free Friday night?"

"Yeah. That sounds like fun."

"I'll stop by Dan and Maggie's house to get you at seven if that works for you."

"Perfect."

Gabe smiled and went back to wiping down the counter.

The bell above the door jingled, and a woman walked inside, removing her sunglasses when she saw me. "Hi, Brooke. Nice to see you again."

Zoe stepped toward me in her heeled clogs and linen pants. Dewy skin and lips painted the color of dusty rose petals completed her look; she was just as polished as the last time I'd seen her.

"Hi, Zoe."

She motioned toward Gabe. "I see you've met the best barista in town."

"That's right." Gabe gave a mock salute. "Brooke and I go way back. What's it been? Almost two weeks?"

Zoe laughed. "Oh, stop."

I took a sip of water, then inched closer to her, dying to ask her a thousand questions about the former classmates she'd known much better than me. "Hey. Do you still hang out with Mikayla and Liz?"

Zoe pulled back, making a face. "Mikayla? No. She hasn't spoken to me in years. Not since prom night. I tried apologizing so many times for that stupid stunt Liz and I pulled, but she wouldn't listen." Her fingers touched her wrinkle-free forehead. "I guess I can't blame her. I mean, what were we thinking? So immature." She paused, opening her mouth, then closing it. "And I don't blame you if you hate me too. I wish we'd done so many things differently."

"I don't blame you for anything that happened. Bailey made a choice that none of us could have foreseen." I looked away, aware that I was sticking to the party line. In truth, I was all but convinced that Bailey's death had been caused by someone else. Someone in this town.

Zoe nodded. "I suppose you're right. We couldn't have known." We stood in silence for a moment. "I still see Liz every couple of months. She does my hair." Zoe shook her head as if starring in a shampoo commercial. Her glossy brunette locks bounced above her shoulders and immediately slid back into place.

"It looks pretty."

"Thanks."

I glanced away, remembering how Zoe and Liz had been bonded at the hip in high school. I wondered if they were closer than she was letting on and if Liz had told her about our uncomfortable encounter in the bike shop. I turned toward a new subject. "I heard you talked to Hannah Mead."

Zoe raised her face toward the ceiling in a painful fashion. "She wouldn't stop calling me until I met with her. I gave her the same information she could have gotten from reading a few newspaper articles from back then. It's not like anyone's story is going to change. I'm not sure what she's trying to prove."

"I'm not sure either. She's persistent."

Zoe forced a smile as she adjusted her collar. "I better place my order because I need to pick up my son from baseball practice."

As we said goodbye. I couldn't help noticing again how refined Zoe was, both in demeanor and appearance. Her presentation reminded me of one of the many pieces of unsolicited advice my dad used to give me: *Be careful of people who pretend to be perfect. They're always hiding something.* I thought back to last week when I'd walked to Willa's shop with Bailey's newly discovered necklace in my pocket. Zoe had appeared out of nowhere. Fear zipped through me at the memory. And now I couldn't help wondering if she'd been following me.

TWENTY-SEVEN

NOW

I said goodbye to Gabe and drove a few blocks to the library to straighten things out with Hannah. When I entered, Lacey had her back to me, hanging a colorful banner that said, "Welcome to Little Library Friends Day Camp" across the wall near the entrance.

"Looks like you're all set for those kids."

She jumped at the sound of my voice, then relaxed when she saw me. "Camp starts in a week, so I thought I'd get a few things set up ahead of time. I hired four high school girls to be counselors, and they're arriving in a few minutes for training. I'm not really sure what I'm going to tell them yet."

"I'm sure you'll figure it out." I pointed to the banner, which tilted downward. "Do you need any help?"

"Oh, no. Thanks, but I'm good." She tucked back her chin-length hair, but it fell forward from behind her ear. "You here to check out a book or to see Hannah?"

"The second one, unfortunately."

Lacey laughed. "She's in her usual room. She never stops working on cracking this supposed case."

"Yeah. I noticed." Lacey straightened the banner as I

headed toward Meeting Room One, spotting Hannah behind the glass wall and giving a light knock. She looked up from her laptop and waved me inside.

"Did you talk to Dan?" she asked.

"Yes. That's why I'm here. It was all a misunderstanding. Someone dropped the necklace in the lost-and-found box at his bike shop. He and Maggie take the box to Willa's thrift store two or three times a year, and he didn't realize the necklace was in there."

She placed her elbow on the table, resting her chin on her knuckles. "Do you think he was telling the truth?"

"Yeah. Of course."

Hannah's face fell. "Shoot." She slid her pink notebook toward her and opened it, jotting something down. "But we don't know for sure if he's telling the truth. The idea of Dan and Bailey secretly seeing each other makes sense, especially if he's had her necklace all these years. We can still raise it as a theory."

My body tensed. "First of all, there is no 'we.' This is your podcast. You basically blackmailed me into helping you. Secondly, you shouldn't be accusing innocent people of things they didn't do."

"Not accusing, Brooke. Just raising questions."

I felt the rage swelling inside me like a summer storm. But I remembered the technique my therapist had given me. Close my eyes and silently count to ten. Breathe in through my nose, out through my mouth. I repeated the familiar exercise.

"You okay?"

"Yes. I'm fine." And perfectly capable of controlling my rage, despite what Hannah thought she'd uncovered about me.

Hannah continued, her voice light. "I haven't heard back from the drama teacher yet, but once I track him down, I'll have enough to record the next episode about Bailey's potential secret lover. Hopefully, I'll get it done by the end of the week."

Hannah tapped her foot, then rocked from side to side, crinkling her nose. "Sorry, but I have to pee so bad. I'll be right back." She rushed away, leaving me sitting there alone.

Hannah hadn't eased my mind about the content of her upcoming episode. I wondered what Mr. Sampson would say about Bailey, and hoped it was enticing enough to take the spotlight off Dan. I remembered how excited Bailey was to go to drama class. Had they met outside of school too? If Bailey had been secretly seeing someone else, Mr. Sampson made a whole lot more sense than Dan. Still, there was no proof of that relationship either.

Hannah returned two minutes later, closing the door behind her. "So much better."

"Just be careful what you say, Hannah. You're pissing off lots of people. People who aren't scared to fight back." The angry faces of Trevor and Jonathan materialized in my mind, plus the blurred faceless figure of whoever had been leaving me notes.

"Don't worry about me, Brooke. I've been through these investigations before. Most people are all bark and no bite. There's no law against raising questions about a suspicious death." She tapped her pink notebook. "Looking ahead, the fourth episode will be about Mikayla, the prom queen who wasn't. It will include the other cheerleaders who betrayed her too, of course, Zoe and Liz. Any thoughts on that?"

"No. I think everyone feels horrible about what happened to Bailey."

"Maybe not everyone, though. Right?" Hannah flashed her straight, white teeth at me. "Not if someone killed her."

My head weighed a thousand pounds, and I rested it in my hands. I hated that she was likely correct, but still no closer to the truth.

She touched her twig-like wrist. "Have you seen my bracelet, by the way? The black one with the beads I always wear. I couldn't find it this morning. It must have slipped off somewhere yesterday."

"Nope," I said without making any effort to recall if I'd seen it. Hannah had exasperated me with yet another conversation that traveled in circles and failed to clarify any actual facts. "I have to go meet with a painter." I stood and left her, scribbling in her notebook.

The fresh air was a welcome relief as I exited the library and crossed the parking lot. But as I approached my car, an object wedged behind the windshield wiper caused my toe to catch on the asphalt. The sunlight bounced off a folded white piece of paper. My pulse pounded in my ears as I surveyed the area for someone who could have left it there. Two women in black jogging suits power walked past me on the nearby sidewalk, gossiping loudly about someone named Carole. A mother exited her car, unbuckling a squealing toddler from a car seat in the back. A half-block down, a man hunched on a bench, sipping from a cardboard cup and looking at his phone.

The note waited for me, feeling more like an undetonated bomb. I forced myself to inch forward and pluck the paper from the wiper, telling myself to breathe, to calm down. Maybe it was only a parking ticket. For the first time in my life, I would have been happy to get one. My fingers trembled as I leaned down, opening the paper and reading the words.

I KNOW WHAT YOU DID!

I reread the words, trying to make sense of them. What had I done? What did someone know? I recalled the previous note, *YOU ARE A LIAR.* Clearly, someone thought I was hiding something.

Just like the night of the concert, I tried to imagine who had the opportunity to place the note on my car during the short time I'd been inside the library. Lacey and Hannah had known

I was here. Hannah had left to use the restroom. But had she really? Or had she slipped out the side door and into the parking lot? Lacey said she was waiting for her counselors to arrive for training. She'd been sitting at a table with them when I left a minute ago, but how many minutes had passed before they'd arrived? I'd told Dan I was coming over here. That was just after confronting him about dropping the necklace at the thrift shop. Then I'd gone to the coffee shop and told Gabe and Zoe I was heading to the library too. For someone who was being stalked, I'd done a terrible job of covering my trail. Then again, maybe it had been none of those people. Jonathan had been so secretive. Mikayla and Trevor so mean. And then there was Willa. I'd never known what to make of her, but I knew she avoided leaving her house if she could, so her name fell to the bottom of my list.

The messages on the notes circled through my head. *Welcome back to Cove Haven, Brooke. You are a liar. I know what you did.* They had to relate to Bailey's death. And as hard as I tried to stop them, the memories from twenty years earlier rumbled through me like a speeding train.

TWENTY-EIGHT

THEN

May 2003

A misty rain dampened my face as I hopped over a puddle, heading in the direction of school. The clothes I'd picked up at The Treasure Cove the night before scratched against my skin. I'd given Lacey a ride to the thrift store so that she could deliver a few groceries to Willa. But I'd returned home with the over-sized flannel shirt, an olive-green army jacket, bell-bottom corduroys, and the high-top shoes I now wore. The items cost next to nothing, and I imagined they'd impress my friends in art class. If Bailey had noticed my new clothes, she didn't say anything. She moped beside me, complaining about how she'd woken up early to study for her first-hour math test.

"It doesn't even matter if I fail. There's no point."

"That's not true."

Bailey huffed. "It's not like the car dealership cares about my math grade."

I stepped carefully, silently acknowledging she was right. But with all of Bailey's missed classes, I worried she was danger-ously close to not graduating from high school at all. "It might matter in a year or two if you decide to go to a junior college or if you want a different job. Something you're more passionate about. You need to graduate, and the higher your grades, the better."

Bailey kept walking with her eyes fixed on the sidewalk, considering my words. But her head hung down and her shoulders slumped, the universal posture of someone who'd given up.

I remembered how the second round of voting slips for prom king and queen had been distributed at lunch yesterday. Bailey's name was one of three girls on the list, the other two being Mikayla and an outgoing editor of the school yearbook named Shelly. "Hey. We voted for you for prom queen," I said, changing subjects in the hope of snapping her out of her funk.

Bailey stopped walking and faced me with a tilt of her head. "Why?"

"It was Dan's idea. He said you deserve it more than Mikayla. Henry and I agreed with him."

She looked at me as if seeing me for the first time, a smile cracking through her frown. "Thanks, Brooke. Mikayla will probably lose her shit if I win. That's really sweet of you, though."

I shrugged. "You're still my friend, right?"

"Yeah. Of course." She lifted the chain beneath her shirt, revealing the tiny puzzle piece.

I touched my neck. "I keep forgetting to wear mine." My voice wavered because I hadn't forgotten. The necklace reminded me of the loss of my closest friend, and I couldn't bring myself to wear it. We traveled another half-block before I spoke again. "Do you have a prom date?"

Bailey made the same face as when she smelled a dead fish on the beach. "Yeah. Unfortunately. Spike ambushed me a few days ago, and I couldn't think of an excuse fast enough."

"I'm sorry. He's such a jerk."

"Yeah. So immature. Not at all who I wanted to go with."

I remembered Bailey sneaking home a few weeks earlier with her hair messed up. "Who did you want to go with?"

"No one. Never mind."

I searched for a clue on her face, but she refused to look at me.

"Who is your date?" she asked before I could prod any further.

I shook my head. "Don't have one. I probably won't go."

Concern pulled down her mouth.

"It's fine," I said, waving her away. "I'm already over it."

A few minutes later, we approached the school's front courtyard. Students gathered in groups, waiting for the first bell to ring and the school doors to open. Zoe spotted us and waved Bailey over to where she stood with Liz, Mikayla, Trevor, and Spike. Not sure where else to go, I followed a step behind.

Mikayla squealed hello to Bailey, then did a double take, cackling as she looked me up and down. "What kind of clothes are those? Have you been shopping in your mom's closet again, Brooke?"

Liz covered her mouth, giggling. "More like her grandma's closet."

I looked down at my vintage shoes and retro pants. "It's called style," I said.

Zoe made a horrified face. "You've got to be kidding me."

"You kind of look like a homeless person." Bailey's eyes seemed to grow smaller as she assessed me, her shallow friends laughing nearby.

"Yeah. A homeless person from the seventies," Mikayla said.

I froze in place, feeling a stab of hatred toward them.

Maybe noticing my face, Bailey added, "Sorry, Brooke. But it's true."

My fingers tightened around the straps of my backpack, my teeth clenching so hard I thought my jaw might crack. I'd spent the walk to school giving Bailey a reassuring speech about her future, and she repaid me by mocking me in front of her new friends. I hardly recognized her anymore. I didn't even want to be around her.

The shrill ring of the school bell ripped through the air, and I was never happier to hear it. I turned from my traitor friend and double-timed it toward art class, toward people who could think for themselves. In the main hallway, Dan, Henry, and Lacey walked several feet ahead, and I raced up to them, forcing back the tears as I motioned them toward a nook by the drinking fountain.

"You okay?" Dan asked.

"Yeah," I said, although my insides felt hollow and shattered. I checked over my shoulder and recounted Bailey's latest "bitch move."

Henry tipped his head back. "Man. Just when I thought she couldn't go any lower."

Lacey's eyes ached with sympathy as she hugged a textbook to her chest. "I think your clothes look nice, Brooke." Lacey wore a version of the same loose jeans and gray sweatshirt she wore several times a week. I was doubtful she knew much about fashion, but I appreciated her support.

Dan nodded. "You look like a million bucks. No joke."

Henry scratched his head, appraising me. "I don't know about a million, but at least ten or fifteen."

I couldn't help laughing.

From behind Henry's head, a bright poster popped against the bland cinderblock wall. It featured images of a tropical rainforest with colorful flowers and a turquoise lagoon and the words, *Senior Prom 2003. Tickets on Sale Now!*

Dan followed my gaze, then looked at Lacey, Henry, and me. "Wanna go? All of us as a group? Brooke and I can be a couple, and you and Lacey."

Prom was only ten days away, and while I assumed I wasn't going, I hadn't considered this option.

Henry's face brightened. "It could be fun."

Lacey looked like she was going to be sick. "I don't want to go."

"Oh, come on, Lacey." Henry gave her a friendly nudge. "You don't have to dance with me or anything. We can just stand in the corner and laugh at everyone. It's the stuff high school memories are made of."

I straightened up, determined to salvage some good memories from my dwindling days at Cove Haven High School. "Henry's right. I think we should do it. They say life begins at the edge of your comfort zone."

Lacey closed her eyes and pressed her lips together. Suddenly, her eyelids popped open and she smiled. "Okay. I'll do it."

I looked from face to face at the small circle of friends who remained steadfast and loyal. And I was grateful I had them near me.

The next day, between third and fourth periods, I crouched in the bathroom stall trying to pee, which always took me longer in public spaces. I envisioned a flowing waterfall, but the mind trick didn't work, and nothing came out. My thoughts drifted to what kind of dress I'd wear to prom. I'd seen some unique options at the thrift shop, but Mom suggested taking me to a department store in St. Joseph on Saturday to look around. The door banged from somewhere beyond my stall, knocking me from my thoughts.

"Okay. Okay. Here's the plan." I recognized the peppy way Zoe spoke. "Don't tell anyone."

"Shouldn't we go someplace more private?" Liz's throaty voice responded.

"We're the only ones in here."

Someone's shoes shuffled closer. I held my breath and lifted my feet off the stained square tiles, hoping that neither of them would spot me. It seemed they didn't because Zoe continued talking, lowering her voice.

"Mikayla has way more votes than anyone else. But you and me are the only ones who know that. We'll invert the numbers on the final count form. On prom night, when we hand the name of the winner to the DJ, we'll write Bailey's name instead."

Liz chuckled. "Mikayla is going to be so pissed."

"That's what she gets for stealing my man." There was an echo of bitterness in Zoe's voice.

I stopped breathing as I remembered how Zoe and Trevor had dated the previous school year.

"What about Bailey?" Liz asked.

"What about her? She won't care. We'll let her enjoy the moment and then tell her later, at the bonfire."

"Yeah. Okay."

The bell rang, and the two of them rushed away. I lowered my feet, feeling sick. These girls were not Bailey's friends. My gut told me to find Bailey and warn her about the scheme Liz and Zoe had in store for prom night so she wouldn't be blindsided. But my self-righteousness outweighed the urge to do the right thing. For the last nine months, I'd acted as the bigger person, and Bailey had been horrible to me. Sooner or later, she needed to learn how karma worked. I pulled up my pants, forgetting all about my full bladder. I slipped from the bathroom and headed toward Spanish class, deciding to keep my mouth shut. Bailey deserved whatever was coming to her.

TWENTY-NINE

NOW

Three days had passed since I'd found the last anonymous note from my stalker. The message, *I KNOW WHAT YOU DID*, had scared me into silence, and I hadn't told anyone about it, not even Dan and Maggie. I wasn't sure who to trust. I'd holed myself up in the guest bedroom, only leaving occasionally to walk to the beach, check for activity at Mom's house, or grab a coffee from Drips. Now, I perched on the edge of the guest bedroom bed, having just ended my call with Ruthie. She'd told me all about her day at camp, how she'd gone out in a canoe with her group, played in a soccer game, got her face painted, and shot some arrows at hay targets. It sounded so much more enjoyable than my day, which had been spent dwelling on the threatening notes I'd received from someone in town. I stared at my favorite photo of Ruthie on my phone, in which she held a giant ice cream cone filled with blue moon ice cream, the unnaturally colored dessert dripping down her beaming face. I'd taken it two summers earlier, a few months before Shane had asked for a divorce. The fissure in my chest opened wider, aching whenever I remembered our perfect little family. Apparently, it hadn't been perfect enough for Shane. But at least I'd always have Ruthie. There were still over five weeks before I'd be with her again, and I wasn't sure I could make it.

The aroma of freshly baked pizza and the melody of chatter downstairs drew me from my room. I ventured down the steps and into the brightly lit kitchen.

"Pizza's ready," Maggie yelled.

Marci and Olivia cheered, their cheeks pink from the sun, and I imagined they'd had a fun afternoon at the park.

"There she is." Dan nodded at me. "Are you hungry?"

"Yes. Thanks so much." I looked at the pizza, breadsticks, and salad that had appeared without any effort on my part, along with the meals from the last few days, and suddenly felt like a freeloader. "I'll order carry-out for everyone tomorrow night."

Maggie waved me off as everyone took their seats at the table. "No need. You're our guest, and we're happy to feed you." She served up a slice each for the girls, adding a few leaves of green salad.

We loaded up our plates, and I stabbed at my salad as the girls told us about their adventures at the park. I couldn't imagine being back in Cove Haven without Dan and Maggie's warm hospitality, especially with all the strange happenings since I'd returned. Guilt tinged my conscience at how quickly I'd suspected Dan of lying about the necklace.

The girls said they were full. Their mom excused them, and they bounded off into the other room.

Maggie leaned forward, her face turning serious. "It seems like you're a little down in the dumps, Brooke. Is it because of the necklace?" She pinched her lips together. "I can't stop thinking about Willa and the lost-and-found box. I still can't believe someone left Bailey's necklace at our store."

I set down my glass of water as the most recent note left on my car edged its way into my mind again. I blinked it away and forced myself back to the present. "I know. Sorry if I've been distracted. I keep wondering who it was." We had discussed the lost-and-found box theory several times over the last three days, but the topic hadn't grown old.

She looked pained. "It's so creepy."

"It really is." I picked up a piece of crust, but then set it down, debating once again whether to share the latest threatening note with them. I knew they would force me to take it to the police, and I wasn't ready to do that. I took a few bites of salad, feeling the weight of eyes, and realizing Dan was staring at me, tracking my every move. I glanced toward him and smiled, noticing he hadn't touched his food. I bit into the cheesy pizza and crispy crust, again feeling myself pinned down by his stare. "Is everything okay, Dan?"

He tapped his knuckles on the table, his demeanor grave. "I was just thinking about something."

"What?"

"The day I took the box over to Willa's. It was the day after you arrived back in town. I'm sure of it."

"Okay."

"You came by the shop your first day back. Remember?"

I shook my head, not sure where he was going. "Yeah. I stopped by to say hello."

"I was busy helping customers outside with their bikes while you tinkered around inside." He angled his face toward the ceiling, then exhaled, focusing on me. "It's just us, Brooke. I mean, you can tell me. Was it you? Did you put Bailey's necklace in the lost-and-found?"

Maggie gasped, her hand covering her mouth. "Dan!"

Dan's accusation derailed me, and I had the sensation of falling out of my chair. My palms found the table, steadying myself. I should never have come back. The whispers about me were happening again, even without me revealing the latest message. *I KNOW WHAT YOU DID.* Now Dan suspected me too.

I found my voice, matching Dan's stare. "No. It wasn't me. I haven't seen that necklace in twenty years. Not since prom night. I can't believe you would think that." The pizza on my plate suddenly appeared greasy and unappetizing, the salad soggy. Heat rose from my chest into my neck and face. Every cell in my body yearned to fling my plate in Dan's direction. How dare he? Instead, I breathed in for five seconds and out for five, then scooted my chair back. Facing Maggie, I said, "Thank you for dinner." I picked up my plate and carried it to the counter next to the sink.

"Brooke, wait..." Dan said, but it was too late. I knew what he thought of me, that he didn't trust me and probably didn't want me around his kids. I would make it easy for him.

"I'm going to pack up my things and get out of your hair."

Maggie pushed her plate away. "Brooke, you really don't have to do that. Please, stay and finish your dinner with us."

"Thanks so much, Maggie. But I've been here a week already, and I can see I've overstayed my welcome." I forced my feet toward the stairs. I'd pack up my things and drive somewhere. Maybe back to my childhood bedroom, despite the construction mess downstairs and what I imagined was the pungent aroma of paint and varnish hanging in the air.

"Just wait!" Dan strode across the room, blocking my path up the stairs. "I don't want you to leave. Can't we talk about this like adults without you overreacting?"

I looked at my hands, reluctantly acknowledging a defect in my personality. How many times had Shane said the same thing to me? My tendency was to hold things in for too long, then flip out. On the other hand, Dan had basically accused me of planting my dead friend's necklace in his store. I wasn't sure my reaction was unwarranted.

"Dan didn't mean to sound so confrontational, Brooke." Maggie looked toward her husband. "Did you, Dan?"

"No. I didn't. I'm sorry." He grimaced, running his fingers

through his hair. "It's just such a weird coincidence. I thought all of this was behind us."

I could see that Dan was upset with the situation and was trying to figure it out. The muscles in my shoulders loosened, and I steadied myself against the wall, realizing I needed to gather myself and talk this through with him. "Yeah. It is weird. But I swear it wasn't me. Even if I had Bailey's necklace—which I didn't—why would I do that?"

Dan set his jaw, a faraway look in his eyes. "I don't know. Nothing makes sense."

I wanted to ask Dan about Hannah's theory about him and Bailey being more than friends our senior year, if only for the purpose of poking a giant hole in it. But Maggie's large brown eyes stared at him, and I worried he wouldn't be forthcoming with his wife present.

"So, as we've all acknowledged, I'm an idiot," Dan said, looking sheepish. "Will you stay?"

"Yeah." I motioned toward my half-eaten plate of food. "Sorry about that. I'll stay tonight if that's okay."

"Of course."

"I'll do the dishes when you're finished eating, and you guys can relax."

Dan and Maggie thanked me and returned to their food. I found the girls in the living room, where I joined their activity of dressing a basket full of dolls for their first day of school. Although the twins seemed happy with an extra playmate, and Dan and Maggie had been polite hosts, I sensed that I'd worn out my welcome. I would look for new accommodations tomorrow.

———

A few hours later, I lay in bed. Above me, the blades of the ceiling fan spun through the shadows. It was 3 a.m., the witching hour, as Bailey used to tell me during our sleepovers. I'd awoken with a start. I closed my eyes and willed myself to fall asleep, but something creaked from beyond my door. A floorboard? I raised my head off the pillow, listening. Only the light whir of the fan met my ears for a few seconds. My head lowered onto the pillow just as another creak sounded, this one closer, causing my head to pop back up.

Was one of the girls out there? Or an intruder? I kicked off the covers and crept toward the door. Pulling in a breath, I turned the knob and flung open the door. Dan stood outside, jumping at the sight of me. A nightlight from further down the hall cast strange shadows across his face.

"Brooke. Why are you awake?" His voice was barely above a whisper.

"I heard a weird noise."

Dan motioned toward the stairway. "I was thirsty. I was just getting some water." He paused, studying me. "Do you need anything?"

"No."

"Okay. Good night." He looked annoyed as he headed across the hall to the main bedroom.

I ducked back inside the guest room, closing the door gently behind me. Pressing my back against the wood panels, I exhaled, replaying the last two minutes in my mind—the two creaks and Dan standing in my doorway. The strange look on his face. Maybe I was paranoid, but I couldn't help wondering why he wasn't holding a glass of water.

THIRTY

NOW

I heaved my last suitcase into the trunk as Maggie watched from the sidewalk. I'd missed Dan, who'd left a half hour earlier to open the bike shop. The twins darted back and forth nearby.

"Thank you so much for letting me stay for so long. I really appreciate it."

"Of course. You're welcome anytime." Maggie crossed her arms in front of herself, and I wondered if Dan had mentioned our middle-of-the-night run-in to her. "Are you sure you're comfortable moving back in by yourself? And with all those renovations going on?" she asked.

"Yeah. All set. I think there'll be enough people around that I won't feel like I'm all alone." I waved to the girls. "Bye, Marci! Bye, Olivia!" The girls hopped up and down, yelling goodbye as I ducked into the car. I hoped Maggie hadn't heard the doubt in my voice. I didn't exactly feel comfortable moving back into Mom's house by myself and wasn't sure if the floors had been completed yet, but I was going to check it out. The thought of staying under the same roof as Dan for another night didn't sit right. I wasn't sure if my unease stemmed from him suspecting me of lying or because I suspected him. Probably a combination of the two.

I crisscrossed town, driving toward my childhood home and arriving five minutes later. Two white pickup trucks with the name First Class Floors printed on the sides were parked out front, the same trucks I'd seen parked there a couple of days ago. Eric's blue truck was parked a little further down. I exited my car and found the contractor on a call around the side of the house.

He nodded toward me, holding up a finger as he finished explaining the pitfalls of copper pipes to someone on the other end. "Hi, Brooke," he said when he ended the call. "We're making good progress. The floors are getting the first layer of finish today."

"Oh. I was hoping that already happened."

"Nope. The prep work and sanding are done, but our head flooring guy had a sick kid. He had to stay home yesterday. Just one of those things." Eric shrugged, seemingly unbothered by the delay. "So we're applying the first coat of polyurethane today."

"How many coats are there?"

"Two or three, depending on how it takes. It will need to dry for a day between each coat. Then we like to wait another four days after the final coat to make sure the floor's cured. So, no sneaking inside after hours. It will ruin the whole thing."

"Oh. I was hoping to move back in as soon as possible."

"Sorry. It's going to be a few days, especially with today being Friday. They'll be back on Monday for the second coat."

I hung my head in disappointment, but there was nothing I could do about the renovations. I wouldn't be staying at my old house tonight. Or for the next week, for that matter.

I thanked Eric for the update and found my way back to my car, where I began looking up nearby rentals. There were a few houses and condos available for rent on Airbnb, but they were out of my budget. I called a well-known hotel called The Inn at Cove Haven, which was basically a glorified Holiday Inn near the beach. They were booked until a week from Tuesday because of the Summer Harvest Festival this weekend. I called three more hotels, hearing the same story from each of them.

Hannah's name buzzed across my phone, sending a spear of panic through me. I'd done my best to avoid her since Monday, when I'd found the note in the library parking lot. I could only imagine what Hannah would think of the message, how she'd twist the words to make it seem like I'd done something to Bailey. On top of that, I couldn't be sure she hadn't written it.

I held a gulp of air in my lungs, reminding myself not to trust anyone, including her. "Hi, Hannah."

"Brooke! I'm so glad you picked up." She sighed. "Guess who I just got off the phone with? The drama teacher, Ron Sampson." She answered her own question before I could respond. "He remembered Bailey very well, down to the part she played in the class performance of *Flowers for Algernon.*"

Flowers for Algernon. A hazy memory of Bailey practicing her lines during one of our rare walks to school together sharpened in my mind. "Did you get any information from him?"

"It wasn't him. He wasn't Bailey's secret lover."

"How can you be so sure?"

"He was in New York City the weekend of your senior prom. With his girlfriend, who is now his wife. He sent me several hotel and restaurant receipts he saved as proof of his whereabouts the night Bailey died, along with a time-stamped photo of him and his girlfriend from the Statue of Liberty. He's telling the truth."

"Oh." I slouched forward as the promise of an easy answer evaporated.

"So if Trevor was right and Bailey had another love interest, someone she didn't want anyone to know about, it wasn't Ron

Sampson. At least, Bailey didn't stick around to meet him after the bonfire got rained out."

"That was kind of a long shot anyway."

"I've got a few other theories, though. Maybe Spike went back to find Bailey after the bonfire. Things got heated. He ripped the necklace from her neck and pushed her off the bridge. Twenty years later, he has returned to town undercover to destroy any memory of that night."

"No. I don't think so. He's not even involved with the decision whether to tear down the bridge, remember? It's the county's decision. And if he was trying to destroy any memory of that night, why would he put Bailey's necklace into circulation?"

"Maybe someone else released the necklace to scare him. Kind of like saying, I know what you did."

I squeezed my eyes shut, not missing Hannah's choice of words. *I know what you did.* Was she toying with me? I wondered again if she was the one leaving the notes.

"Anything's possible right?" Her voice was buoyant as she continued spinning more unlikely theories. I realized her statement must have been a coincidence, and my paranoia had reached a new level.

Hannah stopped talking and took a breath. "Who did Bailey hang around to meet then? Who took her necklace that night? Was it Dan?"

Dan's face flashed through my mind. I felt illogically protective of him, like a sister who tormented her brother but couldn't handle it when anyone else did. He'd acted strangely yesterday, but that didn't necessarily mean anything in relation to Bailey's death. If I knew one thing about Hannah, it was that she wasn't afraid to jump to conclusions. Still, now that the drama teacher was out of the picture, I couldn't help thinking about the night of Lacey's poetry reading, when I'd seen Bailey sneaking home, how she hadn't wanted to tell me who she was with.

PROM QUEEN   185

Something Maggie said during our dinner at The Fish snagged in my memory. She'd wanted to know about Dan's high school girlfriend, the one with whom he'd claimed to have lost his virginity. Dan had refused to tell his wife the girl's name. What if Dan hadn't lied to Maggie about his high school escapades? What if his first lover had been Bailey? Maybe that was why he pushed so hard for her to win prom queen.

A car rushed past me, and I snapped back to the present, to the phone call with Hannah. My imagination was in overdrive, making up sordid facts where I had absolutely zero proof of any wrongdoing. "I have no idea who it was," I said. "Or if anyone else even showed up to the train station to meet Bailey."

"I'm going to raise some possibilities in my next episode. Don't bother lecturing me again. This is the way investigative podcasts work. I just have to record one more segment with the new information about the drama teacher, and it'll finally be ready to drop."

"Please make it clear that the necklace at Willa's store came from the bike shop's lost-and-found box, and not directly from Dan."

"Of course."

I tightened my jaw, resigned to letting Hannah's podcast play out how she wanted. I'd done as much damage control as possible, considering the circumstances. "Do you know if there are any rooms available at your motel?" I asked, changing the subject. "I was planning on moving back into my mom's house today, but it's nowhere near ready. I need a place to stay for a few nights."

"I thought you were staying with Dan."

"I was, but I've been there a long time already. They need their house back."

"You should ask Lacey."

"Her sister is in town for the Harvest Festival. I don't want to intrude."

"Oh, yeah. She mentioned that." Hannah paused. "The motel isn't the greatest, but it's cheap. You should call. And speaking of the Harvest Festival, let's meet up tomorrow and watch the parade together."

"Why?"

"Everyone will be there. I want to observe the town's people in their natural element, especially when this year's prom queen goes cruising past. Body language gives a lot away."

I loosened my grip on the phone, realizing I wouldn't mind catching the parade for old times' sake. "Fine. I don't have anyone else to watch it with anyway."

"Good." She sounded happy, ignoring my unenthusiastic response.

"Meet me in front of Joe's Diner tomorrow at 1:45 p.m."

"Will do." I hung up with her and called the Sandcastle Motel. They were booked tonight but had a last-minute cancelation on a room starting tomorrow and offered a weekly rate that wasn't terrible. I could pay off my credit card once I got the proceeds from selling Mom's house.

The café seemed as good a place as any for a temporarily homeless person to hang out. Leaving my car, I followed the familiar sidewalk for several blocks, at last turning along the street that ran parallel to Main Street. Chief Warner and Lacey stood under the shade of a maple tree, deep in conversation.

Lacey held up a cardboard cup from Drips when she saw me. "Good morning, Brooke."

I approached them. "I see we're all taking a coffee break."

She motioned toward the police chief. "I was just telling Justin about the float The Friends of the Library sponsored in the parade tomorrow."

"I haven't been to a Harvest Festival parade since I was a kid," I said.

"You're in for a treat." Chief Warner smiled. "Sounds like a good lineup this year."

Lacey fixed her gaze on me. "You're going, right?"

"Yeah," I said, thinking of Hannah. "Is your sister here yet?"

"Maeve arrives this afternoon. Leaving on Monday. I wish she could stay longer, but she has to get back to Houston for work. She's a paralegal at a big law firm."

"Good for Maeve." I envisioned the chubby-cheeked little girl with pigtails and fistfuls of animal crackers and could hardly reconcile my memory of her with a professional, adult woman. "I'm sure you two will have tons of fun."

Lacey nodded as she looked down the street. "I should head back to the library. I left one of the new teenage volunteers in charge of the front desk."

"Uh-oh. Sounds like trouble."

Lacey giggled. "See you both later."

I nodded goodbye to the police chief and turned toward Drips, but he stepped toward me. "Brooke, wait. Do you have a second to talk about those notes?"

"Sure." I glanced toward the barber shop on the corner. A part of me wanted to turn the latest note over to him, but a bigger part of me didn't want law enforcement to think I was hiding some dark secret as the message implied.

His face was stern. "I was going to call you this morning, but now that we're both here..."

"What is it?"

"We dusted for prints, but there were none on them other than yours."

The air sucked out of me. "I didn't write them."

"No. Of course not. My point is that whoever left these notes for you was likely wearing gloves."

My fleeting relief that the chief of police hadn't been accusing me of writing suspicious notes to myself was quickly replaced with something else. Fear. The person who wrote those notes knew what they were doing, had put thought and planning into how to scare me while avoiding detection. Now there was definitely no point in turning over the most recent note, which was also likely to be free of prints. Despite the sunny morning, the colorful flags flapping along Main Street, and the children laughing as they rushed down the slide at the park behind me, I couldn't help feeling my day had just taken an even darker turn.

THIRTY-ONE

NOW

I pushed through the doors of Drips, the aroma of ground espresso beans jolting me to attention. Gabe hunched in a corner, looking over some papers. He pushed them aside as I neared. "Hi, Brooke. Are we still on for an evening of mini golf?"

"Yeah. I'm looking forward to it." I forced a smile even as I struggled to rid the tension from my body. My recent conversation with the police chief had left me feeling uneasy.

Gabe tilted his head toward the counter. "Blake's over there if you want a drink."

"Okay. Thanks." I glanced toward the part-time barista who dumped ice into cup, then turned back to Gabe, shifting my weight.

"Everything okay?" he asked.

"Yeah. I, um," I stuttered, unsure how to ask Gabe if I could sleep over at his place without giving him the wrong impression. "I was planning on moving back into my old house today, but the floors are getting redone. I've overstayed my welcome at Dan's house, Lacey's sister is visiting for the weekend, and the only motel in town with a room available can't take me until tomorrow."

He cocked his head, smiling. "I have a pullout couch that's pretty comfy. You're welcome to crash there tonight."

"Really?"

"For real." He winked. "It's a little forward for a first date, but I'm willing to roll with it."

I lowered my gaze, chuckling. "Gee. Thanks."

"I leave here at five." He pointed to the papers. "And I've got to finish reviewing this budget." He dug something out of his pocket and handed it to me. "But here's a key to my apartment if you need somewhere to hang out today. 788 Second Street, unit two. It's nothing fancy, but it's relatively clean."

I took the key, familiar with the street. "Thanks so much. I'm heading to the beach for a few hours, so I probably won't go over until later."

"Suit yourself. And I have a cat in there. His name is Bob. He's a good guy, but he'll try to dart past you when you open the door."

I smiled at the cat's name and the way Gabe described him. "I'm good with cats."

"Cool. Make yourself at home and call me if you have any questions."

I left Gabe to pore over his financials and ordered a coffee at the counter, migrating to a table near the window and watching the passersby. Two girls about Ruthie's age skipped past, with a couple of women who looked like their mothers following at a distance. A man driving a Village of Cove Haven truck dropped stacks of orange pylons every few feet. The parade setup was already underway. I wished Ruthie could be here for the festivities. I'd have to remember to take a few videos for her.

A few minutes later, I found myself back at the beach, where I hoped to spend the afternoon reading a thriller. The steady lull of the waves and the laughter of nearby children soothed my nerves. I spread out my towel, claiming a spot where the sand met the grass under the partial shade of a tree. Leaning back, I closed my eyes, enjoying the warm wind brushing my skin. The utter relaxation of a day at the lake was what I missed the most about Cove Haven. A moment before drifting off to sleep, a notification beeped on my phone. I sat up, reading it. *All the Dark Corners Podcast – New content is here. Episode 3: Who was the Prom Queen's Secret Lover? Listen now!* A link followed the text.

A sickening dread tunneled through me as I wondered what Hannah had recorded. How many innocent people had she accused? I dug my heels into the sand, found my earbuds, and, although every cell in my body told me not to, I listened to the newest episode.

Hi, everyone, and welcome back to All the Dark Corners. *I'm your host, Hannah Mead, and I'm super excited to dig deeper into the mysterious death of the prom queen of Cove Haven. As you know if you listened to the first two episodes, I'm here in the quaint seaside town of Cove Haven, Michigan, where Bailey Maddox, the prom queen, supposedly jumped in front of a train on prom night twenty years ago. I've spent hours at the library digging through old newspaper articles, yearbooks, and a skimpy police file that the local police chief turned over to me after I threatened to obtain it without him via the Freedom of Information Act. I've been conducting in-person interviews with people who were with Bailey the night she died. And here's one thing that caught my attention. Every teenager at the bonfire that night remembered hearing noises in the woods—rustling leaves and twigs cracking—almost as if someone was hiding. Was someone else out there waiting for Bailey? Waiting for the others to leave? Was this the same person who took her necklace? Or caused her death? And if so, who was it?*

My colleague and I had a recent conversation with the 2003 prom king, who still lives in Cove Haven. His name is Trevor, and he stated that he thought that Bailey was romantically involved with someone other than her date Spike, on the night of prom. You see, the prom king propositioned Bailey as they danced in front of the senior class, donning their sparkling crowns. He asked her to meet him at his truck a little while later, but Bailey wasn't interested. Normally, a girl turning her nose up at a boy wouldn't raise any suspicion, but this boy, Trevor, was basically the god of Cove Haven High back then. He claims that no other girl had ever turned him down. (Can everyone hear me gagging right now? I mean, please.) Anyway, Trevor got the feeling Bailey was interested in someone else, and it wasn't her date.

I held a gulp of air in my lungs, hoping Trevor wasn't listening and that Hannah's insights didn't go much further.

Bailey's former best friend, Brooke, stated that she saw Bailey sneaking home late one night a few weeks before prom, her hair messed up, her clothes in disarray, and her makeup smudged. When Brooke asked where she'd been, Bailey told her, "with a friend," but wouldn't say who. These two accounts, coupled with the rustling in the woods and Bailey's missing necklace, might lead a reasonable person to believe that the person waiting for Bailey in the woods was her secret lover, or someone who wished he was her secret lover. But who was it? I've narrowed the list down to a few likely suspects.

My muscles slackened as Hannah talked about Bailey's drama teacher first, but then discounted him based on his receipts from New York City.

Let's turn to the next suspect, Bailey's prom date, Spike.

For a couple of minutes, Hannah spoke of Bailey's reluctance to go to prom with Spike, the cold shoulder she gave him at the dance, and Spike's abrupt exit from the party after Trevor kissed Bailey on the dance floor.

Spike, angry and resentful at having been rejected by his prom date, could have returned to the bonfire after the dance, hid in the woods, and confronted Bailey on the bridge after the others left. Spike and his family moved to the Milwaukee area just days after his high school graduation. Days. Not weeks or months. What was their hurry to leave town? And there's more. I recently discovered that Spike has returned to Cove Haven under a different name. He goes by his legal name, Jonathan, now, and he is one of the partners in a real estate development company from Chicago. And you will not believe which piece of property they're developing into a luxury hotel. That's right. It's the old train station, the same spot where the post-prom bonfire was held twenty years ago.

My stomach sank as Hannah expanded on the idea that Jonathan's purchase of the train station was somehow evidence of his guilt. Once she'd exhausted the topic, she gravitated toward Trevor, conjecturing that Trevor was so angry, either about being rejected by Bailey or about his girlfriend, Mikayla, getting cheated out of her title, that he could have returned to confront Bailey, with or without Mikayla. One or both of them could have lured Bailey to the bridge after everyone left, pushing her to her death.

Hannah's voice continued singing in its carefree melody as she moved to yet another potential suspect.

And now for the most interesting theory, a classmate named Dan. He was part of the group of Bailey's former friends—Brooke, Lacey, and Henry. He would never have caught my

radar, except, a few days ago, the owner of the local thrift store,
an eccentric elderly woman known by locals as Willa the
witch, remembered who brought Bailey's missing necklace
into the shop. It was none other than Dan. When questioned,
he didn't deny dropping it there recently. He claims the neck-
lace was mixed in with lost-and-found items at his local bike
shop, and he didn't see it. But come on. Really? Who doesn't
look through a lost-and-found box before donating its contents?
What if there was a Rolex in there or diamond earrings? It got
me thinking, why did Dan have Bailey's necklace? What if he
was her secret lover?

I hit pause, unable to listen further. While I'd recently had
some of the same questions fleet through my mind, I'd never
sought to announce my unfounded suspicions to the world. I'd
only told Hannah about Dan and the necklace to prevent her
from broadcasting misinformation about my anger issues.
Clearly, I'd made a horrible mistake. Hannah was like an oil
freighter plowing through pristine waters and leaving a path of
destruction in her wake. Dan would be livid with me for sharing
the information with Hannah. Not to mention Jonathan and
Trevor. I could only hope they didn't listen to the podcast.

I hugged my bare knees to my chest and looked around at
the other people on the beach. A group of five teenagers sat on
towels nearby, listening to music. I remembered doing the same
with Bailey, Lacey, Dan, and Henry. I hadn't heard from Henry
in years, although Dan had shared Henry's contact information
with me a few days earlier. Henry lived in Toronto and worked
as a DJ for a radio station, which, given his knack for humor and
smooth talking, didn't surprise me at all.

I stared out at the water, noticing the wind had picked up,
the waves foaming with whitecaps. Something Hannah said in
the podcast touched a nerve. It was Dan's story about how he
came to have the necklace in his possession. I wanted to believe

him, but I wasn't sure if I did. I thought of my old friend, Henry. He'd been out of town on prom night. A blessing in disguise for him. But he had been tight with Dan, maybe even closer than I'd been. What if Henry remembered something about Dan and Bailey being more than friends? Or if he'd picked up on something I'd missed? And for the first time, I couldn't help wondering if Henry knew more about that night than he'd ever told anyone.

THIRTY-TWO

THEN

May 2003

Prom was three days away. I stood in front of the full-length mirror in Lacey's bedroom. A set of bunk beds filled the wall behind us, a bookshelf packed with raggedy paperbacks lined another wall, and a heap of stuffed animals towered in the corner. Lacey shared the cramped room with her sister, Maeve. I pressed the black, satin fabric against my hips and did a little twirl, admiring the line of my collarbone above the strapless dress.

"What do you think?"

Lacey gave a thumbs-up. "It's really pretty. Your mom was right."

"I love it." Maeve hopped in the doorway, licking a blue lollipop. "You look like a princess."

"Oh, great." I made a face because I'd never been the type of girl who dreamed of being a princess, but I had to admit that I felt good wearing it. Mom had talked me into the dress last weekend, saying that I only had one prom and that I should look the part. She didn't know I planned to wear my Doc Martens instead of the heels she'd loaned me. I pointed at Lacey. "Now, your turn."

"Okay. Mine isn't as prom-like as yours. It's my mom's dress." She bent over in the corner and slipped out of her shirt and pants, pulling a navy-blue flower-patterned dress over her shoulders. "Can you zip me?"

I raised the zipper in the back. Lacey faced me, wearing a slim-fitting sleeveless dress with a smattering of colorful flowers that hit her at the knees. It showed off her shapely chest, which she usually kept hidden under oversized sweatshirts. "It looks good on you."

"Willa lent me these shoes." Lacey slipped on a pair of heels that coordinated with the dark background of the dress.

"That's cool that you and Willa are getting along now."

Lacey studied herself in the mirror, touching the ends of her light brown hair. "She's actually really nice. Jasper made her sound so much worse. I feel so bad about what I did to her house."

"At least she's forgiven you."

Lacey stepped back from the mirror, refocusing on me. "Yeah. I'm so thankful for that."

Maeve scooted in front of Lacey, checking out her blue tongue in the mirror. "Can I try on a dress too? Then we can have a fashion show!"

"Maeve! Leave us alone."

It was clear by the cramped living quarters and Lacey's compulsion to lose herself in books that life wasn't easy in the Dunn household. Lacey and Maeve's mom cleaned motel rooms until her hands were raw, sometimes taking on extra night shifts at nearby businesses. A sparkle of hope danced in Maeve's eyes. I didn't want to be the one to extinguish it.

I lowered my head to her. "I'd love to see your dress too."

Maeve grinned and hopped toward the closet. Lacey tugged

at her dress, annoyed. But I gave her a friendly nudge, and she loosened up, going along with her little sister's antics.

The next day, I approached the lunch table where Dan sat by himself, not eating.

"Hey." I claimed my usual seat. Lacey followed a few steps behind, plopping her lunch on the table. I looked around. "Where's Henry?"

Dan rubbed his forehead. "So, bad news. Henry's grandfather passed away last night. He and his parents are flying to Florida tomorrow for the funeral."

"Oh." Lacey blinked, pulling her unopened lunch bag closer to her. "That's too bad."

"He can't go to prom anymore," Dan said.

Lacey nodded, eyes glistening. "That's okay. I don't have to go."

"What?" I straightened up, eyeing Mikayla in the distance, who performed a cheesy dance in front of her table as the others cheered. My blood simmered at the unfairness of it. Lacey had looked so proud and pretty in her dress last night, like a slightly fancier and more sophisticated version of herself. "We need you there, Lacey. Don't abandon us."

Dan held up his hands. "Yeah. Back up a second. We can all still go as a group. The three of us. I mean, who cares if we're not two couples?"

Lacey lifted her chin. "Are you sure?"

I locked eyes with Dan and nodded. "Yeah. It's our last hurrah as high schoolers. It's not like we're a real couple anyway."

Dan gave me a mock salute. "Duly noted."

"Okay. Thanks, guys." Lacey relaxed back into her chair, opening her lunch. "It will be fun to go as a group."

I opened my lunch bag, relieved the crisis had been averted. The conversation I'd overhead in the bathroom between Liz and Zoe churned through my mind, but I tamped down the secret. As much as I wanted to share news of the upcoming scandal, I couldn't risk word of the prank getting back to Bailey. I wanted Bailey to feel the same kind of pain she'd caused me, something she was sure to experience when she realized her so-called friends had duped her.

Three hours later, my feet plodded along the sidewalk toward home. The mid-May sun was hot on my skin, sweat gathering in my armpits as my backpack slid down my shoulder.

"Brooke. Wait."

Bailey jogged toward me. I ignored her and kept walking.

"Slow down." She sounded annoyed. "What's up, anyway?"

"Are you going to make fun of my clothes again? Or do you only do that when the other cheerleaders are around?"

Bailey pinched her lips together. "Really? You're still mad about that?"

I continued on my path, refusing to make eye contact.

"Look. I'm sorry. It was only a joke."

I shrugged. "Okay."

She batted my arm. "Do you want to come over and see my prom dress?"

"Not really."

"Brooke, come on."

"I'll see it on Saturday night."

"You're going?" she asked, not bothering to hide her surprise.

"Yeah. With Dan. And Lacey. Henry was supposed to go too, but his grandpa died yesterday."

"Oh." Bailey's face contorted as if she was trying to work

something out. One silver teardrop earring hung next to her face, but the one on the other side was missing.

"You're missing an earring."

Bailey touched her earlobe. "Yeah. Ms. Greely made me take them off during PE. I set them on the bleachers, and when I came back, one was gone. It must have slipped through the crack. I'm so pissed."

"Check with her tomorrow," I said, trying not to care.

The conversation I'd overheard in the bathroom pulsed through me again. Zoe and Liz had rigged the vote. In two days, Bailey would be named the prom queen of Cove Haven High School. Mikayla would be furious. Bailey would be ecstatic at first, then humiliated when she learned the truth. I could warn her now. That's what a good friend would do.

A motor zoomed behind us, two quick honks of a horn. A jeep splattered with mud pulled next to us, Trevor driving. Mikayla leaned out the open window. "Bailey! Hop in. We're going to Scoops."

Bailey turned toward me, pausing, and for a second, I thought she was going to invite me along. I considered telling them what Zoe and Liz had planned, so they could get the situation corrected before Saturday. But Bailey only lowered her thick eyelashes at me, then she spun around. "Coming!" She bounded toward the jeep, never looking back.

I stood in place, sinking into my heels. How many times would I let her hurt me? I was glad I hadn't warned her. I plodded toward home alone, imagining how satisfying it would be to watch the betrayal play out in real time.

THIRTY-THREE

NOW

I jiggled the key to unit two, double-checking the address to make sure I was at the right place. The lock clicked open, and I cracked the door, ready for Bob the cat to make his move. Only a rug and three pairs of men's shoes occupied the visible slice of floor, so I opened it wider and stepped into the apartment. The scent inside was a strange combination of overripe bananas and Clorox bleach. A black cat sauntered toward me with a drawn-out meow.

"Hi, Bob." I crouched down and pet the cat's head, happy he hadn't attempted to dart past me.

A small kitchen with laminate cabinets opened to a slightly bigger living room. No pictures hung on the stark, white walls. A single couch and coffee table faced a giant, flat-screen TV. A mostly bare bookshelf held a half-dozen books with titles like *The Origins of Coffee Beans* and *Cafés around the World*. Gabe was quite the minimalist.

I still had about thirty minutes until Gabe said he'd be home, so I found my clothes and toiletry bag and located a white-tiled bathroom where I could take a quick shower. A few minutes later, I sat on the couch, freshly showered, hair dried, and dressed for our casual date in my favorite linen pants and comfortable sandals. I scrolled through the emails on my phone, wondering how the museum was doing without me and whether my temporary replacement was keeping things on track. The special historical cars exhibit would arrive at the beginning of August to replace the Dutch Masters exhibit. I itched to get back to it, to design the space, and be involved in the culture of the museum again. I thought my boss would have emailed me by now just to check in, but I hadn't heard from her. My leave of absence ended on August 1st, still nearly six weeks away, though I hoped to return home sooner.

The door clicked open, Gabe's towering body filling the doorframe. "Glad to see you made yourself at home."

I pointed to the cat. "Yep. Bob and I are best friends."

He shut himself inside, looking around. "I haven't done much with the place. I'm hoping to buy a condo closer to the beach when the time is right."

"This is perfect for you." I scooched over, making room for Gabe on the couch as Bob jumped from my lap. "I can help you pick out some artwork if you'd like. Just to brighten up the walls a little."

"Yeah." He studied each empty wall as if seeing it for the first time. "I bet you're good at that sort of thing."

We spent the next hour browsing through discount art sites, selecting two framed prints for the living room, one for the bedroom, and a smaller one for the bathroom.

"You hungry?" he asked after completing the online checkout.

"A little bit."

"I wasn't prepared for company, so I don't have much food here. Why don't we pick up something in town and have a picnic at the park before heading to pirate golf? The village just installed those nice new picnic tables on the bluff overlooking the lake."

"Sounds great."

A few minutes later, we said goodbye to Bob and walked into town, surveying our options for carry-out: Joe's Diner, The Chicken Shack, and the pizza place. I'd had pizza the night before.

"I could go for a chicken sandwich," Gabe said, looking toward The Chicken Shack. "Have you been there recently? The onion rings are so good."

I eyed the white brick building with the black lettering and a red outline of a chicken. The aroma of fried chicken made my stomach rumble. As much as I wanted to avoid Mikayla, I craved a greasy sandwich more. Besides, we were getting the food to go, and she probably wasn't even there. "I haven't eaten there in years. Let's try it."

Gabe held the door for me. A pimply girl of about sixteen stood behind the cash register, wearing a red uniform and a paper hat. A limited menu was written on a chalkboard above her head. Gabe nodded toward me. "Go ahead."

"I'll have the original chicken sandwich, small onion rings, and a Coke."

"Make that two of everything," Gabe said, whipping out his wallet. "I hope I'm impressing you with my big spending." He winked, and I couldn't help chuckling.

Just as my shoulders loosened at having avoided Mikayla, she ambled out from the kitchen, a smirk stretching across her face as she took us in. "Well. What do we have here?" she asked as if our buying dinner was somehow scandalous.

I set my jaw, holding back my lingering questions about the notes and about whether she'd been following me. But both Gabe and the young cashier stood next to her, looking between us.

Mikayla leaned forward, resting her elbows on the counter and revealing a wide gap in her V-neck T-shirt. I caught an accidental glimpse of an ill-fitting bra and large doughy breasts. Her eyes sharpened on me, cold like a reptile. My memory flashed back to the mean girl from high school, the one who'd turned my friend into someone I didn't recognize. She flicked her hand toward me. "I bet that podcaster is coming for you next. I spoke to her, you know. I told her what I thought of you."

I hardened my voice and forced a smile. "I told her what I thought of you too, Mikayla. Hannah's planning an entire episode about how enraged you were when Bailey won prom queen, about how you could have returned to the bridge to get revenge on the person who stole the title from you, and who kissed your boyfriend in front of the entire senior class."

"That's not what happened." Mikayla straightened up as her gaze darted between Gabe and the teenage girl standing next to her. "Why don't you go back to the suburbs, Brooke? You don't belong in this town anymore."

"This is the last place I want to be. Trust me."

The girl working the counter kept her face expressionless as she held out a greasy bag. I grabbed it. Gabe followed my lead, collecting our drinks in a cardboard tray. We exited quickly.

"You okay?" he asked as we reached the fresh air.

I felt Gabe's palm on the small of my back. "Yeah." My heart still pounded, but I was proud of myself for standing up to Mikayla, even if I hadn't had a chance to confront her about the notes.

My pulse returned to normal as we headed toward the park, locating an empty picnic table overlooking the lake. Although I hated to give Mikayla any credit, the sandwich and onion rings were delicious. Gabe steered the conversation away from the past. We talked about movies we'd recently seen and the music we liked. He asked more about Ruthie, who I was happy to talk about. We discovered we both had younger brothers, his in North Carolina and mine in Seattle. Before we knew it, over an hour had passed.

It was a few minutes after seven o'clock by the time Gabe

and I waited in a short line at the Pirate's Bounty Putt-Putt Golf Course. The sense of déjà vu I'd been experiencing so frequently since returning to Cove Haven struck me again. The layout of the little store, the buckets of golf clubs, the rows of colorful golf balls, and the shelves of snacks and merchandise for sale were identical to how I remembered them, although everything looked nicer now with a fresh coat of paint and new branding. The format of the course appeared the same, although the worn turf had been upgraded. Life-sized shiny plastic pirates with disturbingly authentic hair and eyes were positioned around the property. Recordings of blasting cannons and catchy pirate songs echoed through the speakers. A giant pirate ship, broken into two pieces, appeared to sink into a pool of unnaturally blue water, shark fins circling it as two terrified pirates clung to the mast, peering into the dangerous surroundings. The dramatic scene had taken over the grassy area where Bailey and I used to sit on a bench, lowering our voices to critique the other golfers while struggling not to collapse into laughter.

A childlike excitement overtook Gabe's face as he stared at the pirate ship, doing a little jig to the music. "This is better than Disney World."

"It used to look a lot different. There weren't any pirates before."

I looked across the fifth hole to a hole on the second nine, where I spotted Zoe in a striped sundress, pointing to some hills in the middle of the twelfth green. Two teenage boys, who I presumed were her sons, and two younger girls hovered near her. She must have felt me staring because her head flipped toward me. It took her a second to register that Gabe and I were together, but she recovered quickly. "Hi, Brooke. Hi, Gabe," she called across another family playing the hole in between us.

We waved back as Zoe and her group continued forward. A text buzzed through my phone from Hannah, reminding me to meet her in front of Joe's tomorrow at 1:45 p.m. I ignored the text, realizing Gabe and I had reached the front of the line.

Gabe paid the teenage boy behind the counter. I plucked a turquoise ball from a bucket, my eyes traveling upward. A series of old photos portraying the golf course the way I remembered it —with the windmill and the single water jump—lined the wall above the clerk's head. One said 1992 in the corner and showed a family holding their clubs in the air. Another, dated 2005, pictured an older couple standing next to the windmill and smiling. A third, yellowing photo captured three men posing in front of the counter where we now stood. I did a double take. The date in the corner said 1983, but one of the men bore an uncanny resemblance to Gabe, shaggy red beard and all.

I nudged him, pointing upward. "That guy on the right looks like you."

Gabe looked at the picture, chuckling. "Yeah. A little bit. But I can assure you that I'm not that old."

"I know, but it's quite a resemblance." I studied the photo again. The quality was poor, and it was difficult to make out the details of the man's features, but he and Gabe had the same bulky build, a similar square chin, and flat eyebrows.

The teen followed our gaze. "That's one of the previous owners, I think. He sold it like thirty years ago to someone else. Then the current owner bought it a couple of years ago. That's what someone told me, anyway."

Gabe shrugged. "Cool. They say everyone has a doppel-gänger somewhere in the world."

The clerk nodded, turning his attention to the next person in line.

"Let's see. Where do we start?"

"C'mon." I led the way to the first hole, remembering the story Gabe enjoyed telling café patrons, that he'd visited Cove Haven on vacation five years earlier and never left. But the man in the photo shared more than just Gabe's red hair. A pinprick of doubt poked a tiny hole in my gut. I thought back to all the summer afternoons Bailey and I spent here but couldn't remember if I'd ever met the owner. It was the type of place run by teens who needed a summer job. I knew almost nothing about Gabe other than what I'd learned over our picnic dinner —that he'd grown up near Indianapolis and had a younger brother who lived in North Carolina. Gabe's apartment was devoid of any family photos. The photo in the store was forty years old, so the man pictured could have been Gabe's father. Then again, wouldn't Dan or Lacey have told me if Gabe had long-standing connections to our hometown? And like Gabe said, everyone had a doppelgänger. If his father was the previous owner, why wouldn't he just tell me? I set my ball on the first tee, focusing on my shot and banishing the overactive thoughts from my head. Gabe had been nothing but a gentleman to me and had no reason to lie. Recent events had made me paranoid about everyone and everything. I lowered my head and hit the ball at an angle to avoid a treasure chest filled with plastic jewels and fake gold coins. The ball rolled to a stop a few inches from the hole. As Gabe whistled and cheered, I realized his resemblance to the former owner must have been nothing more than a strange coincidence.

THIRTY-FOUR

NOW

I awoke with a kink in my neck and a dry mouth. A hint of morning light swathed the room in a violet hue. It took a second to realize I was on Gabe's living room couch. Bob was curled in a ball, warming my feet. Gabe's bedroom door was partially closed. We'd had a fun date last night, making some unexpectedly good golf shots and some laughably horrible ones. Gabe kept score using a tiny pencil to record our strokes on a card, and I beat him by two. We went to the Dairy Mart for soft serve ice cream, then strolled beneath the streetlamps on Main Street as the summer sky turned orange, then pink, then black. Spending time with him was easy, but I still waited for that romantic spark to hit me, the one I'd felt immediately with Shane, the kind that knocked me off my feet. It hadn't happened. When we'd arrived back at his place, he said he'd had fun, then gathered clean sheets, a comforter, and a pillow for me, setting them on the couch. Then he turned toward his bedroom without trying to kiss me. Maybe he sensed I didn't want him to.

Now it was 5:42 a.m. My mouth was dry, so I kicked off the covers to get a glass of water. Bob jumped to the floor, stretching his back. The man at the motel said I could arrive for an early check-in at 1 p.m., and that's what I intended to do. The parade started at two, which would give me time to get settled and still meet Hannah at 1:45 in front of Joe's Diner, as we'd planned.

Two boxes of cereal sat on the counter. A text on my phone from Gabe read, *I went to the café. Stay as long as you'd like.*

I looked around, realizing Gabe wasn't in his bedroom. How early had he woken up? Drips opened at six thirty every morning, so it made sense that he'd get there ahead of time. I must have been knocked out because I hadn't heard him leave. I poured myself a glass of water and returned to the couch. Out of habit, I picked up my phone again, noticing another text hiding behind the one from Gabe. It was from Dan, sent after midnight.

> *Just heard the podcast. Why did you tell Hannah those things? Bailey was NOT my secret lover and I had NO IDEA her necklace was in the lost-and-found box. Unlike you, I have to live in this town. Don't ever come to my house or my shop again.*

I reread the message, hoping my eyes had gotten it wrong, that Dan wasn't so angry with me that he was ending our friendship. But the words felt even more damning the second time. How could I explain that I'd defended him to Hannah? I told her she was wrong about Dan having had Bailey's necklace all these years and about him and Bailey being secret lovers. But Hannah hadn't listened. She'd done what she wanted and drawn her own conclusions.

I wanted to call Dan, give him the full story, and beg for forgiveness, but it was too early. I typed out a long text instead, explaining my side of things. I lay on the couch, wishing for sleep to consume me. But Dan didn't respond, and sleep never came.

At one o'clock, I checked into Room 108 at the Sandcastle Motel, directly below Hannah's room in the 1960's-style two-story building. The tired room featured shabby carpeting, a cramped bathroom, and a threadbare quilt draped over a double bed. Sunlight shone through the window, highlighting a smattering of beige stains on the gauzy curtains. The place held the odor of stale cigarettes despite a sign on the nightstand that said, "No Smoking." I shook off the room's flaws, relieved to have my own space after staying with other people for over a week.

My body felt as ragged and worn as my surroundings, so I took a few minutes to unpack my toiletries and rest on the bed. The morning's drama with Dan tunneled through me. I'd stopped by his shop a couple of hours earlier, and he'd ignored me, helping a customer as if I was invisible. When the customer left, I asked him if we could talk. Through clenched teeth, he told me to leave before he said something he regretted. I did as he requested, forcing back the tears that gathered behind my eyes.

At 1:30, I hoisted myself to my feet. I'd have to leave now to meet Hannah by 1:45. The way she'd presented the podcast had pissed me off, and I couldn't wait to tell her so.

I lowered my sunglasses and continued toward the sidewalk, blending into the foot traffic that bled into the streets. Tides of people headed in the same direction toward the parade route. Five minutes later, I reached Main Street, passing by Drips, where a line snaked out the door.

I squeezed between two families, set on my course to get to Joe's Diner three blocks down. A large man stepped in front of me, blocking my path. Dark stains dampened the armpits of his T-shirt. I looked up, registering his face.

"I thought I warned you." Trevor's breath smelled of beer. Sweat glistened from his scalp. "You think I wouldn't hear that podcast? You think I was joking when I told her to get outta this town?" He leaned toward me, eyes wild.

"I didn't think she was going to say anything about you. I'm sorry." Trevor was drunk, and he scared me. I worried he might have that knife on him. Or a gun. I was desperate to get away. I tried to edge past him, but he stepped in the same direction, squaring his shoulders.

"Now the whole town knows Bailey rejected me. The whole world. You're playing with fire. No joke." Spittle sprayed from his mouth.

"Got it." I wrapped my arms around myself, feeling threatened by his sheer size, his lack of predictability. But a crowd surrounded us, providing a measure of safety. I hardened myself, jutting out my chin. "It's not my podcast. Hannah said bad things about me too."

Trevor wiped the back of his hand across his forehead, staring toward the crowd, then back toward me. "Was that for real? That Spike is in town?" His demeanor had suddenly shifted, his voice one pitch higher and a note of sadness replacing the confrontational tone.

"Yeah. He goes by Jonathan now."

"Huh." Trevor lowered his head, blinking slowly. For a split second, I felt bad for him. I knew what it felt like to be abandoned by a best friend. Even after twenty years, the loss still tore through me. The two men's lives had turned out so vastly different. Jonathan had made something of himself, a seemingly loving family and a successful career, while Trevor's life appeared to have gone off the rails. I couldn't imagine the two of them hanging out anymore or what they would talk about.

Dan's face flashed in my mind, another friend I might have lost. "I've gotta go." I left Trevor standing there, finding my breath as I cut behind a nearby woman and made a wide loop around the gathering crowd. A mob of people funneled from the nearby streets toward the parade route. Chief Warner stood on the corner with two younger officers stationed across the street. All three directed foot traffic, reminding everyone not to go past the barriers. More visitors had gathered on the grassy hill next to the post office, a high point to view the parade over the crowd. I spotted Lacey sitting on a square blanket up on the hill and waved. She stretched tall, waving back. A narrow-shouldered woman with endless legs sat next to her, wearing a black baseball cap. I realized it was Maeve. I hadn't seen Lacey's younger sister since the night we'd tried on our prom dresses in their bedroom. I'd never imagined what she'd look like as a full-grown woman, and I couldn't help staring at the transformation.

A woman bumped me from behind, then apologized. I pulled my gaze from Maeve and checked my watch. It was 1:50 p.m. As much as I wanted to say hi to Lacey and Maeve, the crowd was too dense to navigate, and it was past the time to find Hannah at our meeting spot. The drums of a marching band beat in the distance, followed by trumpets. Things were in motion. I bobbed and weaved around children with sticky hands and adults coated with sunscreen, moving toward the diner. A familiar figure caught my eye across the street. Jonathan Newson stood near a lamppost with his kids in front of him and his wife by his side. His Chicago Cubs hat was pulled low on his head, and his usual dark sunglasses shielded his eyes. I ducked into the crowd before he spotted me. After my run-in with Trevor and the scathing treatment from Dan, I didn't need yet another person blaming me for the content of Hannah's podcast.

At last, I reached Joe's Diner, staking out an open section of sidewalk to watch the parade over the heads of an older couple sitting in lawn chairs. I scanned the crowd for Hannah, who hadn't arrived yet. I wondered if she'd run into Trevor too, and I could only imagine how that went.

The sun scorched the crown of my head as a dozen horses and riders in cowboy hats followed behind the band. The horses' hooves clip-clopped along the cement as the riders waved to the crowd. Two shiny red firetrucks followed, with friendly firemen hanging off the sides and throwing candy to excited children. I took a video of the horses and fire trucks to send to Ruthie later.

A woman whooped and cheered from the other side of the street. I cut the video, peering above my phone to find the source of the commotion. Beyond the horses and riders, Mikayla hollered with a baby on her hip. Two kids of about ten and twelve stood next to her wearing shirts that looked several sizes too big for them.

The next group in the parade turned the corner, and I realized why Mikayla was so excited. It was the Cove Haven High School cheerleading squad dressed in purple and black. The two girls in front carried a banner that said, *Cove Haven Football—2022 Southwest Michigan Regional Champs*. Several rows of girls behind them moved their silver and black pom-poms in unison, perma-smiles on their faces. I was happy to see one male cheerleader in the mix. Maybe progress had come to Cove Haven after all. "Woo, hoo!" People around me cheered louder as the football team came into view. I cheered too, but it was for the boy with the pom-poms who had the courage to be himself. I could only imagine what would have happened to that boy if he'd attempted the same thing in this town twenty years ago. Jasper's memory rippled through me, and I had to look away.

Once the football team was out of view, several more floats crawled past, including one sponsored by The Friends of the Library, displaying a giant stack of books constructed of flowers. Another, sponsored by the Cove Haven Chamber of Commerce, featured food items from local restaurants, including a coffee cup from Drips, a shrimp kabob from The Fish, and a chicken sandwich from The Chicken Shack. As a float advertising Pirate's Bounty Putt-Putt Golf Course dragged

behind the others with people dressed as pirates and waving
putters in the air, I realized Hannah still hadn't arrived. Again, I
searched the faces around me, but she wasn't among them. I
texted her.

I'm in front of Joe's. Are you coming?

When I turned back to the parade, I nearly stumbled backward at the sight of a gleaming black hearse, a white-haired man
in a black top hat waving from the front window. Cursive
writing on the side of the vehicle advertised the Lakeside
Funeral Home, the same funeral home that had recently taken
care of Mom's burial. I studied the other onlookers to see if
anyone else thought the morbid vehicle creeping past was inap-
propriate for a festive parade, but people only focused ahead
and clapped. A girl scout troop and a boy scout troop marched
past next, followed by a middle school marching band. Then a
slow procession of tractors driven by local farmers for whom the
Harvest Festival was originally intended to honor. Finally, two
shiny red convertibles traveled toward us, side by side. The first
car held an owl-eyed girl with a smattering of freckles who sat
up high in the back, a white sash draped across her shoulders,
and a glittery tiara on her head. The second car held two more
crowned people perched above the backseat, a teenage boy and
a girl. A woman in the front passenger seat spoke into a
microphone.

"Introducing the 2023 Harvest Festival Princess, Ginny
Longshore." The woman paused, leaving space for applause
and whistles. "She is accompanied by the 2023 Prom King and
Queen of Cove Haven High School, Matt York and Phoebe
Mullins!" More applause sounded as the young people in the
back of the cars smiled and waved to the crowd, enjoying their
moment of fame.

My heartbeat hitched in my chest as I took in the sight,

suddenly unsteady on my feet. A similar scene from an alternate universe fought its way into my mind, one where Bailey perched on the back of the convertible in her pale blue dress, waving to the adoring crowd. Or would it have been Mikayla sitting there? The parade was canceled that year.

I widened my stance, my gaze pulling toward Mikayla across the street. She glared at the young prom queen, making no effort to comfort the baby who twisted and screamed in her arms. Mikayla's eyes grew smaller and darker, her lips set. I'd seen that venomous look before, on prom night twenty years ago. It was like a raging storm sweeping in off the lake, searching for a place to aim its fury.

Before I could turn away, Mikayla's stare shifted, landing on me. But she didn't scare me anymore. I leered directly back at her, clenching my teeth. We were gridlocked like that for several seconds.

And I knew we were both thinking about Bailey.

THIRTY-FIVE

THEN

Prom Night 2003

Dan held the door as Lacey and I entered the school, where an Avril Lavigne song echoed through the hallway. We followed the vibrant trail of tissue paper flowers and sparkling fairy lights toward the gym. A talkative girl from the grade below us named Jenna had volunteered as the prom photographer, and she motioned for me and Dan to get together next to a sign that said "Cove Haven High School Senior Prom 2003" in fancy cursive lettering. I pulled Lacey into the photo too.

"Her date couldn't make it," Dan said as Jenna snapped a photo of the three of us: Dan in his rented tuxedo, Lacey in her mom's dress, and me in my Doc Martens.

A kid from my second-hour English class idled near the wall, his hair slicked-back and a bow tie around his collar. I did a double take, barely recognizing the dapper version of my classmate whose hair I'd never seen combed and who normally wore dirty jeans and T-shirts. By the surprised look on his face, I could tell he had a similar thought about me. I touched my hair, which Mom had curled and pulled into a fancy knot on the back of my head. My lashes were heavy with mascara. We nodded at each other, and I followed Dan and Lacey into the cafeteria, where tropical birds hung from the ceiling, and strobe lights pulsed through the shadows. A DJ spun tunes in the corner, seemingly unbothered that no one was dancing. But the night was young. Only about twenty others had arrived, and half of them sat at white-clothed tables that the prom committee had set up around the perimeter of the gym.

Dan eyed a long table against the back wall, large platters of finger food displayed across it. "Let's get some food." He found the small plates and waved me and Lacey in front of him. I took a couple of veggies and mini quiches, joining my friends at a nearby table. Dan left again, ladling out cups of crimson punch, which sat in giant bowls at the end of the food spread.

As I crunched a carrot, stomping and banging drew my attention to the door. Trevor, Mikayla, Spike, and Bailey chanted "Senior Prom, Senior Prom" as they entered the room. Liz, Zoe, and their dates followed behind them, joining the chant. Soon the whole room was repeating the words. The DJ played "Get the Party Started", and it seemed our senior prom was officially allowed to begin.

As people took to the dance floor, I sunk into my chair, my eyes drawn to Bailey. A silky, pale blue dress skimmed her body, strappy heels on her feet, and loose curls falling down her shoulders. A silver chain caught the flashing lights, and I was surprised to see she wore the necklace I'd given her with her strapless dress. It didn't seem fancy enough, although it matched her silver earrings. I would have told her she looked beautiful if I wasn't so annoyed with her. Bailey's ankle twisted atop her heels. She stumbled, and Zoe caught her before she hit the floor, causing them to double over with laughter. It was clear they'd been drinking. Trevor edged toward the punch bowl and glanced over his shoulder toward two teachers enthralled in conversation. He pulled out a silver flask, poured a clear liquid into the punch, followed by the contents of a second flask. Trevor smiled at Spike, who nodded in approval.

As soon as he slipped away, Dan refilled our cups with the spiked punch, handing the plastic cups to us with a shrug. "We had no way of knowing what was in there."

We giggled and sipped our fruit punch which now tasted strongly of vodka. People continued to file into the gym, and soon it was full. Classmates stopped by our table to talk or compliment me on my dress or Dan on his dapper look. Lacey got fewer compliments, but she didn't seem to mind.

I spotted Mikayla wearing a crimson dress covered in sequins and with enormous ruffles on the shoulders. Matching red shoes and lipstick completed her look. A group of girls surrounded her, one of them making a circular motion with her finger, and Mikayla twirled, showing off her gaudy ensemble as the others swooned. Another girl pantomimed placing a crown on Mikayla's head, and Mikayla waved her away, attempting to look modest. Liz and Zoe huddled nearby, whispering, and tossing furtive glances around the room. I knew they were discussing their plot to name Bailey as the prom queen instead of the rightful winner, Mikayla. I fought the urge to sound the alarm on the vengeful cheerleaders. Admittedly, I couldn't wait to see the look on Mikayla's face when someone else's name was called, to see the remorse on Bailey's face when she came crawling back to me tomorrow morning after realizing her so-called friends had betrayed her.

A second later, "Lose Yourself" by Eminem sounded in angry beats over the speakers, people whooped and hollered, and the dance floor flooded. Dan, Lacey, and I wedged our way into the crowd and danced elbow-to-elbow with the others, staying for the Nelly song that followed. The DJ shifted the vibe with a slow song by Enrique Iglesias, clearing at least half the people from the floor.

I retook my seat, along with Lacey and Dan. A few feet

away, Spike tapped Bailey on the shoulder, nodding toward the dance floor. Bailey's expression was blank, but I knew her well enough to notice the curve of her lower lip, the tight clasp of her fingers. She was thinking of an excuse but didn't do it fast enough. Spike grabbed her hand and led her to the edge of the dance floor, where Mikayla draped herself over Trevor nearby. Spike wrapped his arms around Bailey, trying to pull her close. She placed her palms mechanically on his shoulders and extended her arms, keeping her back straight to create distance between their bodies. Spike frowned but stayed strong with his swaying steps. If the prom committee had given out an award for Most Awkward Couple, Spike and Bailey would have been the clear winners.

Their wavering dance steps eventually rotated Bailey in my direction, revealing the miserable look on her face. This clearly wasn't the fairytale prom night she'd envisioned, not to mention Spike. Against the far wall, Zoe and Liz stood shoulder-to-shoulder, looming in the shadows and keeping tabs on the dance floor as if they were chaperones. A sour feeling rose in my stomach, and I was pretty sure it wasn't from the vodka. Something about this night felt off, like I was viewing the party through a narrow crack of a closet door. I had the sickening thought that maybe there was something beyond the rigged prom queen results going on.

The song ended, and another slow song came on. Bailey said something to Spike and peeled away, looking for an escape, but her friends all danced with their dates. She caught me staring. Relief lifted her face as she made a beeline toward our table.

"Hi, guys." Other than waving from a distance earlier, it was the first time she'd acknowledged me all night. "I love your dress, Brooke." Her eyes flickered toward Lacey. "Yours too, Lacey."

"Thanks. Yours is pretty too."

I pointed to her neck. "You're wearing the necklace."

She touched it, staring at my bare neck. "Yeah. It was the right length, and it matched my earrings."

Dan cleared his throat. "Looks like you and Spike have a real love connection."

Lacey giggled, and I couldn't help doing the same.

Bailey lowered her head, the happy-go-lucky veneer falling away. She leaned closer, lowering her voice. "I feel bad, but I just don't like him in that way."

A pang of empathy shot through me as I caught a glimpse of the Bailey I used to know. The old me would have pulled Bailey into the restroom and detailed an elaborate plan to keep her occupied whenever a slow song came on. But I wouldn't give her that effort now.

Bailey glanced toward the food table, where Spike refilled his punch. Then she turned back to me. "Mikayla was so insistent that I go with him. Then Zoe and Liz kept pushing for us to be a couple."

"That's rough."

Dan shrugged. "It's only a dance that lasts a few hours. It's not like you have to marry him."

The slow song ended, and the DJ asked people if they were having fun. A few feet away, Zoe tugged Liz's arm, pointing toward the restrooms.

Bailey noticed them too, and stepped back from our table, smoothing down her hair. "I'm going to run to the restroom. See you later."

I was prepared to let her walk away, but an inexplicable wave of panic overtook me as if she was running toward the edge of a cliff instead of a high school bathroom. Maybe it was the alcohol warming my insides, but I didn't see the friend who'd hurt me. I only saw the friend who used to braid my hair before school, who showed up unexpectedly on my doorstep with freshly baked cookies, and who critiqued my art projects with a snobby French accent. I couldn't let her walk into their trap, to be humiliated. I pushed back my chair and jogged after her, catching Bailey before she reached the others. She flinched when I touched her bare shoulder, spinning toward me.

"Brooke. What is it?"

"Those girls." I angled my head in the direction Zoe and Liz had been heading. "They're not your friends."

Annoyance tightened Bailey's features. "How could you possibly know that?"

A group of chattering girls brushed past us, and I lowered my voice. "Because I do. Just trust me."

Bailey stared at me, something unidentifiable churning behind her eyes. She pressed her glossy lips together and shook her head. "Jealousy isn't a good look on you, Brooke." Her voice had turned cold and sharp. She spun away from me and hurried to catch up with her crew. I watched her leave, feeling a little like she'd knifed me in the gut.

THIRTY-SIX

NOW

The candy-apple convertible carrying Cove Haven High School's 2023 prom king and queen disappeared around the corner, and the parade was officially over. People spilled over the curb and into the street, kids scavenging for stray pieces of taffy, gum, and chocolates. I rechecked my phone, but Hannah still hadn't texted me. It was more than possible she'd received some angry phone calls and was hiding out in her motel room, but she could have told me her plans had changed.

Shrugging off her absence, I made my way toward the hill where I'd seen Lacey and her sister sitting earlier. I wanted to say hello to Maeve and wish them a fun weekend together. But by the time I neared the grassy incline, most people had pulled up their blankets and gone on their way, including Lacey and Maeve.

"Hi, Brooke." Zoe weaved around a young couple. An elegant sunhat perched on her head, casting a shadow across her face. The same two teenage boys and two younger girls who were at the putt-putt golf course with her last night now stood by her side. "These are my boys, Andrew and Matt." The boys nodded politely. "And my nieces, who are visiting from Virginia."

"Hi, guys. Did you enjoy the parade?"

"Yeah!" The girls held up fists full of candy.

"Heading this way?" Zoe pointed in the direction I was going. I nodded, and we walked together, the kids following in a group behind us. "I saw you and Gabe at Pirate's Bounty yesterday."

"Yeah. It's a lot different than it used to be."

"That's for sure."

We took a few steps before Zoe spoke again. "And not to pry, but you're not bothered by Gabe's relation to Willa?"

My feet slowed, and I turned toward Zoe. "Huh?"

"Gabe is Willa's nephew." She raised the brim of her hat, concern clouding her eyes. "Didn't he tell you?"

My mouth had gone dry. "No."

"I suppose it's not something to shout about on a first date. Besides, he seems nothing like her, personality-wise. I mean, who doesn't have a crazy aunt?" Zoe chuckled as she glanced toward her nieces.

I forced myself to keep pace with Zoe, who seemed completely unbothered by the bombshell she'd just unloaded. Again, I remembered the story Gabe told his patrons and me, that he'd visited Cove Haven on a whim five years ago and never left. That story had been a lie. I wondered why Dan and Lacey hadn't told me about his connection to Willa or if they even knew.

"Willa's brother, Mack, used to own the putt-putt course back before our time. He and his wife had two boys—Gabe and his brother—but got divorced when the kids were toddlers. The mom took Gabe and his brother to Indianapolis. Mack died of a heart attack a couple of years later. At least, that's what I remember hearing from someone, although I can't remember who told me that. You know how small-town gossip is."

"Yeah. I do." The photo above the counter at the putt-putt course raced through my mind. The man in the picture *was* Gabe's dad. Why had Gabe pretended to have no relation? I took in my crowded surroundings with a flat gaze as Zoe continued talking.

"It's funny how everyone has the urge to return to their roots, isn't it? So many people who moved away are back in Cove Haven." She motioned toward me. "Even you."

"Yeah." My throat was parched, and I suddenly wished for a cold drink of water.

Zoe pointed down a side street. "This is our turnoff. It was nice running into you."

"You too."

She herded the group of kids in front of her and waved to me. I forced a smile back, but I wasn't sure how long I stood there on the street corner, thinking about why Gabe lied to me. A man's elbow caught my arm, and I snapped back to myself. I wanted to head straight to the café and confront Gabe, but I remembered how busy it was today and knew it wasn't a good time.

My thoughts waded through a swampy haze as I continued toward the motel, never more thankful to have my own space waiting for me. I would grab a drink and some snacks from the nearby gas station, hole up in my room for a while, send the parade video to Ruthie, and eventually locate Hannah. Questioning Gabe about his true ties to this town could wait until tomorrow.

After making a pit stop at the gas station, I greedily gulped a cold bottle of lemonade. When I turned the corner to the motel, I blinked at the unexpected sight, hoping the scene before me was caused by my lingering dehydration or insufficient sleep.

An ambulance was parked in front of the motel with its back doors open. Two paramedics carried a stretcher across the beach, a body strapped to it. They seemed in no hurry. A police cruiser sat a half block ahead, and Justin Warner paced with his head down to meet the paramedics at the ambulance. A small crowd had gathered, exchanging hushed whispers and standing at a respectable distance.

As the paramedics moved toward the ambulance, a lock of black hair hanging from the stretcher caught my eye. I forced myself closer to them. A slim body and a blue bathing suit came into view, only partially covered by a too-small blanket. The face was bloated and had turned a chalky shade of gray. Two lifeless eyes completed the horrifying picture. I doubled over, hands on my knees, struggling to breathe. The EMTs lifted the stretcher—Hannah's unmoving body—into the ambulance as the air went cold. Hannah hadn't met me at the parade because she was dead.

THIRTY-SEVEN

NOW

The white-hot sun blinded my eyes as I tapped the police chief on his arm. "Is she okay?" I asked, already knowing the answer.

He pinched his lips together, his grim expression telling me what the pit in my gut already knew. "I'm afraid not. A swimmer noticed her floating near the shore about thirty minutes ago, but she's been out there a while. Probably since this morning. The beach has been nearly empty this afternoon because of the parade." He took in my face, which surely stretched with horror. "It's a real tragedy. I'm sorry."

"But how could she drown? She was an expert swimmer."

One of the paramedics brushed my shoulder, overhearing my comments. "It looks like she got tangled in a thick section of seaweed. It was wrapped around her ankle."

Chief Warner nodded. "It's happened before. Just last summer, a guy almost drowned because of the same thing. He went out too far and got tangled up. He said he wouldn't have made it if a boat hadn't passed so close to him and stopped to help."

The paramedic spoke again. "Or it could have been a stronger tide than she expected. That's a common danger too."

Black spots swam before me. I squared my shoulders toward Justin and the paramedics, unable to make sense of this. "No. It wasn't an accident." The sharpness of my voice surprised me. "Hannah had enemies. People didn't like the things she was saying on her podcast about Bailey's death. Hannah went swimming every morning. Someone knew her routine and did this to her."

The paramedic hustled into the ambulance, leaving the police chief to rub his forehead. "Brooke, I know it's difficult to lose someone, especially after losing your mom so recently. And after you lost your best friend so many years ago." His voice trailed off as his warm hands grasped my cold ones. "But people die in accidents. Unfortunately, it happens much, much more often than you'd think. Murders, on the other hand, are exceedingly rare. Especially in Cove Haven. The last one was in 1982, and that was a domestic dispute."

"Maybe there's a killer who is smarter than you." The words slipped out before I could filter them. I stared him down, pulling my hands away. "Maybe there has been a more recent murder—or two."

His eyeballs bulged, and he seemed to know I was talking about Bailey as much as Hannah. He must have been aware of all the questions the podcaster had been raising. He looked down his nose at me. "We investigate all deaths thoroughly before making that determination. We did that twenty years ago, and we still do that now. All indicators point to accidental drowning here. We've already accessed her motel room to check for roommates or pets, of which there were none. We took several photos, but there was no sign of forced entry or anything else amiss." He continued explaining the protocol and how the next step was to notify the family and send Hannah's body for an autopsy. At that point, they hoped to rule out any foul play officially.

A movement at the edge of my vision drew my attention to

the far side of the street as a figure moved across the grass and slipped behind the trunk of a tree. Trevor's earlier threats still tumbled through me, and I half expected to see him lurking there. But I'd caught a glimpse of someone else instead. It was Dan who'd been looming in the distance, watching as the EMTs loaded Hannah into the ambulance. A chill skittered up my spine and crawled over my scalp. Why was he hiding over there? He'd been acting so strangely lately, pacing through his house in the middle of the night, somehow having Bailey's necklace in his possession before it arrived at the thrift shop. Had he been angrier than I'd imagined at Hannah and done something to stop her? As much as I didn't want to admit it, I wondered if something in Hannah's podcast had poked a little too close to the truth about what really happened to Bailey.

I half expected the ambulance to speed away with sirens screaming, but it only crept along the street in silence, waiting a few extra seconds at the stop sign. No need to rush because Hannah was dead. The awful realization hit me again. I wondered again who could have done this. And who had sent Hannah the anonymous text claiming Bailey was murdered, prodding the eager podcaster to look into the death of a prom queen twenty years earlier? Why had they lured her to this cursed town? What did they know? And who had wanted to stop her? The questions continued to pile up, far outnumbering any answers.

My heart ached for Hannah's family. She'd mentioned her parents a few times, a pair of social butterflies who lived in a western suburb of Chicago, and an over-achieving brother who was in his final year of college. I imagined they would arrive at the hotel sometime in the next twenty-four hours to retrieve Hannah's personal belongings. They would be in shock, probably inconsolable. Nevertheless, I planned to offer my condolences, praise Hannah's abilities as an investigative podcaster, and tell them everything I knew about Hannah's last few weeks on earth.

My insides were hollow and shaky as I found my way to my room, locking myself inside. Lowering my weight onto the bed, I forced myself to sip some lemonade. Chief Warner said that Hannah had likely been floating out on the lake for hours. That matched what Hannah had told me last week—that she went for her morning swim as early as 6 a.m. I imagined not many people were out and about that early, especially on a Saturday. Someone could have been waiting for her. Once she began swimming, they could have swum out to her and surprised her. Maybe they pulled her under the surface until she drowned. Except for some possible splashing, no one would have heard a thing.

I banished Dan's face from my mind, feeling guilty for suspecting him and determined to uncover a more likely suspect. My thoughts circled over the people in the area who could have wanted to harm Hannah. When I'd run into Trevor at the parade, he'd made no effort to hide his anger about the latest podcast episode. He had threatened Hannah and me. But if Trevor had already killed Hannah, wouldn't he have played it cool? He would have pretended that nothing Hannah said bothered him so as not to become a suspect. Then again, maybe I was giving Trevor too much credit.

Jonathan had been at the parade with his family, still hiding from the locals behind his hat and sunglasses. I wondered if he'd listened to the podcast. If so, how desperate was he to shut Hannah up? How angry had he been about Hannah mentioning his name change and his role in the new hotel? Still, Hannah had only used first names and hadn't mentioned the name of the development company. I couldn't imagine him risking everything he'd built by killing someone. Despite Jonathan's temper in high school, he now seemed more like the type of guy who solved his problems via legal action rather than violence.

What about Liz? She'd been a lifeguard at the public beach for years. She was probably still a strong swimmer, maybe someone who could rival Hannah. But why? Hannah had barely mentioned her as a suspect so far in her podcast. I couldn't make sense of it.

My thoughts turned toward Gabe. Gabe, the liar, as I thought of him since my run-in with Zoe. He hadn't come to Cove Haven on a whim five years earlier. He'd been born here. His dad had owned the putt-putt golf course. Willa was his aunt. While I still couldn't work out the motive for his lying, I wondered if I was missing a more ominous connection. I remembered waking up this morning on Gabe's couch. At barely 5:30 a.m., he'd already been gone. A cold wind blew through me at the memory. Had he really gone to Drips more than an hour before it opened, or had he been doing something else first? Still, I couldn't think of a reason why Gabe would want to kill Hannah. I couldn't discern any connection between them other than Hannah buying an occasional cup of coffee at the café.

I stood up, stepping toward the window as my stubborn suspicions circled back to Dan. I'd told him about Hannah's daily morning swims. Then there was the necklace he'd dropped at the thrift shop and the recent theory that he was Bailey's secret boyfriend. I wondered again which part of Hannah's podcast had been edging too close to the truth. More than anything, I wanted to sit down with Dan and question him, get him to tell me the truth about everything. But I'd betrayed his trust, and he wasn't speaking to me.

There was only one person who'd been closer than me to Dan in high school, someone who might have the answers I didn't have. Henry. I hadn't spoken to him in years, not since Dan and Maggie's wedding.

I shut the gauzy curtain, ignoring the stains and shaking my head at a crinkly warning tag that read, "Highly Flammable." Perching on the edge of the bed, I drew in a breath and pressed Henry's number, willing him to answer.

THIRTY-EIGHT

NOW

"Hello?"

Henry's voice was deeper than I remembered, but it was him.

"Hi, Henry. It's Brooke Webber." I paused, realizing it had been ten years since I'd last seen him. "From high school."

"Oh. Wow. Brooke! How are you?"

"I'm okay. I got your number from Dan and Maggie. I hope that's okay."

"Of course. It's good to hear from you."

I explained how I was back in Cove Haven for a few weeks to fix up Mom's house, that I'd stayed at Dan and Maggie's house for several nights, and that I'd seen Lacey too. Then I turned the conversation toward the reason I called him. "It shouldn't be too surprising, but being back in Cove Haven is forcing me to think about Bailey."

"I'm sure."

"And something terrible happened today." My throat clenched at the thought of Hannah.

"What was it?"

"There's a podcaster that's been in town. Hannah Mead.

She was looking into Bailey's death and kept approaching me with her theories and then accusing people here of possibly having been involved in Bailey's death. She put it all out there on her podcast. Anyway, today Hannah drowned in the lake. They said it looked like an accidental drowning, but I'm not so sure."

Henry's jagged breath met my ear. "Sorry. What did you just say?"

"Hannah—she's a podcaster who's here investigating Bailey's death—drowned in the lake this morning."

"Oh my God." Henry's voice cracked. "Hannah's dead?"

"Yes. And I don't think it was an accident."

It sounded like Henry was panting. "Please tell me you're joking."

My weight sunk deeper into the mattress as I registered Henry's words, the emotion in his voice. "Wait. Did you know her?"

"I... I knew her. Yes." He paused amid a slew of heavy gasps. "What the hell!"

"Henry? What's going on?"

"I'm the one who told her to go to Cove Haven to look into Bailey's death. She's dead because of me."

I leaned back, struggling to comprehend Henry's words. "You sent her the anonymous text?"

"No. There was no anonymous text. Hannah was visiting one of my co-workers a couple of months ago, and he thought she'd like to see the radio station because of her work as a podcaster. She spent an afternoon in the studio, and I was impressed with her, so I listened to a few episodes of *All the Dark Corners* after she left. Her investigations into suspicious deaths got me thinking back to Bailey." His voice trailed off, and then he cleared his throat. "Anyway, I called her a couple of days later and told her how Bailey died. Even though I was out of town on our prom night, I always felt something was off. The scandal. The timing. I only told her to say she received an anonymous text in case anyone questioned why she was looking into it." A muffled sob. "I can't believe I sent her there, and now she's dead."

"It's not your fault," I said, although a part of me was angry with Henry—and Hannah—for not telling me the truth.

"It is. It's all my fault. She wouldn't have been there if it wasn't for me."

Henry was practically hyperventilating. I waited a second before speaking again, my mind still absorbing the new set of shocking facts. "Did you tell anyone else about your connection to Hannah? Maybe Dan?"

"No. I felt guilty about the whole thing. I wasn't sure where Hannah's investigation would lead, if anywhere, and I didn't want anyone tying her back to me."

I lowered my voice. "She must have been getting close to the truth, Henry. Close enough that someone killed her."

"I don't know. It's possible, I guess."

"Have you been listening to the episodes?"

"Yeah. All of them."

"So you heard on her latest episode that she thought Bailey and Dan might have been secretly seeing each other."

"She was way off base on that one."

"I know it sounds crazy. But I was thinking about it, and she might have been right. Bailey could have been dating someone she didn't want anyone to know about. Maybe that's why she stayed behind the train station in the rain after everyone else left."

"Why would she keep it a secret?"

"Maybe she was embarrassed. There were signs she was seeing someone, but I never really thought about it until a few days ago. Did Dan ever mention anything to you about Bailey? Like maybe he was attracted to her or wanted to ask her on a date."

"What?" Henry laughed, incredulous. "No. Not at all."

"Are you sure?"

"I've never been more sure about anything."

"Why do you say that?"

"I mean, I didn't exactly think Bailey was going to win the friend-of-the-year award, but I didn't spend too much energy on her either. Dan was different, though. He worked hard at hating her, almost like it was a part-time job." Henry sniffled, clearly still upset from the news of Hannah's death. "Remember when Dan wanted us to vote for Bailey for prom queen?"

"Yeah."

"That was only because he wanted to see Mikayla's wrath come down on her. He told me that when you weren't around."

I stared at the diamond pattern on the bedspread, my mouth going dry.

"And remember Bailey's DUI?"

"Yeah."

"Dan and I saw Bailey driving—swerving—with a car full of her new friends when we were walking home from late-night onion rings and milkshakes at Joe's Diner. Dan made an anonymous phone call to the police. He tried to make it seem like it was purely a safety concern, but I knew that wasn't his motivation."

My breath lodged in my throat. Dan had been more calculated than I thought, had basically ensured Bailey would get arrested. Still, the line between love and hate was a thin one. "Could Dan have been angry with her because she rejected his advances?"

"No. Nothing like that. He was just as hurt as you that she ditched us. I never mentioned anything to the police when I got back into town after my grandpa's funeral. It was all so overwhelming. I mean, someone who used to be our friend supposedly killed herself. I didn't want to make things worse for anyone or to make Dan feel guilty for calling in the DUI. But the truth was that Dan hated Bailey's guts."

I pulled a knee up to my chest, hugging my arm around it. Dan hated Bailey. I'd known he'd disliked her and had jokingly kept track of her "bitch moves," but I hadn't realized the extent of it. Henry was describing something more intense.

I adjusted my sunglasses, pushing them further up the bridge of my nose. "Bailey's missing necklace magically appeared in the lost-and-found box at Dan's bike shop. I can't stop wondering how it got there. Do you think he could have—"

"No." I could hear Henry's raspy breath through my phone. "Just stop right there. I think you're letting the theories from the podcast get into your head. Dan has always been a good guy. Still is a good guy. You know that. He's not capable of killing someone. Even Bailey."

"Okay." I squeezed a handful of the worn quilt, taking in Henry's words. "But when you sent Hannah on this quest to dig deeper into Bailey's death, you must have had one or two potential suspects in mind."

"Yeah. I did. But it was never Dan."

"Who was it then?" I waited, but Henry didn't speak. "Spit it out."

Henry's breathing was thick and steady. "Honestly, Brooke. I've always suspected you."

I dug my fingernails into my leg, the room spinning around me. "What? How could you even think that?"

"It's just that you and Bailey used to do everything together. Then she completely dumped you and rubbed it in your face. It must have hurt like hell, but you never let it show. I always wondered if you might have snapped, especially when I heard her necklace was missing." A thick silence hung on the line between us. "But I can see now that I was a hundred percent wrong, and I'm sorry I even said anything. I'm sorry I contacted

Hannah too. It was dumb. But I never mentioned my suspicions about you to her, if that counts for anything."

"Oh." My lungs had contracted, but I forced some levity into my voice. "Your theory was way completely wrong, but you didn't know. You were trying to do the right thing."

"Are you okay, Brooke? I don't blame you if you're pissed at me. I have to go on air in about five minutes, but I can call you back later if—"

"Yes. I'm fine. At least you know about Hannah now." Heat crept up my neck, and I gulped back the indignation in my voice. "Take care, Henry." I ended the call without giving Henry a chance to say goodbye. The conversation tore through me again. Henry had dropped a series of bombs on my head, including another accusation against me. One of my few loyal friends from back then had suspected me all along. He was the one who had sent Hannah to Cove Haven, likely getting her killed.

I peered around the dimly lit room, unable to think clearly, the walls closing in on me. Logic told me the person who'd been leaving me the notes was the same person who killed Hannah. I felt numb—detached from myself—even as I wondered if I was next. I peeled off my clothes, pulled on my bathing suit, and grabbed the room key. Stumbling through the parking lot and across the swath of sand, I reached the undulating lake, letting the inky tide swallow my feet and ankles. Hannah's face surfaced in my mind as I stepped further into the frigid water. The waves oscillated around my thighs, then my waist. Closing my eyes, I sank beneath the surface, submerging my head. The water in my ears muted my senses, drowning out the squeals of nearby children. And, for a moment, it was a relief not to have to think about anything but holding my breath.

THIRTY-NINE

NOW

I inhaled the stale air of the motel room as I stared at the ceiling. My bathing suit felt cold against my skin, my feet gritty with sand. Clumps of wet hair fanned from my head, draping across the pillow. I didn't know how long I'd been lying here crying, but my tears had finally dried. Hannah hadn't been a close friend or even a friend at all. She had basically blackmailed me into helping her with her podcast. But she was young and ambitious, and her sudden death had left a hole in me. She had wanted to tell me something. I lifted my phone from the nightstand and scrolled back to the last text she'd sent me, the one I'd ignored while standing in line with Gabe to play putt-putt golf.

I discovered something big. Don't forget to meet me at the parade at 1:45 in front of Joe's.

At the time I'd interpreted her message as an unnecessary and annoying reminder, but my eyes must have skipped over that first part. *I discovered something big.* She'd written the text after her last episode had aired. What had she discovered? I envisioned her empty motel room upstairs. As far as I knew, the police had only entered briefly to check for roommates or pets. Justin Warner told me they'd recovered her swim bag and phone from the beach but were leaving the rest of her things for her family to retrieve, as there was no indication of foul play. No one except for me seemed to suspect Hannah had been murdered. I wondered when her parents would arrive and what they would believe.

Hannah's laptop was most certainly locked in her room, but I knew from having watched her log in that it was password protected. I needed to read her notebook. The pink one that she always had on her and where she wrote all her notes. Maybe I'd been following the wrong trail. Perhaps her death stemmed from this new discovery and not from anything she'd said in the last episode.

I remembered Hannah's car, the beat-up silver Prius that was still in the parking lot. I heaved myself off the bed and changed into dry clothes. The clock on the nightstand read 6:05 p.m. I stared in shock at the number, having lost track of time.

Outside, a breeze whipped off the lake and hit my face, smelling faintly of dead fish. My eyes blinked, adjusting to the sunlight. Hannah's car sat three spaces down from mine. I moved toward it, checking the area to make sure no one was watching before I peered through the front window. A water bottle and a pair of sunglasses rested on the center console. My gaze traveled to the rear windows, finding a few reusable shopping bags lying on the backseat. Hannah's notebook wasn't in there.

My head was heavy, but I lifted my eyes toward the motel, toward the second floor. The blue door of Room 208 stared back at me. The notebook had to be in Hannah's room. Maybe it held some clues about her new discovery. Two doors down from Hannah's room, another door burst open, and I jumped. A man wearing a Hawaiian shirt and sunglasses stepped into the open-air walkway, whistling a happy tune and locking the door to Room 210. He rushed toward the metal stairs that ran down the side of the building. I focused on something behind me, pretending I was minding my own business.

There were too many people around now, but I could return for the notebook in the middle of the night. The locks were the flimsy, old-fashioned kind, not the digital key cards so many hotels used now. I wondered if I could pick it with a bobby pin like I'd seen people do in the movies, but quickly conceded I had no idea how to do that. I thought back to my painfully slow check-in, remembering the lump of a man working in the motel's office, the one with a "Manager" pin on his shirt. A new plan took form.

I combed my fingers through my hair and smoothed down my clothing, hoping I didn't look too unkempt and that my eyes weren't red and puffy. Then I headed to the office, finding the same man slumped behind the counter, reading a sci-fi book.

"Hi, sir. I checked in earlier today. Room 108."

The manager's eyes flickered up, barely acknowledging me.

I edged closer, tasting the salty sweat on my upper lip. "There's a young man lurking near the side of the building, over by the beach. He's blocking the path to the beach and making a lot of the guests feel uncomfortable. I thought you might want to know."

The manager sighed and set down his book. "What a day." He heaved himself up. "I'll go check it out."

"Thank you." I began to follow him outside, pointing in the direction of the made-up culprit. As the man hobbled down the path, I ducked back inside the office. More sweat erupted through my pores as I slunk behind the counter, hoping he didn't return soon and that no one else entered. A cupboard was built into the back of the desk with an open padlock hanging from a metal fixture on the door. He had left it unlocked. I opened the small door, finding six rows of keys in front of me. Each hook was labeled with a room number, and some of the hooks were empty, but 208 held a single key. The manager must have only given Hannah one key, just as he had with me. Or maybe the police had found this one in Hannah's beach bag and returned it. I didn't have time to think about it. My clammy hand swiped the key, tucking it into my pocket.

"The ice machine is around back." The manager spoke to someone just outside the door.

I skittered around to the other side of the counter as he entered, tripping over my feet.

He eyed me suspiciously. "I thought you were coming with me."

"Oh. Sorry." I looked away from him. "I didn't want him to know I was the one who ratted him out."

"There was no one there."

"Really? That's funny." I touched the back of my neck, slick with perspiration. "He was just there."

"Well, he's gone now. Problem solved." The manager picked up his book and sat on his stool.

"Thanks for checking." I hurried out the door, grateful that he hadn't detected my dishonesty. Or, if he had, he didn't seem to care. When I reached my room, I fumbled for my own key, breathing a sigh of relief as I closed myself inside. Tonight, when it was dark and everyone was asleep, I would let myself into Hannah's room and read her notebook.

I passed the hours by talking to people. First, Ruthie, who had been at her friend Isabelle's birthday party all afternoon. She sounded happy and was getting ready to watch a movie with Shane, so I didn't mention Hannah's death. When she asked how I was, I only told her I'd had a long day, and I couldn't wait to see her again.

As I ended the call with Ruthie, a text came through from Gabe:

I just heard about Hannah. Are you doing okay?

I read it twice, but questions about his past loomed in my mind, preventing me from responding right away.

A call from Lacey interrupted my thoughts, and I answered it.

"Oh my gosh, Brooke. Did you hear about Hannah?"

"Yeah," I said. "I watched them load her body into the ambulance. It was horrible."

"I can't believe it. She was at the library yesterday." Lacey paused. "I mean, we had our differences, but she was just starting to grow on me."

I coughed out a laugh because I knew what Lacey meant. "Yeah. Me, too. And her poor family."

"It's so shocking."

I picked at my nail, debating whether to ask the next question. "Do you think someone could have been so mad about Hannah's podcast that they killed her?"

"What?" Lacey huffed out a puff of air. "Hannah raised a lot of baseless theories, but I can't imagine someone would kill her for that. People die swimming in that lake almost every year. That's one of the reasons I never go in the water, at least not past my knees. Liz tells me harrowing stories from her lifeguarding days whenever I get my hair cut. People don't realize how far out they've gone, and then they can't get back. I'm actually surprised there aren't more fatalities out there."

"Yeah." I pressed my fingertips into my temples, remembering a similar explanation from the police chief and the paramedics and wondering how paranoid I'd become. "You're probably right."

"Do Gabe and Dan know?" she asked.

The mention of their names unleashed a flurry of doubts. "Yeah. They know." I blinked away the vision of Dan hiding behind the tree. Then I sat up in bed, steadying myself against the pillow I'd propped in the small of my back. "Did you know that Gabe is Willa's nephew?"

"What?"

"Zoe told me today. Gabe's dad used to own the putt-putt golf course way back when we were kids, or even before that."

"No way. Why didn't he ever mention that?"

"I don't know."

"That's a big piece of information to leave out. You should ask him about it."

I agreed with her. Then Lacey invited me to join her and Maeve at another concert in the park tonight or drive with them to an art fair in Saugatuck tomorrow, but I declined both invitations. Hannah's unexpected death occupied all my thoughts, framing everything around me in suspicion and paranoia. There was no room for anything else. I only hoped the notebook in Hannah's motel room held some answers.

It was going to be a late night.

FORTY

THEN

Prom Night 2003

A song by Fifty Cent echoed through the hallways as I hovered near the drinking fountain, watching Bailey, Mikayla, Liz, and Zoe exit the restroom. I'd been stunned—literally frozen in place—by Bailey's reaction to me warning her about her fake friends. I turned my back to them as they rushed past, squealing about the bonfire planned for after the dance. Once they'd cleared out, I returned to the gym and found a spot against the wall, where I watched Dan and Lacey dance in a circle with a larger group of people.

The DJ stepped forward as the song came to an end. "Alright, class of 2003! This is your prom night!" he said in his overly animated voice. A smattering of cheers sounded across the gym. "I said, this is your prom night!" the DJ yelled again, drawing louder cheers and applause from the students.

Dan and Lacey joined me on the perimeter, making faces at each other at the DJ's over-the-top antics.

The DJ continued speaking into the microphone. "At the

request of Principal Lawson, I would like to take a moment to
thank the prom committee, headed up by Zoe Johansson and
Liz Rhemy." Zoe and Liz waved to him from the edge of the
dance floor. "Zoe and her team have worked so hard to trans-
form this gymnasium into a magical rainforest. They have
provided excellent food and drinks, and of course, they hired
the best DJ money can buy." He paused, waiting for laughter.
"Let's give your prom committee a big round of applause."
Everyone clapped. "And now, the time has come to announce
the king and queen of the prom. As you know, they will also
have the honor of riding in the Harvest Festival Parade next
month."

A few people squealed in anticipation. At the edge of the
dance floor, Zoe grabbed Mikayla's arm, her face stretching in
fake excitement. Trevor winked at Mikayla, preparing to see his
girlfriend walk to the front and receive her crown.

"Can I get a drumroll, please?" The DJ grinned and pressed
a button that sounded like drums. Liz approached him, walking
awkwardly in her heels and handing him a white envelope,
which he opened. "The 2003 prom queen of Cove Haven High
School is..."

Mikayla straightened her shoulders, already taking a step
forward.

"Bailey Maddox! Congratulations, Bailey."

A collective gasp sucked the air out of the room. But the
stretch of silence was quickly shattered by cheers. "Yeah,
Bailey!" someone yelled as others whistled.

Bailey looked around, confused. She touched her chest,
shoulders falling forward as if to ask, "Is it really me?" Spike
stood next to her, clapping and pointing her toward the front.
The cheers grew louder as Bailey took her first step forward, a
pink blush creeping up her neck and into her face. She reached
the DJ, who lifted a sparkling tiara from a box and held it high,

dramatically placing it on Bailey's head as if coronating the next Queen of England. Bailey covered her mouth with her hands as the crowd went wild at the unexpected turn of events. I forced myself to clap, even as a cold dread spread through me.

Jenna, the prom photographer, crouched low and snapped several photos of a happily stunned Bailey touching her jeweled tiara.

A few feet away, Mikayla stood rigid, hands on her hips. Trevor attempted to hug her, but she shoved him away. When she turned toward me, her eyes had hardened into stones, and her bottom lip quivered with rage. I saw Zoe and Liz watching Mikayla too. And when they thought no one was looking, they smirked at each other.

The DJ pinched the white card between his fingers. "And we can't have a prom queen without a prom king. So, without further delay, I'm pleased to announce that this year's Cove Haven High School prom king is... Trevor Baker!"

More cheers and whistling filled the gym as Trevor lumbered forward, waving to the crowd with an easy smile, and obviously much more comfortable than Bailey in his role as the winner. The DJ placed a second crown on Trevor's head.

The DJ motioned toward a trembling Bailey and a grinning Trevor. "Your prom king and queen, ladies and gentlemen."

Trevor grabbed Bailey's hand. Then he pulled her to him as if to peck her on the cheek, but his lips landed on her mouth instead. Hoots and hollers erupted. Bailey laughed it off as her cheeks grew redder. Trevor looped his arm around Bailey, and she leaned into him.

Mikayla pinned her arms to her sides, sneering. Spike also watched from nearby, shaking his head at the public display of affection. He turned on his heel and strode past me and into the hallway with the look of a dog who'd been kicked one too many times. A tearing sound caused me to peek around the corner, where I found him ripping streamers from the walls. Next, he grabbed a strand of fairy lights and yanked it to the floor, stomping on the tiny lightbulbs. Then he stormed to the end of the hallway and out the double doors.

"And now the royal dance," the DJ said, drawing my attention back to the dance. He cued up the song, "A Moment Like This" by Kelly Clarkson.

"I hate this song," I whispered to Dan and Lacey, who laughed.

But like everyone else in the room, I couldn't pull my eyes from Bailey and Trevor dancing in the middle of the floor as the photographer snapped away. Even Mikayla looked on with a murderous glare as the royal couple swayed back and forth. About thirty seconds into the song, Trevor leaned his face close to Bailey's and whispered something in her ear. She shook her head but kept dancing. Her eyes glistened with tears, and I knew she thought she'd won, that her ditching me for the popular crowd had been worth it for this moment.

The song ended, and everyone clapped again as Trevor and Bailey took a bow. The DJ said something about the party not being over yet and played a song with a techno beat.

A half-dozen girls clamored around Bailey, congratulating her. Mikayla's lower lip protruded as she watched the commotion. Trevor approached her, but she batted him away, then hurried from the gym.

"Wait, Mikayla. Just wait!" Trevor pleaded as he followed her toward the hallway. "What about the bonfire?"

"We're not going!" her voice shrieked from outside.

Lacey shook her head.

"This is too much drama for one night," Dan said.

"Yeah. You guys want to go to Joe's?" I asked.

Nothing more was needed to convince them. Dan, Lacey, and I hadn't been invited to the bonfire behind the train station and probably wouldn't have gone even if we had. The three of us left as a group, walking through the darkened streets in our nice clothes. As we reached the bright lights of the diner, I wondered how much longer it would be before Bailey's storybook ending was shattered, how much longer before she collided with the cold, hard truth.

FORTY-ONE

NOW

By 2 a.m., the occasional noises outside faded into the night. I'd heard no voices or conversation since a group of teens staying a few rooms away had returned about a half hour earlier from what I imagined was a drunken party on the beach. I sidled next to the motel window, looking for any signs of life. There were none. I zipped up my navy hoodie, pulling the hood over my head to disguise my hair. My fingers opened slightly, revealing the key to Hannah's room. I'd been squeezing it so hard that it had left a mark on my palm. Tucking my phone into my pocket, I slipped from my silent room and tiptoed past several more blackened windows, climbing the stairs to the second floor. When I reached Hannah's room, I pulled in a long breath, relieved to see her curtains were closed. I slipped the key into the lock, half expecting an alarm to sound. But only the dank scent of damp clothes filled my mouth as I stepped inside, shutting the door gently behind me.

I turned on my phone's flashlight, scanning the walls and ignoring the way my muscles twitched. Hannah had left her space relatively neat, considering she'd been living here for over two weeks. A canvas laundry bag sat near the wall next to her suitcase. The bed was roughly made, with the outfit she'd planned to put on this morning still laid out. The pair of beaded sandals she always wore sat near the door. I gulped back my sorrow, telling myself to find the notebook and get out of this room before I got caught.

My eyes followed the weak circle of light as it wandered around the room. The beam landed on Hannah's laptop case, which sat on a chair near the tiny table in the corner. I rushed toward it, unzipping the bag. The first pocket held Hannah's slim black laptop and some cords. As I unzipped the second pocket, a flash of pink caught my eye. A strange combination of excitement and dread prickled through me as I grasped the notebook and perched on the nearby chair, angling my phone on the table to cast light toward me. I flipped through the pages, unable to control the trembling in my fingers.

The first few pages detailed information Hannah had discovered from her research at the library and some of the information she'd gotten from me after my conversations with Jonathan and Trevor. There were two pages about Mr. Sampson, which now had Xs through them. She'd written a whole page explaining why she didn't believe either Zoe or Liz had been responsible for Bailey's death. According to the police file, the two pranksters had gone back to Zoe's house together immediately after the bonfire, where Zoe's younger brother and his friend were watching TV in the living room. The girls made popcorn and burned it. They watched a zombie apocalypse movie together. Zoe's mother confirmed the night's events. *Five people aren't lying*, Hannah wrote. *Zoe and Liz weren't on the bridge when Bailey died.*

Hannah had titled the following page:

People with Weak Alibis:

1. *Trevor*

2. *Spike*
3. *Mikayla*
4. *Brooke*
5. *Lacey*
6. *Dan*

Their alibis came from one or both parents. What parent wouldn't lie for their child? One of them could have been the person who met Bailey.

The next page said:

Was Dan Bailey's secret lover? Why did he have Bailey's necklace?

I pulled my eyes from the page. After talking to Henry, I was confident Hannah had gotten the secret lover theory wrong. Dan had hated Bailey. It was still strange that her necklace came from Dan's lost-and-found bin. Love and hate were equally strong emotions, and I couldn't help wondering which one was a more powerful motivator for murder.

I flipped the page again, immediately wishing I hadn't. Hannah's next line pointed at me like an accusatory finger.

BROOKE IS HIDING SOMETHING! Find out what it is.

I exhaled when I saw that nothing was written underneath. Maybe this was when she'd called up the museum and searched old blog posts written by former art school students. I hoped my history of angry outbursts was all she found.

I turned the page again, rethinking my plan to leave the notebook. Maybe I should take it. Burn it.

I forced myself to look at another page, and my eyes popped when I read it.

Justin Warner = Bailey's secret lover

It makes sense! This is why Bailey couldn't tell anyone about her boyfriend. He was a police officer. Skimpy investigation into Bailey's death because HE killed her!

Someone else must know about the secret relationship!!!

I reread the lines several times, trying to process the information. This must have been the big development Hannah wanted to share with me. My thoughts tumbled back in time to the night a young Officer Warner escorted an intoxicated Bailey up to her parents' front door, then skipped ahead to when he stopped us on the way to school, giving us each his card. Had Bailey called him? Met with him? Was he the "friend" she'd been messing around with the night I returned home late from the poetry reading? Was he the reason she'd stuck around in the rain after the bonfire? The scenario had never occurred to me before.

A motor rumbled outside, bright lights shining through a crack in the curtains. My heart pounded as I crouched down, covering the light on my phone. What if Hannah's family had just arrived? They would find me lurking here like a burglar. I wondered if I could go to jail. The urge to run overtook me, but my knees were locked into place. Just as panic and desperation took over, and I resigned myself to a life behind bars, the same headlights passed again, and the sound of the motor disappeared down the road. The car had only been turning around.

I focused on my breathing and flipped to the next page, finding it empty. All the pages after it were also blank. The entry about Justin Warner had been Hannah's last one.

The surprise of the car headlights confirmed I'd been in the room too long. I debated swiping the notebook so no one would ever see the damning things she'd written about me. Then again, she'd written similar things about everyone else, some of them much worse. And the police had already checked the room, taken a few photos. I wasn't sure if they'd done a more detailed inventory, but I decided to play it safe. Gritting my teeth, I zipped the notebook back into the pocket of her bag.

I slunk toward the door, pausing at the sight of the outfit lying on the bed. "You did good work, Hannah," I whispered, and I hoped, somehow, she could hear me. Gripping my phone and the keys, I crept outside as I locked the door and scurried down the stairs. I kept my head down as I approached my room.

A gust of wind blew, and a slight movement in my peripheral vision caused my head to turn. My car was parked there, two spaces down from Room 108 and three spots from Hannah's car. I peered through the shadows toward my vehicle, my skin tightening around my bones. In the light of the moon, another white note pinned under the windshield wiper fluttered in the wind.

FORTY-TWO

NOW

I slunk deeper into my hood, the blackened landscape of the motel parking lot surrounding me. I had the sensation of sinking to the bottom of a cold and murky lake, unable to breathe. My stalker had left another note on my car. I didn't know if it had been there all along or if someone in the vehicle that just pulled into the parking lot had pinned it to my windshield. I forced myself toward the unwelcome object. My fingers trembled as I plucked the paper from behind the wipers, slowly opening it.

SOME PEOPLE DESERVE TO DIE.

The words sucked the air from my body, confirming that Hannah hadn't drowned in an accident. That Bailey hadn't died by suicide either. And again, I suspected that the same person was responsible for both deaths. It seemed more than likely that I was next on their list.

Fear sped through me as I crumpled the note, squeezing it in my palm. I pictured Ruthie's smile, her chubby cheeks, and the way she always braided her hair slightly off-center. I thought of how hyper she got before soccer games and how her eyes lit up whenever she saw a butterfly. I needed to get back to her and be the mom she deserved, to let her know it was okay to make mistakes like the ones I'd made in the past. People could learn from their bad decisions and grow from them. That's what I'd tried to do for so many years. But coming back to Cove Haven had churned up too much painful history. I couldn't escape the cyclone of past mistakes that followed me here.

I rushed toward my motel room, frantic to get inside. The key fell from my hand, and I bent to pick it up, struggling to control my shaking body. The lighting was dim, and there were too many hiding places. Someone could emerge from the shadows at any moment and grab me from behind. Would they make my death look like an accident too? I straightened up, scolding myself for freaking out. I focused on the lock and the key, and at last, the key slid into the hole. I lunged toward the safety of my room, turning the lock behind me, and sinking to the floor.

I was scared and confused, and it wasn't clear what my next move should be. I couldn't trust anyone, not even the police chief. Dan wasn't speaking to me. Both he and Gabe had probably lied to me. Spike and Trevor both had strong motives to shut Hannah up. Mikayla was a wild card. I could confide in Lacey or Zoe, but both had family in town. I barely knew Liz, and she'd made it clear she didn't want to be friends. Any of them could be responsible.

Slowly, I rose to my feet, checking all the corners of my motel room, peeking in the closet and behind the shower curtain to make sure no intruders were lurking. Satisfied that I was alone, I kicked off my shoes, climbed into bed, and forced my eyes shut. It had been such a long and horrendous day. Paranoia had consumed me, tangling my thoughts. I would try to get some sleep and figure out my next move in the morning.

Things felt less scary with the morning light filtering through the flimsy curtains, although the crumpled note still sat where I'd left it on my bedside table, confirming the events of the night before had actually happened. As I showered and brushed my teeth, I recalled the last words in Hannah's notebook, hoping for a moment of clarity. Was it really possible that Justin Warner and Bailey had been seeing each other? It was a lot to process, and I reminded myself that Hannah's theories had been wrong before. She'd caused me to suspect everyone at one point or another and the constant scrutiny was exhausting. A craving for a cup of coffee rumbled through me, and I realized I wanted nothing more than to stop by Drips and have an honest conversation with Gabe.

I headed into the sunlight, deciding it was time to confront him. My car sparkled against the asphalt as I walked past it toward Drips, and I was relieved to see no additional notes stuck to the windows. I continued along the waterfront, looking over my shoulder and refusing to let the steady rise and fall of the waves lull me into a false sense of security. I arrived at the coffee shop ten minutes later, convinced no one had followed me. It had only been a little over a day since I'd seen Gabe, but so much had happened. It felt like a year had passed.

Gabe handed a drink to a woman at the counter, wishing her a good day. His eyes sagged when he looked up. "Hey, Brooke." He lowered his head and shook it. "I can't believe the news about Hannah."

"I know. I'm sorry I didn't respond to your text yesterday. I was in shock."

"No worries. I just wanted to make sure you were okay."

"Yeah. I'm still processing everything."

He motioned behind him. "Can I get you something?"

"Yes. Coffee. Black. And a blueberry muffin, please." My

stomach twisted and I realized I hadn't eaten any real food in almost twenty-four hours. Gabe handed me the coffee and muffin. I noticed the other barista making an espresso drink. "Do you have a minute to talk? Privately?"

"Oh." Gabe looked around at the café, which was only mildly busy compared to the day before. "Sure. Let's grab a table."

We sat near the window. I pushed my coffee to the side and leaned back, prepared to rip off the Band-Aid. "I ran into Zoe at the parade yesterday. She said that Willa is your aunt and that your dad used to own the putt-putt golf course. That was him in the photo I pointed out."

Gabe dropped his head. "Shit. I'm sorry."

"So, it's true?"

Gabe pressed his lips together, glancing toward the door, then back to me, and looking like he'd been caught with his hand in the cookie jar. "Yeah. Crazy old Willa the witch is my aunt. My dad died when I was very young. I don't really remember him."

"But you told me you came here on a whim five years ago and never left."

"That wasn't exactly the truth. I'm sorry." He pinched the bridge of his nose between two fingers, then flattened his hands on the table. "I did come here for the first time five years ago, but it wasn't on a whim. I was searching for a connection to my dad, who I never knew." He stared out the window. "It was so hard growing up without a father. I was desperate to learn anything about my dad, but my mom wouldn't talk about him. My mom married a guy who was a total jerk about six or seven years ago. I refused to go to the wedding, so I came up to Cove Haven to visit my aunt instead." Gabe motioned toward the wall. "That's when I found this prime space for sale, already remodeled and ready to go. I'd been the manager of a coffee shop in Indianapolis, so it wasn't too big of a leap to quit that job and move here to start a new business. Dad was already long gone by then, of course, but I thought living in the same town where he'd lived would somehow help me feel closer to him." A sad smile pulled at his lips. "It's stupid, I know."

"No. It's not," I said, noticing the watery sheen in Gabe's eyes.

"I'm not anything like my aunt. I mean, I love her, but she has some issues. I know how people in small towns are sometimes. They would have a preconceived idea of me if they knew of our relationship. So, I made a decision to keep it quiet. Once I told the first lie about how I ended up here on a whim, it was hard not to keep it going."

I cupped my hands around the warm drink. "Oh."

"I'm sorry I lied to you. I should have told you when you saw the photo at the golf place, but, like I said, I'd already lied about other things by then."

His face looked haggard, and I felt bad for judging him so harshly. "It's okay. And I won't tell anyone if you don't want me to."

"You don't have to lie, but there's no need to bring it up in conversation." He winked, and I felt mostly at ease again. I could see how Gabe's little white lie to distance himself from Willa and protect his reputation had trapped him. Now he'd told me the painful truth about never having known his dad and he seemed genuinely sorry for misleading me. I couldn't ask for much more. I was about to confide in him about the threatening note I'd received and my suspicions about Hannah's death, but Gabe pushed back his chair, eyeing a line that had formed in front of the counter. "I better get back to work. The parade crowd hasn't left town yet."

I nodded as he left, then I devoured the muffin and finished the coffee. The writing in Hannah's journal continued to scrawl through my mind. *Justin Warner = Bailey's secret lover*

Could it be true? I was tired of throwing around theories

like wild splatters of paint, seeing where they landed, and merely hoping they'd form a coherent picture. It was better to be clear and upfront with people and see how they responded, as I'd just discovered by talking with Gabe. So I left the café and headed to the police station to speak to Justin Warner.

FORTY-THREE

NOW

The police station sat on the other side of town, and like most of Cove Haven, it was walkable. I hiked past the shops and restaurants and toward the outskirts, past the fire station and an abandoned factory, finally landing on the red-brick building. The doors were unlocked, and the same receptionist I'd met a couple of weeks before sat at the front desk, her cropped gray hair cut shorter than last time. I couldn't help wondering if Liz cut her hair too.

"Hi." I motioned to myself. "It's Brooke Webber. I'm looking for the police chief."

The smile faded from the woman's face. She sucked her lips into her mouth and shook her head. "He's not working today. It's Sunday. I can radio someone on duty to meet you here in a few minutes."

"Can you ask Justin Warner to meet me here? I don't mind waiting."

"I'm not going to do that. He had a hell of a day yesterday with the parade and then the drowning. The poor guy was here until nearly midnight. He needs a day off." She tapped the end of her pen on the desk, puffing out her chest. "I'm happy to leave a message for him. Or, if it's something urgent, I can call someone else to meet you."

I could see the woman wasn't budging. "There's no need. Thanks for your help." Luckily, Dan and Maggie had pointed out the police chief's house on one of our after-dinner walks around town. I slipped out the door, still set on my mission.

About fifteen minutes had passed, and the soles of my feet ached, as I approached a white colonial on a small but well-kept lot. A shadow passed behind a window as I rang the doorbell, and a moment later, a boy of about fourteen opened the door, sharing his dad's oval face and hazel eyes.

"Hello?" he said.

"Hi. Sorry to bother you on a Sunday morning. I'm Brooke Webber. Is your dad home?"

"Just a second." The boy looked toward a kitchen further back just as Justin stepped down the stairs dressed in plaid flannel pants and a T-shirt. He froze, doing a double take at me.

"Who's there, honey?" a woman's voice yelled from upstairs.

"No one. I got it," Justin called over his shoulder. He waved his son away and stepped outside, aiming a cold stare in my direction and closing the door behind him rather than inviting me in. "Brooke. What brings you to my house on a Sunday morning?"

I looked at my hands, suddenly second-guessing my decision to come here to confront a middle-aged police chief in his pajamas. But there was no turning back. "Hannah discovered something before she died. Something explosive about Bailey. That must be why someone killed her."

Justin placed his fingers on his forehead, chuckling in disbelief. "Hannah drowned, Brooke. There's no reason to think otherwise. She wasn't the first person to swim too far out from that beach, as I told you yesterday."

I gritted my teeth, shaking my head. "No. This death wasn't

an accident. Hannah figured out that Bailey was your girlfriend. She was going to talk about it on her podcast."

His smile faded, arms falling to his sides.

I could tell I'd hit a nerve, so I continued. "I remember that day my senior year when you stopped us on the way to school and gave us your card. Bailey called you, didn't she? You guys must have hit it off."

His glare tightened on me. "Stop it. You don't know what you're saying."

"Bailey was young for our grade, still only seventeen until August. She couldn't tell anyone about you because if things had gotten serious between the two of you—if you'd had sex—you'd be charged with statutory rape. You'd lose your job at a minimum."

"No." His nostrils flared.

"You're the person she stuck around to meet after the bonfire. It all makes sense. There was virtually no investigation done into her death before you and your colleagues decided it was a suicide. The state police never even got involved." I felt something gripping my arm and found Justin's hand there, squeezing.

"You need to stop talking. Now." His eyes were wild as he glanced toward the house, then back to me. "You got it wrong. I'll tell you what you want to know, but not here with my wife and kids two steps away."

"Where? When?"

"Meet me at midnight behind the train station. There won't be anyone there."

"Why midnight?"

"Because I don't want anyone to see us. I'll tell my family I got called in for work."

I took a second to process the meeting place and time, which seemed strange. But at least he was willing to talk.

"Okay." I shook my arm away from his grip, but the intensity of his stare held me in place.

"And don't speak a word of this to anyone. Do you understand?"

I nodded, but a frightening sensation rattled through me. "I'll meet you at midnight."

At 11:55 p.m., my car eased to a stop in front of the train station. Under the moonlight, the outline of the old stone building resembled a haunted castle. I closed my eyes and pressed my back against the seat, wondering if I'd gone mad. Why had I agreed to meet a man I barely knew in this remote location in the middle of the night? I was like one of those dumb teenagers in horror movies who finds two of her friends murdered in the living room and decides to check on a strange noise in the basement. What if Justin Warner was the person who killed Bailey and Hannah? I may have set myself up to become his next victim, and no one would ever know. I pulled out my phone and considered texting someone. Ruthie? No. I didn't want to alarm her. I couldn't tell anyone in Cove Haven where I was because I still didn't know who to trust. And if Justin found out I didn't keep my word, he might not talk. I clicked off my phone and hid it in my pocket.

Peering through the car window, I searched the shadowy surroundings, reminding myself not to jump to conclusions. There was something the police chief wanted to tell me. Perhaps I'd only uncovered a sliver of the truth and not the whole picture. And if he required us to meet here to tell me, the truth must be something dangerous. I exited the car, confirming that no one else was around. Further down the street, only a dim light glowed from behind a curtained window in Willa's house. No police cruisers sat nearby, and I guessed Justin was walking from somewhere to meet me.

I crouched low and pushed my feet forward, navigating through the night. Beyond the stone building and a line of trees, crickets buzzed. An owl hooted. I approached the train station, ducking behind the sign for Harsons Real Estate Group for a moment to get my bearings. A muffled cough echoed from the other side of a building. Justin was already here. I edged toward the noise, praying I wouldn't find him waiting for me with a butcher knife and a roll of duct tape. As I rounded the corner, I made out his silhouette.

"Over here." He waved me forward.

Although it was difficult to see, he appeared to be empty-handed, so I moved closer. The badge on his police uniform glinted in the dim light, and I imagined he'd worn it to go along with whatever story he'd told his wife.

"I'm going to talk to you only to stop you from heading down a dangerous road." He was mere inches from me. So close, I could feel his warm breath.

"Okay."

He blinked, the whites of his eyes glowing. "What you said earlier about Bailey and me. You were right." He paused, his chest filling with air before he released a long breath. "We'd been seeing each other for a couple of months back in 2003, and we both kept it a secret."

A scandalous picture revealed itself as a sense of paralysis overtook me, my thoughts swirling. Hannah had been correct. How had I missed it?

The police chief shook his head. "We never had sex, but we messed around from time to time. Of course, there was no way to prove the truth if someone ever accused me. And in any case, a police officer dating a high school student wouldn't have sat well with anyone, including my boss at the time." He glanced toward the night sky, wispy dark clouds shape-shifting across the moon. "Bailey's parents would never have allowed her to see me, so she was happy to keep it quiet too."

I nodded, knowing he was right about her parents. They were completely absent in some areas of her life, but when it came to dating, Mr. Maddox had been strict.

I cleared my throat, finding my voice. "Are you the person she stayed to meet after the bonfire?"

"Yes. And no." He dropped his head, covering his eyes. Then he started over. "We had planned a secret date after the prom to have our own private dance beneath the stars. I was supposed to show up around eleven thirty and break up the bonfire. Bailey said she'd hang back and tell the others her mom was picking her up. When everyone was gone, I would come back again. I was on a routine patrol that night, which usually meant driving the streets and doing nothing. Ninety-nine times out of a hundred, it wouldn't have been a problem for me to skip out early and hang out with her. But that night, I got called to a domestic disturbance out on Route 16 just as the rain started pouring down. The call came right before I was supposed to show up at the bonfire. I had a cell phone back then, but she didn't. I had no way to reach her to tell her my plans had changed."

"So, she was waiting for you, but you weren't there."

"I arrived twenty minutes after our meeting time, not really expecting Bailey to be there because of the rain. I hoped she'd gone somewhere to stay dry. Still, I grabbed my flashlight and walked toward the tracks. That's when I heard sirens in the distance." He covered his eyes. "I was already too late. I couldn't believe what I saw. Pieces of her dress. Her hair. Her foot was —" He bit his lip, unable to go on. He drew in a long breath to compose himself. "The sirens kept getting louder, and I realized someone—the train conductor—had already reported the accident. When my chief arrived, he assumed I'd been in the area and was first on the scene. But I hadn't known anything about it until I got there. My scanner must have picked it up when I was dealing with the other disturbance." He raised his eyes to meet mine. "I didn't kill Bailey. But if she thought I'd ditched her after everything else that happened, maybe I'm partly to blame for what she did." The sheriff sniffled, and I realized he was crying.

I found my balance, still processing his words. It was a story I'd never imagined. I heard the hitch in his voice as he spoke, watched his face crumple with guilt. His emotion seemed real. I touched his arm, suddenly feeling terrible for forcing him to expose the pain he'd kept tucked away for so long. "We all could have done things differently back then. You're not to blame."

A twig cracked under his foot as he squared his shoulders at me, taking a few deep breaths in an effort to regain his composure. "Now you know the truth about me and Bailey, but you can't speak a word of it to anyone else. I'm someone people in this town look up to. I've spent years working my way up the ladder. The last thing I need is you spreading a rumor that I dated Bailey, much less that I killed her. People are quick to condemn someone in my role. My entire livelihood is at risk."

I squeezed my hands together, looking toward the bridge, the path beneath, and the surrounding woods. "I won't say anything."

The police chief and I stood shoulder-to-shoulder in the darkness, and I was unsure what to do next.

More questions swarmed my mind, and I finally broke the charged silence. "And the night Bailey died, you didn't see anyone else there?"

He rubbed his jaw, taking an uncomfortably long time to answer. "Yeah."

"Yeah, you did see someone else?"

"No. I mean, no. No one else was around."

I steadied my feet. "Are you sure?"

"Yes."

"Why did you hesitate? It was a simple yes or no question."

He released a dry chuckle. "Because I'm stressed out. I don't like being secretive like this. Lying to my wife, all that."

I wanted to believe him, but something about his answer felt incomplete. "Is there anything else at all you remember when you first found Bailey? Maybe a distant voice? Or a noise in the woods?"

"I remember a movement in the woods that scared the daylight out of me. But when I looked closer, it was only a couple of deer running away."

"Oh."

His eyes looked black as he held my gaze. "My relationship with Bailey doesn't change anything. Bailey was depressed. We both knew it then, and we both know it now. She told me two days before she jumped that sometimes she wished she was dead, that things would be easier that way. She dreaded a future working at the car dealership. Then those girls made her think she won prom queen. It must have all been too much when she found out it was a prank. I can only imagine how humiliated she was. And then I didn't show up for her. Bailey jumped just like Jasper jumped the year before."

I held a gulp of air in my lungs, squeezing my eyelids closed. This couldn't be the answer I'd been waiting for. "Did you take Bailey's necklace?"

"What?" He cocked his head, surprised by the question. "No. I was too traumatized by the scene. I couldn't get anywhere close to her."

"Maybe there was someone in the woods. The person who scared the deer."

Justin placed his hands on his head and sighed. "No. I don't think so. I shouldn't have even mentioned it."

I edged closer to him. "Someone is still leaving threatening notes for me. I've gotten more since I came in to see you. The same person who took Bailey's necklace. The same person who killed Hannah. Please."

Justin frowned. "Bailey killed herself. Hannah drowned. You probably have an enemy or two left over from high school. Mikayla, if I had to guess. You'll be back with your daughter in Ferndale soon enough, and you can leave all this behind."

"But—"

"I've said everything I have to say. And I'll do whatever it takes to ensure that it stays between us."

I froze in place.

"Remember, Brooke, I can make things worse for you." He paused, letting the words sink in. "I saw that YouTube video of you attacking the woman at the museum. I'm not above making a phone call to your director and fanning the flames from your past. That's a threat."

I rocked back on my heels, unable to respond.

He motioned toward the street. "Good night, Brooke. This meeting is over. I'll wait here until you're safely inside your car."

Stunned, I turned away from him and stumbled to my car, aware that I'd pushed my interrogation as far as it would go. I'd uncovered one more piece of the puzzle, but I felt no closer to the truth. Bits of our conversation swirled through my head as I fumbled for my keys. Justin had acted recklessly back when he was a young officer, dating a seventeen-year-old high school student. He'd lied about his plans to meet Bailey by the train tracks the night she died. What else had he lied about? Or covered up? No matter how he spun it, he was the reason Bailey's death was never properly investigated. I didn't owe him anything. An urge to report him to his superiors pulsed through me, but I couldn't risk losing my job. I had a daughter to think about and a mortgage to pay. And if Justin Warner wasn't the one who killed Bailey or Hannah, as he claimed, then I needed to keep him on my side.

FORTY-FOUR

THEN

Prom Night 2003

I slurped the final sip of my chocolate shake through the straw as Lacey plucked the last onion ring from the plate between us, the harsh overhead lights of Joe's Diner shining down.

Dan pushed an empty plate away from him. "Well, ladies. This has been my favorite part of prom."

Lacey and I nodded in agreement. We'd been sitting in the booth for over an hour, reliving the most memorable parts of our prom night, from the ridiculously frilly sleeves on Mikayla's red dress to Benjamin Logan's bad dance moves. My side ached from a combination of having eaten too much greasy food and laughing too hard at Dan's imitations. Still, images of Bailey's shocked smile kept popping into my mind. She'd been so happy. But had she learned the truth yet?

"I still can't believe Bailey is the prom queen." Dan shook his head, grinning. "I wonder what Mikayla will do to her."

We sat in silence for a second as I imagined a vengeful Mikayla slashing the tires of Bailey's car in the middle of the night. I could see from the somber looks on Dan and Lacey's faces that they were having similar thoughts.

"I have to tell you guys something." I lowered my voice, glancing toward two nearby tables and finding them empty. "I should have told you before, but I was hoping to talk some sense into Bailey first."

Lacey leaned closer. "What is it?"

"A few days ago, I overheard Liz and Zoe in the bathroom, saying they were going to write down Bailey's name as the prom queen, even though Mikayla got way more votes."

Lacey's eyes widened as she studied my face.

"Are you serious?" Dan angled himself away from me.

"Yes. Bailey didn't really win." I took in their stunned expressions. "I'm worried about how she'll feel when she learns the truth."

Dan wadded his napkin into a ball. "Man. That's messed up."

"I know. I tried to warn her at the dance, but she was so mean when I tried to bring it up."

"Maybe she'll never find out." A hopeful note lifted Lacey's voice.

I looked at the empty plates, remembering the exact words I'd overheard from my cramped position in the bathroom stall. "No. They said they'd tell her it was a prank at the bonfire. As if it wouldn't affect her."

Lacey gazed out the window at the red taillights of a car disappearing down Main Street. "So, she probably already knows the truth by now."

"Probably."

"That's rough," Dan said.

I placed my hands on the table, looking from Lacey to Dan. "I know she hasn't been a very good friend lately."

Dan raised his chin. "Ha. That's the understatement of the century."

"But I hope she's okay."

Dan slumped back. "Yeah."

"Me too," Lacey said. "We can check in on her tomorrow."

I stifled a yawn, the long day and night catching up with me. "Anyone else stuffed and exhausted?"

We decided it was time to go, pooling our cash on the table and exiting the diner. The clouds blacked out the moon and stars, and a drop of rain hit my arm. "Let's go. The rain is coming."

We hustled down the street, away from the lake and toward our houses. At the corner of Fourth and Cottage Street, Lacey headed left for the long walk toward her address, and Dan and I went straight. A few blocks later, Dan peeled off toward his house. I walked alone for the last three blocks. A light from Bailey's parents' bedroom lit a single window of the house next door, but Bailey's room was dark, along with the rest of her house. She hadn't returned home yet.

I climbed the front steps to my house and knocked. Mom opened the door almost as soon as my knuckles hit the surface, and it was clear she'd been waiting up for me.

"How was it?" she asked.

Rufus sniffed my legs as I told her the highlights and lowlights, including Bailey winning prom queen.

"Well, good for her," Mom said, her voice lacking even a hint of excitement. I couldn't help chuckling at her cold reaction. Dad had already gone to bed, so I hugged her good night and went up to my room, eager to pull off my scratchy dress and replace it with some comfortable sweatpants. A few minutes later, I heard the click of my parents' bedroom door closing across the hall. Derek was sleeping over at his friend's house and wasn't home.

I perched on the corner of my bed, wondering if Bailey was still at the bonfire. I hoped she'd learned the truth and that she was finally telling those girls off. But I knew Bailey too well, and it was more likely she was being stoic, smiling off the prank as if it was no big deal while her heart shattered. I'd made a mistake by not warning her, and now guilt swept through me. I needed to make it right. I waited a few minutes, then peeked into the darkened hallway. Slipping from my bedroom, I tiptoed down the stairs, pausing and checking over my shoulder with every step to make sure my parents didn't hear me. When I reached the first floor, I patted Rufus on the head and told him he was a good boy.

Then I sneaked out the front door to find Bailey.

FORTY-FIVE

NOW

I'd been so lost in my thoughts after leaving the secret midnight meeting with Justin Warner that I found myself sitting in my car in the Sandcastle Motel parking lot without having remembered driving there. As I cut the ignition, Justin's words cycled through my head yet again. He and Bailey had been seeing each other. Hannah's secret lover theory had been correct. The young officer was the reason Bailey had stayed in the pouring rain when everyone else had left. Justin claimed he hadn't taken the necklace, but I couldn't be sure if he was telling the truth. He'd hesitated a little too long when I asked him if he'd seen anyone else in the woods, his story about the deer ringing hollow. Even if a couple of deer had darted through the trees, as he'd described, something or someone may have startled them. Surely, he would have investigated the surrounding area for anyone lurking nearby.

I glanced toward the door to my motel room. A movement in the shadows caused the tiny hairs on the back of my neck to stand on end. I reminded myself to stay calm; this was a natural reaction for a single woman alone at night in a parking lot. Still, my muscles tensed as I peered through the windshield into the dimly lit surroundings. The figure moved toward my car, illuminated by the lights lining the motel walkway. A familiar face turned in my direction. I exhaled in relief. It was only Lacey, who clutched a bottle of red wine to her chest, her mouth stretched with worry.

I emerged from my car and waved toward her. "Lacey!"

"Oh, there you are. I was getting nervous when you didn't answer."

"What are you doing here?"

"I'm really sorry. I know it's late. Did you see my texts?"

I pulled out my phone, remembering how I'd turned it off before meeting with Justin. I powered it back on, finding several unread text messages from Lacey lighting up the screen.

Hi. Are you still up?

Maeve and I got into an argument, and she left.

I could use a friend. I'll bring wine ☺

I redirected my attention toward Lacey, again noticing the distress on her face. "Are you okay?" I ushered her inside my motel room, where the scent of stale cigarettes still hung in the air.

"Yeah. I'm so sorry to show up this late. When you didn't respond, I should have taken a clue."

"Not at all. I had my phone turned off by mistake." I motioned toward the bed, and Lacey sat down on the edge, looking uncomfortable. "I'm sorry about the smell in here." A sandalwood-scented candle I'd purchased at the dime store sat on the nightstand, and I moved it to the table by the window and lit it.

"It's fine," she said, crinkling her nose. "I also wanted to check in and make sure you were okay after Hannah's tragedy."

"That's nice of you."

Lacey glanced toward the window. "Where were you just now?"

"Oh. I was out driving around." I shrugged, forcing a smile, the police chief's bombshell confession still twitching through my nerves. Part of me wanted to spill everything to Lacey, but I couldn't. Justin had threatened my career. There was too much at risk. "I drive sometimes when I can't sleep."

Lacey nodded, but I wondered if she'd detected my lie. She handed me the bottle of wine and a corkscrew. "I brought an opener, but we need glasses."

I retrieved two clean water glasses from the bathroom and set them on the small table by the window. Lacey joined me, relocating from the bed to one of the two chairs pushed under the table as I opened the bottle and poured wine into each glass.

"Sorry to ask, but do you have anything to eat?" she asked. "I didn't eat dinner, and I meant to bring some chips, but I left them on the counter."

"I have crackers somewhere. Hold on." I crossed the room and rummaged through my suitcase for a minute, locating an unopened box of Club Crackers. I handed the box to Lacey, who tore it open as I took my seat across from her. The wine was a godsend. Exactly what I needed to unwind so that I could, hopefully, sleep tonight. I tipped back my glass, letting the first sip pool on my tongue. It tasted cheap, but Lacey had been nice to bring it over, so I told her it was good. "What's going on with you and Maeve?"

Lacey shut her eyes and sighed. "I don't know what's wrong with her. I spent so much time planning this long weekend, and she's so ungrateful. She acts like she can't stand to be around me, like every activity we do is the worst." Her voice quivered, and it was obvious the day's events had taken a toll on her.

"Well, the parade *was* pretty lame." I smiled, letting her know I was joking.

Lacey chuckled, despite herself. "Yeah. It never gets any better, does it?" She took a swig of wine, and I did the same.

"And Maeve didn't want to go to the concert either?" I asked.

"We went, but she pouted the whole time. I finally told her she was acting like a jerk. She started bringing up a bunch of stuff from our childhood, about how I'd wronged her and this and that. She sounded like a crazy person. When we got back to my place, she just took off. Didn't even tell me where she was going. Now she's not answering my calls."

"Wow. I'm sorry. Maeve looked so grown up when I saw you at the parade."

Lacey rolled her eyes. "Looks can be deceiving."

I swallowed another sip of wine and crunched into a cracker, realizing my stomach was empty too. Lacey continued talking about all the planning she'd put into her ungrateful sister's visit. Finally, she paused to retrieve another cracker. "I still can't believe Hannah is gone."

"I know. This might sound paranoid, but I can't help wondering if her death wasn't really an accident."

"You mentioned that." She made a face, lips twisting as if she was leery. "I'm not sure I can make that leap."

I leaned forward, the image of Dan hiding behind the tree yesterday flickering through me. "Hannah was a strong swimmer. Her podcast pissed off a lot of people."

Lacey's gaze bounced toward the window, then back to me. "It *is* kind of strange that people keep dying in this town."

"Yeah." I nodded, eager for her to see things my way, to have someone on my side.

"Not just Hannah. Bailey died here too. And Jasper." A shadow passed across Lacey's face at the mention of Jasper, and I set down my wine glass. Her skin had turned even paler than usual. "It's almost like this place is cursed," she added.

"It does seem that way, doesn't it?"

Lacey reached across the table and touched my hand. "I remember how mean Bailey was to you. It broke my heart. You were such a good friend to her, but she was horrible to you, to all of us, really."

"She was depressed, and she wasn't herself."

Lacey leaned so close that I worried the candle flame might ignite the ends of her hair. "I've been wanting to tell you something. It's something I should have told you a long time ago. Please forgive me for not telling you sooner."

"What is it?"

"I saw you on prom night after we left the diner. You must have gone home for a few minutes like I did, but then curiosity got the better of you. You went to the bonfire because you wanted to see the fallout after Bailey learned she wasn't really the prom queen." Lacey's eyes looked bigger than normal, the whites glittering with something dangerous. "I've kept your secret for all these years, Brooke. But the truth is, I was there too, hiding in the woods. I know what you did."

FORTY-SIX

THEN

Prom Night 2003

The rain intensified as I pulled my black hoodie over my head and scurried along the sidewalk with my flashlight off, trying to blend into the shadows. Bailey had most likely learned the truth by now; her prom queen title was merely a cruel joke. Surely, she'd finally see that those girls weren't her friends. I needed to find her and tell her that we could put the past few months behind us, no hard feelings. I was there for her no matter what. I hoped she was still at the bonfire.

My breath was jagged by the time I reached the train station, my sneakers squeaking with each soggy step. The rain pummeled my head as I rounded the stone building in a wide loop, flicking on the flashlight and taking refuge in the nearby woods. Through a gap in the trees, I could see the bonfire embers smoking in the rain, empty beer cans scattered around it. Bailey and her crew had already left.

"Crap." I dug my hands into my pockets, wondering where Bailey had gone. Maybe we'd crossed paths, and she was back at her house.

A shift at the edge of my vision drew my eyes toward the train tracks. In the distance, a dark smudge moped across the bridge. I hurried toward it, noticing the glint of a shiny object as I aimed my flashlight toward the person's head. She still wore the tiara. "Bailey," I said under my breath as I ran toward her. The rain let up again as I neared the bridge, but it was a temporary calm. I climbed the metal stairs, thankful she'd stopped moving and hoping no lightning would splinter the sky and strike us. "Bailey." This time I projected my voice. I followed the weak circle of light from my flashlight to Bailey's pale dress, a denim jacket covering her shoulders.

She stopped and turned toward me as confusion stretched over her face. "What are you doing here?" Her face looked thinner than usual with her wet hair plastered to her head. The rhinestones on her tiara had lost their sparkle, appearing dull and black in the night. The necklace I'd given her lay crooked on her neck, the silver puzzle piece angled against her collarbone.

I stepped closer, raising the flashlight. "Why are you up here? Are you okay?"

Bailey wiped the back of her hand beneath her nose, sniffling. "I was taking the long way home."

She was lying. Her eyes were puffy and red, and it was obvious she'd been crying.

"I was trying to tell you. At the dance." I motioned toward the burned-out bonfire. "Those girls aren't your friends."

"Really, Brooke? You came all this way to a party you weren't invited to, so you could tell me that?"

I shifted my weight, looking at my feet. "I'm your friend."

"You're jealous, and I don't like it." Her lips curled into a sneer as her words cut through me. "I don't like you."

I waited for her to realize the hurtful thing she'd said and take it back. To apologize. But she only crossed her arms in front of her chest and glared at me.

I could feel my temperature rising. My anger began as a slow simmer, thickening like molten lava bubbling up from my core. The hot fury surged into my limbs, my neck, burning through my veins as it filled my body. I'd always been there for Bailey. I remembered all the times I'd listened to her complain about her dysfunctional parents, or comforted her as she cried over a boy who dumped her, or took her side when she bitched about a teacher she didn't like. And all the times, like tonight, when I risked my own well-being to save her from her poor decisions. Now, the scorn on her face caused something in me to snap, and months of compressed rage to burst outward in an unexpected blast. I lunged toward her, fueled by vengeance. Her mouth dropped open as the fingers of my free hand tightened around the necklace I'd given her last August. Then I yanked it from her neck.

FORTY-SEVEN

NOW

The candle flame oscillated on the table between us, its scent making me woozy. Lacey's eyes fastened on me. "I said, I saw you on the bridge after the bonfire, Brooke. I know what you did."

My mouth had gone dry, and I couldn't speak. Had she really been there watching as I confronted Bailey? *I know what you did.* Those were the words on one of the notes.

She gave me a reassuring look. "Don't worry. I never told anyone."

"Why not?"

"Because we're friends. Right?"

"Of course." My head felt dizzy as I studied the eerie calm on Lacey's face. There was something unsettling about the flat way she asked the question.

"I was always jealous of you and Bailey. You were like two peas in a pod." Lacey swirled the wine in her glass, looking sad. "I don't have many friends."

"I'm sure that's not true."

"Mark had lots of friends, but they all went with him when

we got divorced. I only really had Maeve. And now she's gone too."

"I'm your friend, Lacey." My tongue felt thick in my mouth as I said the words.

Lacey rolled her eyes. "Jasper was my friend."

"I'm so sorry you lost him. I'm sorry for Willa too."

She stared at the flame, lost in thought for a second. "Remember when I spray-painted the side of Willa's house?"

"Yeah. You were in pain."

"I used to blame Willa for Jasper's death, but that was before she showed me his diary during one of my court-ordered visits. I always thought the horrible stories Jasper told the last few weeks of his life were about his mom. He was so vague about everything—almost nearing a comatose state. He never used her name, just called her 'that bitch.' He said she made promises she didn't keep, that she hated his music, and made him feel like he'd always be alone. He started to believe that he'd never fit in. I assumed he was talking about Willa because he spent most of his time with her."

"Wasn't he?"

"After I read his journal, I realized I'd gotten it wrong. He'd been talking about Bailey."

It felt like Lacey had yanked the chair out from underneath me, and I shifted my legs, laying my palms flat on the table. "What?"

"Jasper was in love with Bailey. His crush started when they were paired together for the science fair junior year. He worked up the nerve to ask her out for ice cream. She said yes, but then never showed up. He waited for almost two hours, sitting alone at Scoops." Lacey shook her head. "So rude. But Jasper didn't give up. He wrote her a song and sang it to her. She mocked him for that, made him feel like he was worthless. He never told me any of this when it happened, but all the details were right there in his journal, the one Willa let me read. Two weeks later, he gave away his most precious belongings, wrote a short note, and jumped in front of the train."

"Oh my God." A thousand thoughts collided in my head. "But he must have had other issues. There must have been other things that happened to—" I started to say before Lacey interrupted.

"And then I saw Bailey doing the same thing to you. She used people up and threw them away. Week after week. Month after month." Her voice had grown louder, frantic. "I always wondered why someone like her had a friend like you. I was a better friend to you than Bailey, but you never gave me a necklace."

I took in the disdain on Lacey's face as my thoughts tumbled back to prom night, to the feeling of the chain clenched between my fingers, the rain pelting my skin, and the faint sound of a distant train whistle. And I wished I had done everything differently.

FORTY-EIGHT

THEN

Prom Night 2003

The chain slid around my fingers, and I could hardly believe what I'd done. Wind whipped through the nearby treetops, but Bailey froze in place, astonished. Her lips parted as she touched the hollow of her neck, but no words came out. My rush of anger had subsided, and I fought the urge to hand the necklace back to her and apologize. Instead, I steeled myself, returning her icy stare. I was determined to hurt her as much as she hurt me. "You're a horrible friend, and you don't deserve this."

A distant train whistle jolted me into action. With a swoop of my arm, I tossed the necklace through a dangerously wide gap in the slats beneath the railing. By the light of my flashlight, I glimpsed the silver chain as it landed in a metallic heap on the gravel bordering the tracks below. Before Bailey had a chance to yell at me, I sprinted back across the wooden planks and down the steps, leaving her standing alone on the bridge beneath a gathering storm.

FORTY-NINE

NOW

I blinked the candle smoke from my eyes, studying Lacey over the tops of our nearly empty wine glasses. "Did you take the necklace, Lacey?"

She gave a slight nod. "After you ran away, I left my hiding place in the woods and grabbed the necklace off the ground. There was a train coming, and I didn't want it to get ruined. Like I said, I always wanted one like that. I've kept it all these years." Lacey's finger traced her collarbone. "You broke the chain, but I replaced it with a new one. Sometimes I wore the necklace under my shirts and pretended that you gave it to me instead of Bailey. She didn't deserve it, just like you told her on the bridge."

"Did you see Bailey when she..." I couldn't bring myself to finish the sentence.

"I saw her up there." Lacey shifted in her chair, snapping out of her trance and locking her stare on me. "Why weren't we friends, Brooke?"

"We were." I dipped my chin toward her as my vision blurred at the edges.

"That's what I thought at first, too. But it wasn't true. I

thought we'd keep in touch after high school like real friends do. But I came to visit you at college once, only because I invited myself. You said you'd come to see me next time. But you never did. Not even when I invited you."

I wanted to stay focused on what else Lacey had seen the night Bailey died, but now she'd changed course. My mind tunneled back to freshman year of college, to the November weekend Lacey had crashed in my dorm room. She was right that I hadn't wanted her to come, that I'd settled into my college routine in a new city with new friends, desperate to leave the painful memories of Cove Haven behind me. Lacey had stayed for two nights, and I missed out on a party hosted by an older art school classmate because Lacey didn't want to go. We hung out at a dingy café instead, and we hadn't had much to talk about. I assumed we'd grown apart, and so when she invited me up to Alma a few months later, I told her I was busy.

"I invited you to my wedding even though you didn't invite me to yours," Lacey said, her voice piercing my thoughts.

I shook my head at her statement, at the warped way she was remembering things. "Ours was small. We only had fifty people, total."

"Still, you didn't come to mine."

My temples throbbed, and I pressed my fingers against them. Lacey and I were both divorced now anyway, so I didn't see why any of this mattered. "I was nine months pregnant with Ruthie when you got married. Remember, I called you?"

Lacey ignored me. "And when my marriage imploded less than a year later, I reached out to you, desperate for a friend. You were too busy to talk to me. I could barely get up off the floor, and I didn't have a single person to help me other than my sister."

I wanted to circle back to the necklace, to whether Lacey had talked to Bailey after I'd left her on the bridge, but there was a distressing quiver in Lacey's voice. She was barely holding it together. "I'm sorry, Lacey. You're right. Ruthie was still a baby, and I was working full-time. It was overwhelming, but I haven't been a good friend. I apologize for that."

"You could have made things right when you came back to Cove Haven, but you didn't. When I saw you at your mom's wake, I was so hopeful. I thought maybe you'd move back into your old house, and we could pick up where we left off. I even planned to show you the necklace one day so you could see how I'd saved it for you. I hoped you'd finally understand that I was the best friend you deserved. But you barely said two words to me."

"It was my mom's funeral, Lacey." My body felt heavy as I took in her face, noting the feral look in her eyes.

Lacey continued as if I hadn't spoken. "After you went back to Ferndale, I heard from Dan that you were coming back in a few months to renovate your old house. You didn't even have the courtesy to tell me. I thought I'd give you a little scare by putting the necklace back into circulation and leaving you a couple of cryptic notes just to let you know you're not smarter than everyone else." A deranged grin spread across her colorless lips before morphing into a frown. "But you continued to kick me while I was down. You stayed with Dan instead of me. You took everyone out to dinner but not me. It confirmed what I already knew—that you and Bailey are the same. Both terrible people who will ditch your friends whenever it suits you."

Details from the night we ran into Lacey after leaving The Fish surfaced in my mind. I'd had no idea she'd been offended. I shook away her troubling take on the evening and turned the conversation back to Bailey. "Did you talk to Bailey after I left her on the bridge?" I forced the question out, although the wine was hitting me hard, and the words left my mouth slowly. I'd been blaming myself for Bailey's death for years, and I needed to know what happened after I left her standing alone.

"I climbed up the bridge to talk to Bailey, pretending I was going to return the necklace. But once I was standing up there, I told her what I thought of her. I told her she was the reason Jasper died. Do you know what she said?"

"No."

"First, she laughed. Then she said I was delusional. I waited for the train to get closer, and then I pointed to an imaginary animal down below—a bunny that didn't exist. I said I hoped the poor thing would move before the train got there. I pretended to walk away, then waited a second for her to lean over and look. And when the train was almost to the bridge, I shoved her from behind through the gap in the railing."

My hand flew to my mouth, and I felt as if my body was swallowed by the room. All these years, I told myself Bailey had jumped, that it had been my fault, even as my gut rippled with doubt. Of all the hundreds of scenarios I'd turned over in my mind, I'd never once suspected Lacey of doing anything.

I struggled to focus on Lacey's face, but now two of her sat across from me. "Why did you kill her?"

"I did it for Jasper. And for you."

The room seemed to spin around me. "For me?"

"Yes. Because I wanted to be your friend. I was protecting you from her. But you never appreciated what I did for you. You even started helping Hannah." Lacey paused. "I looked at her notebook and laptop sometimes when she went to the bathroom or out for lunch. She was getting too close to the truth, so I had to shift my plan into the next gear."

Lacey stood up and paced back and forth. My eyes tracked her, but my arms and legs were locked in place. Fear took hold. What was she doing? I viewed Lacey in a new and terrifying light—a deranged woman who had killed Bailey and caused me to suspect my former classmates, including my good friend, Dan, of multiple crimes. As she paced back toward me, I imagined tackling her, but my limbs weighed like anchors. I couldn't move. Had she drugged me?

Lacey returned to her seat, humming.

"Why did you frame Dan?" My question came out in a slur of words, and I knew for sure that she'd slipped something into my wine.

Lacey tilted her head, smiling as if she were explaining something to a toddler. "I dropped the necklace in the lost-and-found box at Dan's store because I'd been in there the day before, and I overheard them saying they were due to take it to Willa's shop. I could have given the necklace directly to Willa, I suppose, but that woman says the darndest things sometimes." Lacey made a face and chuckled. "I couldn't trust her to keep a lid on it."

"Why did you—"

"At first, I just wanted to scare you, Brooke. I wanted to get back at you for hurting me." There was now a sharp edge to Lacey's voice. "I planned to send you to The Treasure Cove on a made-up errand, so you'd see the necklace there and get spooked. But Hannah found it first. That stupid bitch has been interfering with my plan every step of the way."

My mind struggled to process the information again. Lacey had killed Bailey. Had she killed Hannah too? Lacey had left the notes for me to find. She might have been inside my house while I was sleeping. I wanted to jump from my chair and run outside, but my body was a lump of clay; it wouldn't budge.

I closed my eyes, and when I opened them, Lacey was gone. A stream of water splashed from the bathroom, and it sounded like she was filling up the tub. The flame melted the candle on the table, and a strand of drool hung from my mouth.

"Oh, boy. Looks like the drugs are hitting you hard." Lacey returned, gripping my hand and closing my fingers around a pen. She placed a motel notepad underneath it. "I need you to write something here. *Goodbye. Sorry. I'm an awful person.* It doesn't really matter. Just a few words, so there's no question you took your own life."

This couldn't be how things ended. Lacey was dangerous, someone who had killed before and wanted to do it again. I needed to get back to my daughter. I had to reveal the truth about what happened to Bailey. I'd inadvertently welcomed a total sociopath into my room, and I wasn't sure I was going to live to tell. Through my blurry vision, I eyed the flickering flame again, the cheap, gauzy curtains hanging to the side of the table, the ones with the "Highly Flammable" warning. Although my arms and legs weren't responding, I was able to lean back in my chair. I still had some control of my core.

A sudden attempt to fling myself toward the candle failed, resulting in only the slightest movement. But the sound of Lacey humming nearby ignited my ire and caused my muscles to twitch. There was still some life in them. I needed to gather my rage and use it against her. I forced my thoughts to the unspeakable thing Lacey had done, shoving Bailey in front of the train when she was already at her lowest. I felt the gaping holes of opportunities lost because of Bailey's death. Lacey had stolen the chance for Bailey to live out her life, for us to repair a lifelong friendship, and for me to apologize for the things I'd done wrong, for Bailey to apologize to me. Lacey was the reason I'd lived under a cloud of suspicion my entire adult life, unable to visit my parents in the house where I'd grown up. I wanted to jump from my seat and strangle her, but my legs didn't work, and she was somewhere on the other side of the room. I held the fury in my chest, letting it writhe and pulse, expanding and threatening to break free. Counting to three, I heaved my torso toward the candle, knocking the flame toward the curtains before I fell off my chair and onto the floor. A second later, a whoosh lit up the room as the gauzy fabric ignited. I lay help-less, unable to roll away from the flames and hoping someone from outside would see the smoke and come to my rescue.

"Dammit!" Lacey scurried to the far corner of the room. "Is this how you'd rather die? In a fire?" She sounded more like a teacher scolding a wayward student than a deranged murderer. She grabbed her things, moved one of the wine glasses back to the bathroom, rinsed it out, and coughed as smoke filled the room. "Suit yourself."

I tried to scream, but only a murmur came out. She was going to leave me here to die and pretend she'd never been present.

Lacey exited the motel room, closing the door behind her. The heat from the burning curtains intensified, scorching my skin. A long moan released from my lungs as I inhaled a mouthful of smoke. I'd only made my situation worse by lighting the fire, speeding up the circumstances of my own demise. I was going to burn to death alone on the floor of this dingy motel room. And I only hoped Ruthie would know how badly I wanted to stay alive.

FIFTY

NOW

When my eyes cracked open, I found myself sprawled on the floor beneath a ceiling of black smoke, unable to move. I'd lost consciousness for a minute, and the fire had spread, the flames licking closer to my head, the smoke darker and thicker. An alarm shrieked from somewhere near me. Voices shouted from outside. I imagined the other motel occupants evacuating their rooms. No one knew I was here, completely incapacitated.

"Brooke! Are you in there?"

"Open up, Brooke!"

A man and a woman screamed from outside, banging on the door. I couldn't respond. The door was unlocked. All they had to do was open it. The fire crept closer, and my lungs were short on oxygen. Finally, a figure hovered above me, coughing.

"She's here! On the floor! Help me drag her outside."

Through the smoke, I made out the faces of the man gripping me beneath my armpits and the woman grasping my ankles. It was Justin Warner and Maeve. And as I teetered at the edge of consciousness, I couldn't make sense of why Lacey's sister was rescuing me.

The next time I woke up, I was lying in a hospital bed, the glow of fluorescent lights stinging my eyes. My vision was blurry, and my entire body hurt. The police chief sat in a chair nearby, wearing his uniform. Touching my stomach, I looked down, realizing I wore a hospital gown. There was a tube connected to my nose. Daylight filtered in through the partially open blinds. The terrifying nightmare hadn't been a dream, but I was alive.

"They have you on oxygen," Justin said. "You were in a fire, but you're going to be okay."

I nodded, absorbing the fact that I'd escaped certain death. He looked almost as haggard as I felt. "You saved me," I tried to say, but my voice was hoarse.

A nurse stepped into the room and smiled at me. "How are you feeling?"

"Not great." I reached for my throat, which burned. Now hot tears leaked from my eyes. "Can I call my daughter?"

The nurse patted my arm. "Your family has been notified, and they're on their way to see you."

My muscles relaxed at the news that I'd see Ruthie soon. I assumed Shane was driving her, and I no longer cared if Mandy was with them because I'd be with my daughter again.

"Let's get you some water. I'll call the doctor."

Justin waited patiently while the nurse and a doctor attended to me, asking a series of questions and reassuring me that the damage to my lungs wouldn't be long-term because I'd been rescued in time. All the while, Lacey's disturbing confession rumbled through me.

When the doctor and nurse left the room, Justin scooted closer. "I'm here because I wanted to fill you in on what happened last night."

"Lacey killed Bailey," I croaked before he could say more.

"She pushed her in front of the train. She admitted to the crime, and then she tried to kill me."

He held up a hand as if telling me to save my voice. "I believe you. At least, I've been piecing things together since Maeve showed up at my house last night."

"She did?"

"Yeah. She was very upset. I finally got it out of her that she suspected her sister of killing Hannah. Maeve said she got up early on Saturday to go for a run and noticed her sister was gone. Lacey came back later with wet hair, saying she'd gone to the beach, which was strange because Lacey had never enjoyed swimming, especially in the lake. Maeve wrote it off as a weird occurrence until after the parade, when she heard about the podcaster drowning. She said she had a terrible feeling, especially after some older memories came to light."

My eyelids lowered as I took in the information, almost afraid to ask the next question. "What memories?"

"She remembered seeing Lacey sneaking out their bedroom window the night of your prom. Said Lacey swore her to secrecy. Threatened her, even." He clucked and shook his head. "At first, I couldn't understand why Lacey would want to kill Hannah, but then I realized her podcast must have been close to something. Like you told me the other day when I didn't listen."

I laced my fingers together, sorry that I'd been correct.

"After we got you safely out of the burning motel room, the firefighters arrived and quickly put out the fire. I asked the motel manager to let me into Hannah's room again so I could retrieve some evidence—Hannah's bag and her notebook. After reading her notes, I realized that she suspected me of being Bailey's secret boyfriend. She was most certainly planning on confronting me next, of putting whatever she found out there on her podcast for the world to hear. Somehow, Lacey must have found out about it too."

The last words written in Hannah's notebook scratched

through my mind – *Justin Warner = Bailey's secret lover...* *Someone else must know about the secret relationship!!!*

Lacey had told me last night that she often looked through Hannah's things when Hannah was in the bathroom or out for a walk. She'd had a front-row seat to Hannah's next move. I looked at Justin. "Okay. But what does your secret relationship with Bailey have to do with Lacey?"

"There was something I didn't tell you when we met last night, but I've come clean with my wife, and I'll tell you now." He drew in a long breath and slowly exhaled. "I lied to you yesterday. I did see someone else in the woods the night Bailey died. It was Lacey."

I pressed my spine into the hospital bed, wondering if I'd heard him correctly.

He bit his lip before speaking again. "Lacey had stumbled upon me and Bailey messing around in the back of my patrol car one night a couple of weeks earlier. We'd parked in the woods not too far from Willa's house, and I guess Lacey often walked home that way. I got out of the car and had a desperate conversation with her. She promised not to tell anyone, but I didn't feel good about it. Lacey knew too much. When I saw her in the woods the night Bailey died, she said she'd just returned a pair of shoes she'd worn to prom to Willa and was taking her usual route home when she came across what was left of Bailey's body. Lacey looked so scared. She begged me not to tell anyone she was there. She said she'd already been through so much after confessing to the vandalism at Willa's house, and she couldn't go through all the questioning again. She couldn't face all the smug looks from the townspeople. When I didn't agree to her request, she threatened to tell everyone about Bailey and me if I mentioned her name. She started running, and I assumed she was freaked out by the suicide she'd just encountered, that she'd been in the wrong place at the wrong time as she cut through the woods. I questioned Willa the next morning, and she confirmed that Lacey had stopped by late at night to return some shoes. So, I believed the reason Lacey gave me for being in the woods. She was a good kid who'd been through some hard times, and I never thought she had done anything wrong. I never mentioned Lacey's name to my colleagues because I didn't think there was anything to investigate there. But—to be perfectly honest—I also felt I had too much to lose if she talked."

"Oh."

"It was a mistake to withhold that information, but I really believed Bailey took her own life. After she was gone, I remembered so many red flags that I should have taken more seriously. She'd been so down about her future. She'd told me more than once that she'd rather die than stay in Cove Haven. She started drinking heavily and not caring about her grades. And her parents were horrible, her new friends so mean. And she was obviously very jealous of you."

I cocked my head at the last revelation but let him continue.

"I assumed what those girls did to her on prom night was the final straw. Bailey must have been so humiliated when they announced the prank to everyone at the bonfire. She learned she'd been used as a pawn by people she thought were her friends and had to sit there and act like it was no big deal. And then I didn't show up to meet her. She didn't have anyone to confide in other than me." He pinched his lips together. "I felt so guilty. But I was also terrified of what would happen if Lacey told anyone about the relationship between Bailey and me. I got it in my head that Lacey could destroy my career, maybe ruin my family once I was older. But the thing is, it wasn't a crime to kiss a seventeen-year-old girl, especially when I was only twenty-three. It was poor judgment, but that was about it."

"I understand."

"And now my wife knows the whole story too. I even reported myself to the department. So, everything's out in the open. But I'm sure Lacey was worried that once Hannah uncovered my scandalous affair with Bailey, I'd no longer have any reason to hide that I'd seen her near the bridge that night. I'd almost certainly mention my encounter with her if only to deflect blame from myself."

I tipped my head forward, finally putting together all the missing pieces. "So Lacey stopped Hannah from talking to you. She killed her before the conversation pointed back to her."

"Seems overwhelmingly likely." Justin frowned. "We arrested Lacey about two hours ago for Hannah's murder. I suspect after you tell me everything that happened last night, they'll add a second charge for Bailey's murder."

The truth fluttered through me, and I felt a little as if I was levitating off the bed. People always said the truth set you free, and this must have been what they meant. Bailey hadn't jumped to her death because of me. Lacey, the jealous friend, had murdered Bailey, pushing her in front of an oncoming train before Bailey and I ever got the chance to repair our friendship. And now Lacey was finally going to pay for what she'd done.

FIFTY-ONE

NOW

Four weeks later

We huddled around the table on Dan and Maggie's back deck, the heat of the late afternoon sun glazing my forehead with sweat. A mismatched crew had accepted my invitation to gather and listen to the final episode of *All the Dark Corners* podcast, which I'd recorded over the last several days after getting permission from Hannah's parents. Dan, Maggie, Gabe, Zoe, and Jonathan were there, perched around the table. Even Liz had shown up to listen. Liz and I had made amends a couple of weeks ago with Zoe acting awkwardly as our liaison, eventually getting both of us to admit we'd acted childishly and were eager to put the past behind us. Now my phone rested on the center of the table, a recording of my voice playing through the speaker.

Dan caught my eye from across the table and tossed me an encouraging look, even as my voice told the listeners that Bailey's missing necklace had come from his bike shop. Dan had visited me at the hospital the day after the fire, where he and I had immediately apologized to each other, both of us feeling ridiculous for our mutual suspicions. Dan had been shocked to learn about my phone call with Henry, and that Henry was the one who'd sent Hannah to Cove Haven. Now my gaze shifted to Gabe, who winked at me, apparently riveted by every word spoken by my recorded voice. For the last four weeks, I'd been taking Ruthie for daily visits to Drips, where Gabe continued to be his jovial self. He and I had settled into a permanent friendship mode, which suited me fine. The episode continued playing, as Liz shifted in her chair and Zoe widened her eyes with each new revelation. Jonathan stared at the phone. He'd dressed casually, and without a hat or sunglasses. Now that Lacey had been arrested, he had no reason to hide from this town.

For nearly twenty minutes on the podcast's final episode, I'd been explaining the details of what actually happened on prom night, including owning up to having ripped the necklace from Bailey's neck on the bridge. I explained how Lacey blamed Bailey for her best friend, Jasper's, death the year before and how Lacey had been jealous of my years-long friendship with Bailey and of the necklace I gave her, which represented our bond. I even exposed the secret relationship between Bailey and Justin Warner, the relationship Hannah had been so close to uncovering, and which Lacey had most likely feared would lead the chief of police to crack and reveal that he'd seen her in the woods. Finally, I described the events of four weeks ago, when Lacey showed up at my motel room at one in the morning with a bottle of red wine and a sob story about her sister who'd abandoned her.

I'll end the podcast with one final summary. Bailey Maddox was murdered twenty years ago by her classmate, Lacey. It is a relief for so many of us to learn that Bailey didn't kill herself as we'd been led to believe, but a different kind of grief arises when one learns a friend has been murdered. When your beloved podcaster, Hannah Mead, got too close to the truth, I believe Lacey killed her too, making it look as if Hannah drowned on her morning swim. Then she tried to kill me. Thankfully, Lacey's sister and a quick-acting police chief named Justin Warner came to my rescue, and Lacey is now under arrest for two murders. So thank you, listeners, for letting me fill in for Hannah for one last episode of All the Dark Corners. *I know I'm a poor substitute for your beloved host, but I've done my best to honor her and Bailey's memories. Hannah would have wanted to see this investigation through to the end, and without her dogged determination, we may have never learned the truth about the tragic death of the prom queen of Cove Haven.*

The podcast ended, and I clicked off my phone as the others clapped and offered their praise for my work on the episode. I tipped back my head, hoping I'd finally closed the most harrowing chapter of my life. Several feet away, Ruthie ran across the backyard with Olivia and Marci, deeply entrenched in a never-ending game of tag. We'd been staying at their house since I'd been released from the hospital, and Shane and I had renegotiated our summer custody agreement, allowing Ruthie to spend an uninterrupted month with me in Cove Haven. Maggie had lent me some things, and I'd ordered some new clothes and shoes to replace everything I'd lost in the fire. It had been a joy to watch Ruthie become fast friends with Dan and Maggie's girls. But now that the work at Mom's house was complete, I'd listed the property with a real estate agent, already receiving some serious interest.

Clouds drifted past the sun as the others chattered around me. I glanced at my wrist out of habit to check the time but found it bare. I'd misplaced my favorite accessory: a gold and silver Coach watch I'd splurged on after getting a raise from the museum two years earlier. The last time I remembered seeing it was when I'd moved out of Dan and Maggie's house, and I'd hoped that meant it had survived the motel fire. But they'd helped me turn their place upside down, searching for it with no luck. Gabe had combed through his apartment too, but couldn't find it. The watch was nowhere to be found. I suspected it had gotten lost in the fire after all.

Dan tipped his glass toward me. "I hope you and Ruthie will come to visit before another twenty years passes."

"We definitely will. She really seems to love it here."

Tomorrow morning, I'd return to my life in Ferndale more grateful for the extended time I'd been granted to be Ruthie's mom and the unexpected experiences we'd shared over the past month, from showing her my childhood bedroom to playing putt-putt golf to lazy afternoons on the beach. I'd return to work soon, indebted to my supervisor at the art museum, who'd held my position for me despite my behavioral mishap a few months earlier. I closed my eyes, grounding myself and noticing that my insides, which had been so tightly wound for years, had finally uncoiled, perhaps loosened by a deeper understanding of my past. And at this moment, there was no place I'd rather be than in Cove Haven surrounded by friends.

EPILOGUE

WILLA—NOW

In a darkened room at the back of her house, Willa placed two shiny objects next to each other on a stone altar: a cufflink from the real estate developer Jonathan Newson and a slim gold watch from Brooke Webber. She envisioned Lacey rotting away in jail. Lacey, Willa's last living connection to her son, Jasper. The injustice of her friend's fate and her son's death weighed Willa down. Performing her rituals was the only thing that made her feel better. Lacey had claimed that Willa's chants were ridiculous and didn't affect anything, but Willa liked to remind her friend that there was often no outward proof of things not of this realm. Most followers of any religion would agree that some explanations couldn't be found in a book.

A cat wound itself around Willa's ankles as her mind traveled back twenty years ago to when she'd spied young Lacey leaving bags of canine droppings on her front step and spray-painting the devil's words on the side of her house. Willa understood that a person's pain could show many faces. So when the vandal turned herself in and apologized, Willa forgave Lacey and welcomed her into her home. Willa even shared Jasper's journal with Lacey, including the entries about Bailey Maddox and the cruelty she returned to Jasper in exchange for his crush. She successfully redirected Lacey's grief and rage toward Bailey, the one who deserved it, the one who, according to Lacey, continued to disavow her former friends. Willa and Lacey became a team dedicated to getting revenge for Jasper.

Things were calm for years after Bailey met her fate. Willa's cats multiplied, and business ticked along. Lacey departed for college. It was a happy surprise when Lacey returned to Cove Haven a few years back. But then the developers drifted into town like a dark cloud. Next, the podcaster arrived, followed by Brooke Webber, whose presence upset Lacey.

Willa's knotty fingers hovered over the stolen relics as a dangerous spell bubbled through her mind. This curse, the same one she'd cast on the prom queen and the podcaster, required a piece of jewelry recently worn by the intended victim. Lacey had done Willa's dirty work two decades ago when she'd swiped Bailey's teardrop earring during PE class two weeks before pushing the horrible girl off the bridge. More recently, Lacey had spotted Hannah's beaded bracelet in a meeting room in the library and delivered it to Willa a few days prior to Hannah's final morning swim. But Lacey had complained that stealing the jewelry was too risky and unnecessary to accomplish their goal. Willa disagreed. There was an order to things of this nature, and certain steps shouldn't be ignored.

Now Lacey awaited trial and was no longer available to propel Willa's curses into action, but Willa had someone arguably better. Her nephew Gabe was eager to reconnect with his roots, anxious to learn about the father he never knew and to win his aunt's approval. He had already helped Lacey ambush the podcaster as she swam, pretending he was drowning as Hannah approached to help him, then turning on her as he and Lacey held Hannah beneath the surface. Gabe was more than capable of acting on his own.

Per Willa's request, Gabe had already delivered a cufflink the real estate developer had dropped at the café and a gold watch he'd swiped from the living room table as Brooke Webber slept on his couch. Willa's palm hovered over the cufflink, then the watch, thinking about how Jonathan Newson's greed threatened her home and how Brooke Webber's stubbornness had stolen Lacey from her. Willa closed her eyes and chanted the words that welcomed death, feeling the objects' energy snake through her.

Gabe stood opposite her, arms crossed and eyelids low. Then he whispered the question Willa longed to hear.

"Which one of them is next?"

A LETTER FROM LAURA

Dear reader,

I want to say a huge thank you for choosing to read *Prom Queen*. If you enjoyed it and want to keep up to date with all my latest releases, just sign up at the following link. Your email address will never be shared, and you can unsubscribe at any time.

www.bookouture.com/laura-wolfe

I have a confession—I remember virtually nothing about my senior prom, which took place decades ago. I know I attended because I've seen a photo of myself and my date on our way to the dance in a shiny red convertible, but I don't remember anything after that, not even where the event was held or if my school elected a prom queen and king. I've reached out to some friends to help with my memory, and their recollections are equally as vague. Perhaps the uneventfulness of my own prom was the reason I felt compelled to write this story of a MUCH more memorable prom night. And, because I write psychological thrillers, the fictional prom night had to include murder and plenty of dark secrets.

I've had several recent experiences of returning to a place where I haven't been in many years and finding certain things—and people—looking exactly as I'd remembered, while others had been completely transformed to the point of being unrecognizable. (Anyone who's moved away from their hometown and returned to attend a high school reunion knows what I'm talking about.) Finding a place or a person you once knew as unrecognizable can be disorienting and unsettling, a feeling I hoped to capture with Brooke's return to Cove Haven. Cove Haven is a fictional town on the shores of Lake Michigan, very loosely based on a few Michigan towns where I've spent portions of my summers over the years—South Haven, Port Austin, and Harbor Springs.

Finally, the painful subject of suicide is mentioned throughout my story and is something I don't take lightly. If you or anyone you know are suffering from suicidal thoughts, please call 988 in the US or visit www.supportline.org.uk in the UK for additional resources.

I hope you loved *Prom Queen,* and if you did, I would be very grateful if you could write a review. Reviews make such a difference in helping new readers discover one of my books for the first time.

I love hearing from my readers – you can get in touch on my Instagram, Facebook page, or my website. To receive my monthly book recommendations in the mystery/suspense/thriller genre, please follow me on Bookbub.

Thanks,

Laura Wolfe

 facebook.com/LauraWolfeBooks

 instagram.com/lwolfe.writes

bookbub.com/profile/laura-wolfe

ACKNOWLEDGMENTS

While writing a novel is mainly a solitary endeavor, there have been many people who supported and assisted me in various ways along the journey of writing and publishing this book. First, I'd like to thank the entire team at Bookouture, especially my editor, Harriet Wade. She helped to smooth out my novel's rough edges and reminded me to raise the stakes. Her insights into my story's structure, pacing, and characters made the final version so much better. Many thanks to Isobel Akenhead for giving me the idea for the title. Additional gratitude goes to copyeditor, Dushi Horti, and proofreader, Shirley Khan, for their keen eyes, and to Bookouture's top-notch publicity team led by Noelle Holten. Thank you to my intern, Catherine van Lent, who kept me company at library visits and read through my manuscript at various stages. Many thanks to the handful of friends who continuously support my writing and provide inspiration and encouragement. Thank you to the many book bloggers who have helped spread the word about my books. Thank you to my parents, cousin, siblings, mother-in-law, and other family members who have supported my books. I appreciate everyone who has taken the time to tell me that they enjoyed reading my stories, has asked me, "How's your writing going?", has left a positive review, or has sent me a personal message. I also owe gratitude to my canine "writing partner," Milo. He sat by my side (and only occasionally barked) as I wrote every word. Most of all, I'd like to thank my kids, Brian and Kate, for always cheering for me and for finding creative ways to occupy themselves so that I could have time to write, and my husband, JP, for supporting my writing. As always, I wouldn't have made it to the end without his encouragement.

Printed in Great Britain
by Amazon

42317459R00179